THE Lyons DEN

THE *Lyons* DEN

CAROL ANN CULBERT JOHNSON

THE LYONS DEN

iUniverse books may be ordered through booksellers or by contacting:

iUniverse
1663 Liberty Drive
Bloomington, IN 47403
www.iuniverse.com
844-349-9409

Because of the dynamic nature of the Internet, any web addresses or links contained in this book may have changed since publication and may no longer be valid. The views expressed in this work are solely those of the author and do not necessarily reflect the views of the publisher, and the publisher hereby disclaims any responsibility for them.

Any people depicted in stock imagery provided by Getty Images are models, and such images are being used for illustrative purposes only. Certain stock imagery © Getty Images.

ISBN: 978-1-6632-0884-2 (sc)
ISBN: 978-1-6632-0885-9 (e)

Print information available on the last page.

iUniverse rev. date: 10/09/2020

The Meeting (The Lyons Den)

M adison was so nervous as she stared at herself in the mirror. She was a size six now, and she couldn't believe it. She was wearing a long green maxi dress, and it showed off her remaining curves. She was still stunned as she continued to stare at herself. Losing weight had been a battle for her, and now, finally, she was a perfect size.

Madison's life has changed as men were now breaking their necks to date her, but a year ago, men ignored the hell out of her. She was invisible. With her size six body and beautiful face, she could get any man she wanted and then some. Her stomach was flat, and she finally lost her fat legs and thighs. She can wear jeans now. She can now stand to look at herself in the mirror. She was just as hot as Beyoncé and any other woman. She was thirty years old and hot.

Madison hasn't dated that much with this new body. She resented men because they ignored her when she was fat, treating her like she didn't exist in this tarnished world. To most men, she was fat and ugly, and this is how they treated her.

She smiled as she continued to stare at herself in the mirror. She remembered taking an Uber somewhere because she didn't want to drive. She had this Uber driver before, but he practically ignored her, but when she got into his car this particular time, he was smiling all over himself. She can remember the conversation as if it was yesterday.

***

"Wow, you look great, "he said.

Madison smiled.

"You are fine as wine now," he commented.

She frowned, feeling her Taurus the bull coming out. So, I was ugly and fat before," she snapped?

The Uber driver stared at her. "You weren't ugly, but you were obese. I'm glad you lost the weight. With your pretty face, and your beautiful hair, it was a damn shame you let food get the best of you. I would like to date you now."

She laughed. "I don't think so."

"And why not?" he snapped.

"I don't date bastards."

"Excuse me?"

"I'm the same person that you now want to date."

You are fine as wine now. Who wants to date a fat woman?"

"You don't, so let's cease this conversation."

"So, you're fine now, and you think you are all that."

"No, but I will never date a bias ass as yourself for discriminating against weight instead of getting to know a person and their inner beauty."

He laughed. "How many men did you date when you were fat?"

Madison ignored the bastard. Who did he think he was?

The Uber driver continued to stare at her with an angry frown on his face. He had the nerve to be mad at her. He is the one that hated fat women and now wanted to take her out. She refused to go out with any man who ignored her when she was fat. She knew this was wrong thinking, but that is how she felt. She was a new woman with a new attitude. If she did decide to date, it would be with an unconditional man. Other than that, she will be single for the duration of her life. Sometimes men can go to hell and back. Who needed men?

As Madison continued again to stare at herself in the mirror, she smiled. It was time for her to leave her condo and surprise her two best friends. They are going to be very surprised to see the new Madison. Her two best friends, Sylvia and Helen, lived in New York City, and this is their weekly meeting where they get together in Chicago. She couldn't wait for her best friends to see her. They are going to be shocked to see all the weight she had lost. Although Madison talked to them all the time, she never told them that she was losing weight. Sylvia and Helen are size six, and they never put her down, call her fat names, or ask her to lose weight. They were her unconditional friends for life.

The three of them grew up together as they met in the third grade. Madison was always the chubby girl in the bunch. Helen and Sylvia welcomed her with open arms, and they became the three Musketeers. Of course, they put her on diets, and she lost the weight, but she gained it back. Madison loves to eat, and eventually, they left her alone. Helen and Sylvia are like sisters to her. She loved them to death and would die for either one of them. They felt the same way about her. The three made a pact to be friends for life.

Helen is the registered nurse of the group. She loves nursing. Helen is married to her husband, Joseph, who she met in elementary school. They have two children Michael and Fatima. Helen has been married for over twenty years. They love each other very much.

Sylvia is the famous fashion designer of the group with Sylvia's fashions. All the celebrities, men and women, have worn her styles. Sylvia now has her own fashion house, where she employs five associate fashion designers. It's her dream to find the next fashion designer and make their dreams come true. Madison was so proud of her two best friends.

Now Madison is a paralegal of the group. She's a freelance paralegal, and she works for four Law Firms. She has two other paralegals working for her, and they get the job done. She lives in a four-bedroom condo in Lombard, Illinois, and is single. She loves her job, and she loved helping others achieve their goals and dreams.

The three of them were very successful women. They love each other very much, and they don't envy each other. They support each other, and whatever decisions they made terrible or good, Madison knows she could depend on Helen and Sylvia whenever she needed them. Sometimes, Sylvia and Madison would butt heads, but they still adored each other, of course. They also knew that they could depend on her too. They are a team.

Her best friends were visiting Chicago, and she couldn't wait to see them. They would get the surprise of their lives when they laid eyes on her. She stared into the mirror one more time, and then she turned away. It was time for her to see her two best friends.

Madison grabbed her large tote bag and her keys. She also held her cell phone. Her iPhone 6 Plus was large enough to find. She touched the home button with her fingerprints, and the phone came to life. She then searched her apps for the Uber app and called for a ride. She didn't drive anymore, which was a pain, but there was a reason for it. She smiled because it was time to see her best friends.

As Madison sat in the Uber car, she was glad that she had a new driver. He spoke and then minded his own business. She played on her iPhone as they drove to the Lyons Restaurant in Wheaton, Illinois. This restaurant was the most expensive and debonair in Illinois. Of course, Sylvia wood spring for the best. She had never been to this restaurant in her life, but she had read about it and seen plenty of pictures. This restaurant was the best, and she couldn't wait to walk in. This was a dream come true. She loved to read, so she clicked on her Kindle app and started reading one of her many books. She noticed the Uber driver staring at her from time to time, but she ignored him. Men were the last thing on her mind. She could not stand them.

After maybe twenty minutes, they pulled up to the lavish restaurant. She was speechless as she thanked the Uber driver who was going to get a big tip.

A black man in a uniform greeted her at the door with his note pad. "May I help you?" *He was very handsome and belonged in a modeling fashion show, but she was sure he was getting plenty of money working at Lyons Restaurant. She read once in a magazine that they paid their staff so very well that no one ever quit their jobs unless they got fired.*

"I am meeting the Sylvia party."

He consulted his clipboard and smiled as he checked off something and then opened the door for her. "Janet will check you for weapons, and then Bob will show you to your table."

Madison smiled as she walked in, and Janet went to work on searching her from head to toe with a wand or something, and then she had to open her large tote bag for her. She stared inside, and then Bob took over, and they walked to Sylvia's table. This restaurant was classy as hell and very safe. She still couldn't believe that she was here. Bob was white and very handsome.

When Madison approached Sylvia's table, she heard them talking as she stared at the rich people who looked up at her and then carried on with their business.

Madison reached the table, and Sylvia and Helen stop talking to stare at her in shock. They were speechless and amazed all at the same time. Bob left after he seated her. She smiled at her two best friends. There was silence as the smile lit up her face. She then took out her cell phone to snap their pictures. It was a moment she would never forget for as long as she lived. Finally, after five minutes, the silence was broken by Sylvia. "Are you freaking kidding me? You look amazing."

"You look so beautiful," Helen cried.

"Surprise?" she cried.

"Wow," Sylvia cried. "I don't know what to say."

"So, this is the secret you were keeping from us," Helen cried. "I remember now why you never wanted to face time or skype with us. Why didn't you level with us about losing weight? We never bothered or nagged you about it."

Madison sighed. "I just wanted to surprise you both. You know we cannot keep secrets from each other, so I do not consider this a secret, girls. I just wanted to do this on my own, and then surprise you two."

"I do understand," Sylvia said. "You are more beautiful than ever." *Sylvia stared around the room.* "Look at the men staring at you, girl. You could be a model or something."

"She's right about that, and the women are looking at you with evil in their eyes," Helen cried. "I told you so many times that you were a gorgeous woman, and now you proved me right."

"I'm too skinny, but when you lose the weight, you lose everything," Madison cried.

"That's the truth," Helen cried. "I was fat when I gained weight with my children, and Joseph nagged the hell out of me until I lost the weight. How did you do it?"

Madison wanted to lie, but Sylvia and Helen knew her like sisters, and since she did not have any of her own, they were her sisters. "I watched what I ate, exercised a little, and used diet pills."

"What?" Helen cried. "Didn't I tell you about diet pills?"

"But you used the Garcinia Cambogia to lose the weight. I'm skinny now, and I'm never going to gain any weight again, so let's just be happy for me. I feel great about myself, and now I can stare in the mirror."

"I'm thrilled for you," Sylvia. "Now, you can date and get married."

She frowned. "I don't think that's going to be happening real soon. A regular Uber driver wanted to date me, and he had been ignoring me, and now all of a sudden, I'm attracted to him. I wanted to shoot him in the balls if I thought I could get away with it."

"Are you going to punish all men now," Sylvia said. "I see where your logic and thinking is going, Madison. Men don't date fat women, and that's something we have to handle. You can't blame the men for not finding you attractive."

Madison frowned again. "I was invisible where men were concerned, Sylvia. They didn't look at me or give me the time of day, and most of them ignored me. I felt so ugly and fat."

"Now you're fine as wine," Helen said. "You don't have to rush into a relationship, Madison, but the way the men are checking you out now, you will have to screen them or something because they will be raining on your parade."

Sylvia frowned. "Why did you lose weight?"

"So, I can't be invisible anymore."

"And you do want to meet men," Sylvia stated.

"I want to meet an unconditional man, and someone who will bring those butterflies in my stomach, and ringing in my ears. Until then, I am focused on my career, and nothing more or less. Let's change the subject, please, ladies, and we need to embrace each other. I know I shocked the hell out of you both, but it was only eighty pounds."

All three ladies stood up and embraced, and then sat back down. "I want a salad," Madison cried, and some lemonade.

"Not a diet soda for you," Helen asked.

"I'm off diet soda for a while," Madison confirmed. " I might have one from time to time, but I'm not betting on losing weight again. I want to maintain my size six and move on."

"I was just going to introduce my plus-size line, and I had you in mind for doing it," Sylvia said. "I was going to convince you to model for me. Now I have to put out a casting call for a plus-size model."

Madison *laughed.* "Sorry!"

"I'm sure you are," Sylvia laughed.

"How did you get a reservation at Lyons Restaurant, Sylvia?"

She smiled. "I know the Lyons, and I work for his three sisters in giving them the fashions that they crave and need," Sylvia bragged. "I get most of my money from the Lyon's family. They are Tanyann, Tammyann, and Toniann. I'm also doing a men's line for their brothers, Toxic and Tumor."

Madison laughed. "Are you kidding me?"

Sylvia laughed. "Their names are funny, but they are the richest family in this world, and then some. I love working for the sisters, and they respect me as I respect them. Tanyann is the oldest, and she's married to a black man. His name is Guy Rough."

Madison was stunned. "He's the actor with his sitcom."

"Yes, he is," Sylvia cried. "Tammyann is a nurse, and Toniann is a fashion model, and she models for most of my fashions."

"What do Toxic and Tumor do?" Madison laughed.

Helen laughed out loud. "I just can't get over their names."

"Is their mother a comedian or something?" Madison asked.

"She's a doctor with a sense of humor," Sylvia laughed. "Toxic is an attorney, and he's famous for winning all his cases. He just got that actor off, Owens, for murdering his wife and her male best friend."

Madison frowned. "I thought he was guilty."

Helen shook her head. "He's innocent, or Toxic would never have taken his case. Toxic is a stickler for finding out the truth, and he has a team who can find your dead mother if you want them too."

"Some of the cases I handled as a paralegal, the client was guilty as sin, but got off."

"That happens, but with Toxic Lyons, they'd be in jail right now. I admire the man and the family. Toxic is thirty, and he's searching for a wife, and he wants children, but he can't find a woman who loves him more than his money and name."

"What about Tumor?" Madison asked.

"Tumor is married to his high school sweetheart, Tricia, and they have two children. Tumor is a real estate agent and a rich one, and his wife is an anchorwoman for the news here in Chicago. They live here, of course."

"Wow," Madison cried. "They are always in the magazines."

"For positive things," Sylvia stated. "I can come here whenever I want, and the meal is free. We can eat what we like, so I think you should order your rib tips and get off the diet for today. The three of us have been so busy. It isn't easy to have weekly meetings. This is the first one for two months."

Madison frowned. "I miss you guys living in New York City. I thought I was going to hurt myself. I did eat like a pig when the two of you decided to leave me here in violent Chicago. I couldn't believe it."

"I had no choice," Sylvia pointed out. "My fashion career is out there in New York. I went to the School of Parsons, and made a name for myself. Sylvia's fashions are all over the world, and then some."

"I have some of your shoes," Madison said. "I'm so proud of you."

"We all are," Helen said. "I do most of the sewing for Sylvia, and she pays me well, which is why I'm out there with her. I also run a hospital unit for the nurses, and I love my job, girls. I wouldn't trade it for the world, but you two know how I use to make our clothes all the time when we were younger."

"You did have a gift," Sylvia cried.

"I still do have the gift," Helen said.

The black waitress walked over to them. "What can I get you three? Everything is on the house, and Toxic Lyons is here, and he says enjoy yourselves. He's going to come out and talk with you three later."

"Thank him for us," Sylvia cried. "I'm going to order for us. I want the rib tip dinner, the catfish dinner, and the meatloaf dinner."

The waitress smiled. "Coming right up, and what would you three like to drink?"

Sylvia retook the lead. "I'm going to have an Island Long tea, a Matai, and a rum and coke."

The waitress smiled. "I'll be right back."

"She is delighted," Madison pointed out.

"If you knew how much she made working here as a waitress, you'd be happy too," Sylvia pointed out.

"How much?" Helen asked.

$40.00 an hour," Sylvia cried.

Madison was stunned. "Are you for real?"

Sylvia shook her head. "No."

"Wow!" Helen exclaimed. "I guess I would love my job too."

The three ladies laughed. The waitress came back with their drinks, and she took a very long sip of her Matai. It was delicious and made the way she liked it, and it was in a very tall and large glass. Madison then stared around the restaurant. She felt that someone was watching her, and continued to look around, but everyone minded their own business, but the back of her black roots was standing up at attention for some reason. What was going on with her?

"Are you okay?" Sylvia asked.

"I'm having the time of my life, "Madison replied.

"We're on the first floor of this lovely establishment," Sylvia pointed out. "The building has everything you need and more. When you come into this building, you never have to leave."

Madison was stunned. "Have you had the tour?"

"We both have," Helen cried, and we went bowling and played tennis. I got my nails and feet done and had a great massage."

"Can anyone just come off the street here?" Madison asked.

"No," Sylvia replied. "But you can make an appointment and have your day here. The Lyons aren't just for the rich. They have deals for low-income people who can't afford their high services, but they screen all people, and the ones who are criminals, won't get in. They have over two hundred men and women working for security, and the Lyons employ a lot of people."

Madison took another sip of her wine and then again felt like someone was watching her. She looked around the room and finally spotted a white man talking to another white man, but his eyes stared at her. For some reason, she wanted to look away, but she could not tear herself away from his gorgeous green eyes, her favorite color, of course, with purple being her second favorite. Their eyes met, and then the butterflies and the ringing took over her soul. She felt like she was about to burst from something or faint from his intensive glaze.

Madison had to look away because she thought or believed that she was losing her mind. She loved reading romance novels, and this was probably one of the last books she was reading. She looked away, sipping her drink, and then turned back around, and again the handsome white man was still staring at her.

Madison took another sip of her wine and then noticed that Helen and Sylvia were eyeing her. "What?" she cried.

"What's going on with you?" Helen said, and don't bother lying."

"Someone is staring at me," Madison pointed out.

Helen and Sylvia laughed. "You need to get used to that," Helen said. "You're a stunning woman Madison Johnson. Men and women will be staring at you for a long time."

"Where?" Sylvia asked.

"Look toward the bar, and he's talking to another white man, but his eyes are on me. I've never seen him before in my life, but he does look familiar to me for some reason."

Sylvia and Helen followed Madison's directions, and Sylvia screamed, causing attention to herself, but covering her mouth in shock. "That's Toxic Lyons," she cried.

"She's right about that," Helen said. "The man he's talking to is his cousin, Bart, who works in the restaurant. My God, his eyes are on you."

Madison was speechless. Toxic Lyons was staring at her. This was like a dream, and she was never going to wake up. Why was he staring at her, and he was still staring? She peered at her best friends, who had shocked expressions on their faces.

"Should we leave?" she cried.

"Of course not," Sylvia cried. "Are you crazy? He's going to come over here in a few minutes, and you better act confident and like you got some class. Don't let him see you sweat."

Madison frowned at her. "I beg your pardon."

"She was just joking?" Helen said.

She focused on Sylvia. "You don't think I have class."

"Girl, your self-esteem is very low," Sylvia pointed out.

"She lost the weight, Sylvia, so I don't think you have to worry about Madison any longer. This chick will carry her own with Toxic Lyons, or even the President of the United States."

Sylvia shook her head. "I didn't mean it like that, Madison. You know how shy you can be, and Helen and I had to drag you out to go anywhere with us. All you wanted to do was stay in the house, and never go anywhere."

"She's so right about that," Helen agreed. "You used to get on my nerves at times. Sylvia and I went to a lot of clubs, but you only went once and never went back with us."

Madison rolled her eyes at the two of them. "You two were skinny, and men ignored me at the club. I had to sit there and watch the two of you meet men after men, and no one gave me the time of day. I wasn't about to humiliate myself ever again. I know you two are my best friends, but you two could be cold-blooded bitches at times."

Sylvia and Helen were shocked as they stared at me with their mouths opened. It was the truth, and the truth will set you free.

"So, tell us how you really feel?" Sylvia shouted.

"Let's not make a scene here," Madison pointed out. "I wouldn't want to embarrass you with your damn rich family."

"I'm not a cold-blooded bitch," Sylvia whispered.

"You are too," Madison shouted.

"She does have a point," Helen advised. "You're a Hispanic woman, and I'm not saying that Hispanics are cold-blooded, but sometimes the things you did to us was questionable. I remember the time that Madison and I were going to drop you from our friendship group. We didn't like your ways."

"Well, I'll be damn," Sylvia shouted. *She stood up.*

"I think I need to go to the ladies' room." *She grabbed her little purse and stormed off.*

Madison stared after her and then took another sip of her Matai. "I think I'm going to need two more of these," she pointed out. "I'm glad to have gotten that off my chest," Madison cried.

"Sylvia means well," Helen said.

"She told me often to lose weight, Helen. I used to hate her so much."

"I'm so sorry this had to happen," Helen stated. "We're BFFs."

"I love Sylvia, but her nasty remarks is something I won't take from her any longer. I've known her since we were eight, and I let her remarks pounce off my back, but this is it, Helen. Sylvia will no longer use me as her punching bag. The fact that she just insulted me because of her white, rich friends is proof that she's a cold-blooded bitch. She told me to get some class. I am a head paralegal at four law firms, and she thinks she' is better than you and me. I can't stand the bitch at times."

"Wow," Helen said.

"She didn't even appreciate you being a nurse."

"I know," Helen said, but I'm a head, nurse."

"Thank God, you didn't listen to her."

"I think Sylvia is having issues at home, but she's not leveling with us about them. I wondered if her husband cheated on her. We're not supposed to have secrets in this friendship, but I believe Sylvia broke the rules."

"Then she needs to talk to us and get it out in the opening instead of putting me down and letting her anger attack us. It's not fair, and I won't stand for it. I have backbone now, and if she attacks me again, Helen, there's going to be hell to pay, and I don't give a damn about this restaurant or her rich friends."

"Hello, ladies," the male voice replied.

Madison thought she was going to faint at the sound of his voice. Her eyes stared at him as his eyes focused on her.

"I'm Toxic Lyons and welcome to my restaurant. Helen, it's good to see you again, but who is this lovely lady I haven't had the pleasure of meeting? I'd never forgotten such a beautiful creature."

Madison blushed as she stared at Helen. What was happening to her?

Helen smiled. "Hi, Toxic, and it's good seeing you again. This is our best friend, Madison Johnson; we are visiting her for our monthly meeting. Sylvia is in the ladies' room. How is everything going with you?"

Everything is perfect," Toxic replied. "Madison, such a lovely name, for a lovely woman."

He reached for her hand and kissed it, and the heat that accosted her was mind-boggling. Madison thought she was going to faint or something. She immediately grabbed her hand. She was on fire by this man's touch, and she could tell by the smile on his face that he felt the vibes too. Madison had to find her voice. "It's nice meeting you, Mr. Lyons, and this restaurant is fabulous and then some. This is my first time here, and I'm very impressed." *She had more confidence, after all. Maybe losing weight was going to change her life for the better.*

Toxic smiled. "Would you like a tour?"

Madison stared at Helen, who smiled at her. "Yes, she would."

Lyons took her hand as she stood up like a robot.

She stared at Helen, who smiled at her, and told her with her eyes to have fun. Madison's body was on fire as he guided her to the elevators, with red carpeting as the doors opened and they walked in. He was still holding her hand, and the electricity was out of this world.

"You are the most beautiful woman in the world," he spoke. "I know you hear this all the time."

Madison was speechless like a damn teenager on her first date. The doors opened, and they were on the floor of McDonald's for heaven's sake. She was stunned. "You have a McDonalds?"

He laughed as he guided her off the elevator. "I do, and it's one of my favorite restaurants. I own this one, so by all means, help yourself to a big mac, or fish fillet. The fish fillets are my favorite."

Madison followed this handsome man as they walked into McDonald's and took a seat. One of his employers hurried over to the table. "Mr. Lyons, hello."

"Hi, Tommy, and how are you doing and the family?"

Tommy smiled. "I'm fine, sir, and yourself?"

"I'm terrific. This is Madison Johnson and Madison; this is Tommy Greene. He's one of my brightest employees. How is college going?"

"It's nice to meet you, Madison and college is wonderful."

"I'm glad to hear this. Madison, what would you like to eat?"

She was speechless and could kick herself.

Toxic smiled. "Get us two fish fillet meals and two apple pies."

"Yes, Mr. Lyons," Tommy said.

"I told you to call me Toxic."

Tommy blushed. "Yes, Toxic coming right up."

She finally found her voice. "I'm sorry."

"This building surprises everyone, and you're not the first nor the last. I hope the fish fillet is okay for you. I am so attracted to you, and this hasn't happened to me before. I'm astonished by your beauty and that beautiful green maxi dress."

She shook her head. "I'm beside words."

"I can't believe I haven't met you before."

Madison frowned. "I don't go out a lot."

"And what is your line of work, pretty Madison?"

She could not get used to anyone calling her pretty. It was unbelievable. "I'm a paralegal."

He laughed as they were sitting at a private table, and it was only the two of them away from the other guests. "I knew we had something in common. I'm an attorney."

"Sylvia told me," she snapped.

"Is something wrong?"

"Of course not," she lied. "I'm just new to this."

"I'm praying that you're not married or seeing someone."

"You don't waste time, Mr. Lyons."

"Toxic," he demanded. "Life is just too short."

He was so right about that. Their meal came from Tommy, and he smiled as Toxic reached into his expensive jeans and took out a bill. The bill was one hundred dollars, and handed it to Tommy. "Keep up the good work."

"Thank you so much, sir."

Tommy left, and Madison stared at Toxic. This man was full of surprises. "Let's eat and dig in. There's nothing like McDonald's fries."

Madison didn't want to get fat again, but she couldn't possibly turn this man down. Besides, she had missed her fish fillets. She reached for the fish fillet and took a long bite, closing her eyes. It was heaven and then some.

"You have a gorgeous smile."

"Your compliments are going to give me a big head."

He stared deep into her eyes. "I have a feeling that you need these compliments because you're not used to them. I will keep them coming because something is nagging at me with you, and I'm going to find out what it is. I have never had these feelings for another woman before, and the butterflies and ringing in my ears are very evident. Is the same thing happening to you?"

Madison could not deny the attraction or whatever was going on with them, and something was going on. "Yes," she whispered.

Toxic bit into his delicious fish fillet as it cured his appetite. "I'm glad we're on the same page. We also have a Popeye's, burger king, pizza hut, and Wendy's on this floor. My other siblings insisted that I get other restaurants besides McDonald's."

She chewed a few fries and then washed them down with her sweet tea. How did this man know that she wanted sweet tea? "This building is unbelievable."

"It's the dream I had in mind when I wanted to make this happen. I'm an architect by night when I'm not in court, and this was my dream. I employ a lot of people, and this is keeping them off the street. I'll continue the tour with you in a few minutes. I'm going to have a serious talk with Sylvia."

She took a long sip of my sweet tea. "Why?"

"How could she keep you from me?"

"It's not her fault, Toxic. I was fat and didn't go anywhere." *Why did I just burst that out? Now I would lose the man before I found out what could happen between the two of us.* "Wow," he said. "Do you have pictures?"

"A few to remind me never to get that fat again."

"I'd like to see them."

"No, you wouldn't," she cried.

"Yes, I would, Madison Johnson. I asked God to send me a woman who can love me and only me and unconditionally, and I have to abide by the same rules. I didn't ask him for size or color and looked at what he sent me?"

Of course, the tea went down the wrong pipe, and she began coughing like a fool. Toxic was beating her back, and the electricity was about to kill her. After a few minutes, the coughing stop and Toxic took his seat. "I'm sorry."

"I'm flattered, Toxic, but we're from two different worlds, and I don't want to date men right now."

"Are you into women?"

Madison frowned. "No, but men are dogs."

"Some of them, but not me. I see something or someone that I want, and then I go after it. This voice keeps telling me that you're the one, and I'm not going to disobey God."

Was he for real? This was indeed one of her romance novels.

"Give me your phone so that I can program my number into it, and then I want you to call me, and I'll have yours. This is no game, Madison Johnson. I will pursue you, and then you and I will get married and have plenty of gorgeous babies. I am up for the challenge, and soon you will hear the voice, telling me that you are the one. So, let's finish our meal, and get back to that tour, and then I'll get you back to your friends. I need your phone now."

She did not even remember grabbing her purse, but it was there, and she opened it and took out her iPhone. Madison handed it to him, and the electricity was apparent, and she could not deny it any longer. She watched as the handsome, white man programmed his number, and then handed her the phone, as the electricity was so deep that she dropped the phone on the floor under the table where they were sitting.

Toxic reached for it, and then laid it on the table, and Madison was grateful.

"Our connection is evident, Madison Johnson."

She found his number and called it, and he reached for his phone, which was a Samsung, and said hello. She smiled. "Hi."

Toxic disconnected the phone. "Now, let me see those pictures."

She did not want too, but she found the photos under the gallery and laid the phone on the table, moving it over to him. She did not want to risk the electricity killing them. He smiled and went through the ten pictures from her beginning when she was fat, to her weight. "You're still a gorgeous woman, and you weren't that fat."

She frowned. "I was fat and ugly, and men ignored me."

"They ignored you because you and I had to meet, and God had to keep them away. There is no way with that fabulous ass of yours and those great breasts that men don't want you. You chose not to have confidence in yourself, and we can spot a woman with no self-esteem in a minute. Most men take advantage of them, but you probably scared them away with that frown on your face, I'm witnessing now."

She laughed. "Right!"

"I have a lot of work to do with you, but there's a season for everything, Madison. I met many women, and two of them I thought would be my wife, but they showed their true colors, and thank God, I found out. I realize when I saw you sitting there with your friends, I knew God was on my side. You and I will be the power couple. I can feel it."

This man was crazy. "I don't think so."

"Do you not feel the sexual vibes between us, the electricity, the ringing in the ears, the butterflies," he snapped.

Madison saw the frown and anger on his face. "I guess you rich white men can have and take whomever you want without any consequences. I am not the one, Mr. Lyons. I'm ready to go back."

"After we finish our meal," he insisted.

"I'm not hungry any longer."

"But I am," he stated.

She rolled her eyes and stood up. "I think I can find my way back to my table, and thanks for lunch."

"If you don't sit down, Madison, I'm going to make a scene."

Was he for real? "Excuse me?"

"Not only will I make a scene, but I will remove you and your friends from this restaurant, and you'll never come here again. I don't mean to throw my power around, but you're about to let a good thing getaway because of your insecurities, but I'm not going to let it happen."

Madison was stunned by his words. She also knew Sylvia would kill her if she disrespected the family who paid her damn bills. She sat back down and took a long sip of her sweet tea, and then she finished off her fries and the rest of her fish fillet. She then reached for one of the Apple pies and ate that too. She always ate when she got angry or depressed, and this was not good. Who did Toxic Lyons think he was?

"Good girl," he said.

She rolled her eyes at the man as he finished his meal staring at her. She was going to teach Mr. Lyons a valuable lesson, and this time she was going to have the last word.

Madison Johnson

I t was an hour before she found herself sitting back with Helen and Sylvia, who had a frown on their faces.

"I will call you later on," Toxic stated.

Madison frowned at the man. "Whatever!"

He smiled. "Have a great day, ladies."

She stared after the wealthy goon—the nerve of him.

"What did you do to him?" Silvia shouted.

She rolled her eyes at Sylvia. Oh, you decided to come back to the table."

"What did Toxic want with you?"

"I hate you, Sylvia, and those are my facts."

"I can't stand the sight of you either at the moment," Sylvia said.

"Will you two cut it out?" Helen said. "Why didn't you two ever get along? I was always trying to break up arguments and fights with the two of you. What in the hell is going on?"

"Sylvia thinks she's better than me, "Madison pointed out.

"I never said this," Sylvia shouted.

"Your actions speak louder than words," she shouted.

"We're going to get kicked out of this restaurant if you two don't tone it down," Helen said.

"I'm ready to go," Sylvia said. "Don't sleep with Toxic."

"Do you want him for yourself, Sylvia? I can't believe you're jealous of used to be fat old me, but that's what it comes down too. I evaluated our relationship since the third grade, and you always put me down, but you pretended that everything is okay. I got your number."

Sylvia laughed at Madison. "You were fat as hell, so why would I be jealous of you. I got all the men in elementary and high school."

"Oh, my goodness," Madison cried. "You hate me because I went out with Dean Jones in high school for two years, and you had a crush on him. But he wanted my fat ass because he liked meat on my bones."

"What?" Helen exclaimed.

"This is why Sylvia hated me all these years."

"You're a lying ass," Sylvia snapped. "I hated Dean Jones."

"You always talked about him," Helen said. "But for some reason, he wouldn't give you the time of day. I think he said he did not date Hispanic chicks. Madison dated him for two years, and then she broke up with him when he cheated on her with Sandra Gaines. You were truly better off without Dean. He was a dog on four legs."

"You two are crazy," Sylvia said. "I was never in love with Dean Jones, or jealous of Madison Johnson. Let's move on."

"Not until you admit it," Madison snapped. "You wanted Dean Jones."

"I didn't," Sylvia snapped. "Let's change the subject."

"Then why did you always put me down, Sylvia? We are sisters since we are the only children in our families, and I would die for you, and I thought you would do the same thing for me. I'm beginning to think Helen would, but you'd let me die."

"You did talk about Madison's fat ass behind her back," Helen pointed out.

"But you never said it to my face too," Madison cited. "I love you, but not your ways."

Sylvia took a long sip of her drink. "Okay, I was in love with Dean. He knew it and used me. He slept with me and then dumped me for you, and I was livid with rage. I got pregnant with his child and told him about it. I was fifteen years old, and he laughed at me and told me that it wasn't his baby. I had to get an abortion."

Helen and I stared in shock at Sylvia.

"How could you keep this from us?" Helen exploded.

"I never knew," Madison cried. "Dean never said a word."

"You never told us that you slept with Dean?" Helen said. "I guess we had secrets after all. I thought we were best friends, but I'm beginning to see that I lived a lie the entire time since the third grade. I'm deeply hurt."

"So am I," Madison replied.

Sylvia stared at the two of us. "I'm sorry, but I was humiliated, and I couldn't tell anyone. I felt so lonely and almost took a bottle of my mother's pills. I was so in love with Dean, and he wanted you. I just couldn't understand it."

"Dean was a dog, and I'm glad you didn't take your life over him," Madison confirmed. "Do you know how that would have made Helen and me feel? We love you, and the fact that you would be dead, probably burning in hell for taking your own life, would have killed us here on earth. People that commit suicide are so selfish. They do not give a damn about the people that they leave behind. It's a sin."

"I agree," Helen said. "What's going on with your marriage now, and don't you dare lie to us."

"My husband is cheating on me with a man."

Madison was stunned as hell as she stared at Sylvia, and then Helen and Madison exchanged glances. "Are you serious?" Madison asked.

"I'm not joking here," Sylvia cried as the tears fell. "My husband was working late, but I just had this feeling. George kept calling looking for him, and I told George he was not home. I could not stop thinking about George, so I took a ride over to his house, and my husband's car was parked over there. I was going home and kicked myself for being stupid, but I heard the laughter at the pool. I knew George lived by himself, so I slowly walked over to the pool without being seen. I was having heart palpations because my sixth sense was telling me that something was wrong. George had many trees, so I hid in front of two and watched them in the pool. Girls, they were naked as sin and making love in his pool. They kissed for a few minutes, and then George turned my husband onto his stomach and put that big dick inside of his booty, and I wanted to scream. My husband was enjoying it and screaming all over the place with his moans of passion."

"I couldn't move as they continued to make love, and then when George dropped from pleasure, my husband turned George around and put his penis inside of his booty where he put inside of me, and the game of lovemaking went on until they were both spent. Did they stop to catch their breaths? They got out of the water and laid right down there on the side of the pool. George kissed my husband for a very long time as their tongues mated. I took pictures of them with my cell phone. They were so into the lovemaking that if I made a noise, they would not have heard me. My husband had his tongue inside of me like that, and now he was kissing a man. I threw up in the bushes, and they still didn't hear me."

"I couldn't move, girls. I just stayed there hoping they would retire to the house, but they continued to make love for hours as if they could not get enough of each other. I made a video of the two of them, and they didn't even know it." *Sylvia reached for her phone and found the video and then handed it to Madison. She watched some of it in shock, as Sylvia's husband was sucking George's dick and having a grand time. I gave it to Helen, and she watched with amazement on her face and then handed it back to Sylvia.*

"How long has this been going on?" Helen asked. "Did you confront him?"

"It's been a month now, and no," Sylvia cried.

"Are you sleeping with him?" Madison asked.

"No," Sylvia shouted. "Don't be stupid. I took an AIDS test, though, and it was negative. I have to retake it in six months. I wanted to kill my husband, and I thought about it with the gun I have hidden for safe protection. He violated our marriage with a man I thought was our friend. I never suspected that my husband would cheat on me with a man. He always likes to make love in my booty, but I just thought he wanted to experience the different ways. I'm so angry."

"What are you going to do?" Helen asked.

"I don't know, but I can't be with him. My husband wants a man."

"George is a very handsome man," Helen said.

"George is fucking gay," Sylvia said. "We both knew this, but I never thought that my husband would be sleeping with a gay man. Didn't he give a damn about his two children or me? George has been sleeping with men for a long time and could have AIDS and don't even know it. My husband slept with me, and then George."

"This is unbelievable," Madison cried.

"That's the truth," Helen said. "We're so sorry, but you should have told us. Your husband was probably on the down-low when he married you, denying his feelings for George."

"You think," Sylvia cried. "I'm going home."

"How do you stay with him or even look at him?" Madison asked.

"I love him so very much, and I don't want to divorce him," Sylvia cried.

"He's sleeping with men and damaging your health in the process," Helen cried. "You need to tell him that his secret is out, and he needs to make a choice, it's George or me."

"He's going to choose George over his children and me. You can see the way he's enjoying himself when he's making love to a man. We never had that passion. I love him."

Madison shook her head. "I don't understand how you can still love him."

"When you fall in love, you will understand," Sylvia pointed out.

Madison thought about Toxic for some reason. "I am never falling in love."

Helen laughed. "I think Madison may have just found her one true love."

"With?" Sylvia asked.

"Toxic Lyons," Helen sang. "The two of them have the chemistry, and I noticed it, and I'm sure others did too. He took our girl here on tour, and what else happened?"

"We went to McDonald's and ate, so I'm not hungry anymore," I stated. "We had a tour of the place, and then I came back to our table. Mr. Lyons thinks he owns people, and I told him to take a hike."

Sylvia laughed. "I hope it works out for you two."

"Really," she said.

"I love you, Madison. I told you to lose weight for your good because it made you miserable and unhappy. What kind of friends would we be if we didn't tell you about your weight?"

"You have a funny way of showing your love," Madison snapped.

"I have so much going on in my life. I took my frustrations out on you. Toxic is a good man, and if I knew he'd fall for you, I would have set it up a long time ago."

Madison shook my head. "A man like Toxic wouldn't be giving me the time of day when I was fat, so it worked out the way it was supposed to work out. I know he's not going to call me, and I'm not going to let myself think anything about it. I do feel the butterflies, and the ringing in my ears and the electricity when our hands touched was toxic, excuse the pun," she laughed.

Helen and Sylvia laughed. "Toxic is a very successful man because when he sees something or someone, he goes after it, and something tells me that you're about to see how the rich works."

Madison frowned. "I can handle Toxic Lyons."

Sylvia laughed. "I doubt that very much, but good luck with that."

"I agree," Helen said. "You two are only just beginning."

Madison stared at the two of them and frowned again. "I need another Matai for the road."

"I need a vodka tonic," Sylvia said. "I don't know what I'm going to do about my husband. He's going to figure out something is wrong when I stop sleeping with him."

"You need to level with him and see what he wants to do," Helen said. "If he wants to be gay, then you have to let him go. I can't see you staying with him, and he's sleeping with a man."

"Me either," Madison cried. "Let him go."

"How can you say that to me," Sylvia cried. "He's my husband, and I love him. I'm so relieved we don't have any children. This is going to ruin our marriage and my existence."

"Your husband is going to continue to live like this until George gives him an ultimatum or something," Helen said. "He's trying not to hurt you, but he is when he's sleeping with a man who supposedly was his best friend. I'm still in shock."

"I read about this in novels, but not in real life," Madison cried.

"Reality is a bitch," Sylvia snapped.

The waitress brought their drinks, and everyone drained their glasses because it was a lot to handle in one day. It was another hour later when they all stood up, ready to go their separate ways.

"How long are you two in Chicago?" Madison asked.

"We're going back tomorrow," Sylvia said. "I have a fashion show coming up. It was good to see you and spend some time in Chicago. You are beautiful and sexy now, but you were always sexy to me."

"Even when I was fat," Madison cried.

"You had that ass and those breasts going on," Helen laughed.

"I agree," Sylvia said. "If you used them to your advantage, men would have been knocking down your door. What men don't like a big ass and big breasts."

Madison frowned, which she was often doing. "A lot of men, now look at the suckers staring at me."

Sylvia and Helen smiled as they stared around the restaurant. "I think all three of us can find a man right here and now if we wanted too," Sylvia cried. "Maybe I need to go out there and cheat and see how it feels."

"Are you going to sleep with a woman?" Madison asked.

Sylvia frowned. "No, but another man is just as damaging."

Helen shook her head. "Don't play those games because they're going to backfire on you. Your husband is playing a dangerous game, and if you had not found out, you would never know, but they forget about a woman's instinct. If he thought his secret would die when he went to his grave, he didn't know a woman."

"I agree with Helen," Madison cried.

"Let's just get out of here," Sylvia cried. "I don't know what I'm going to do, but I will keep the two of you posted this time since you know the truth. And as for you, Madison, if Toxic calls, and I'm sure he will, you need to give him the time of day. Yes he's a white man, and he has money, but so do you, so you don't need his money."

"I don't have nearly as much as he does," Madison replied.

"But he's not looking for a woman who wants him as a sugar daddy," Sylvia stated. "Be truthful with him, and the two of you will last a lifetime. Don't make a mistake in your marriage as my husband is doing to me. Toxic is a good man, and he gives back to the community here in Chicago and New York City. I don't believe you'll find a better man."

"Right on, sister," Helen said.

The three of them embraced and then left the restaurant. Madison searched around for Toxic, but he was not in sight. She then heard a vibration on her iPhone and reached for it as they walked outside the Lyon's restaurant. She smiled for some reason.

"I will call you in a few hours," Toxic text.

Madison did not reply as she looked at Helen and Sylvia. "Do I get a ride home, or should I call Uber?"

"I'll take you home," Sylvia said. "I'm not in a rush to go back to New York or my hotel."

"I'll see you both later," Helen said.

I got into Sylvia's blue range rover and buckled my seatback. This car was costly, and Sylvia was rich in her own right, and might just be up there with Toxic Lyons. She did not have to put up with a cheating husband. She could take him to the cleaners and move on with her life. Of course, that was easier said than done. I stared out the window. It was June and a lovely summer day. I could not stop thinking about Toxic as Sylvia discussed her marriage and what she would do about it.

Toxic Lyons

───────── ❦ ─────────

Tumor smiled at his brother as they went over the accounting books to make sure the numbers added up. Tumor was a pro in accounting, so Toxic was glad he was available. His mind was on the gorgeous black female, Madison Johnson. She was fine and then some, and he wanted to rock her world. What was happening to him? He met women every day for a booty call, and they were willing to give him anything he wanted as long as he paid their rent or took them on a shopping spree. Why did women want to sell their bodies for money that they didn't earn, but believed they had a right to it? He wasn't born with a silver spoon in his mouth, and his riches were made with hard and dedicated work, as his mother and father instilled in them. They didn't suffer from hard work.

"Hello, Toxic," Tumor sang.

He focused on his handsome older brother, who was thirty-five and very successful in the real estate business. He was also good at math. "How are the books? Is anyone cheating me?"

"The books are fine, but what's going on with you? Does it have something to do with the fine woman you gave a tour too? Now, if I were not married, I'd be all over the beauty, and she's fine as silk."

Toxic frowned. "Just remember you have a fine as silk wife."

"I think my brother has finally found the woman of his dreams."

"I don't know, Tumor. Ms. Madison has so many demons I do not know if she will be worth the effort. I know she does not give a damn about my money, and maybe me, either."

"You've finally found your match."

"Maybe and maybe not, but the butterflies and the ringing, and the voice told me that she was the one."

"Wow!" Tumor said. "Then you have no choice in the matter. Ms. Madison is black, so we have to deal with that, but our sister has a black husband, so we're just keeping this in the family. Love doesn't have age, size, or color."

"Ms. Madison used to be fat."

"I couldn't tell," Tumor laughed. "You know my wife is fat."

"Your wife is healthy and fine as wine."

"And I love that ass on hers. When she lost weight, I made sure she gained it back. I love a woman with meat on their bones. Now Ms. Madison is fine, but she is too skinny for me. I bet you she was beautiful overweight but didn't know it."

Toxic shook his head. "I'm wondering if you were adopted or something because you're the oldest brother, and you're crazy as hell."

Tumor laughed. "I love you too. Now the books are in order, so I have to take care of some houses to sell, and then I'm going to take my beautiful wife out of town for her birthday. She wants to go to Las Vegas."

"That's not a bad idea," Toxic exclaimed. "I should take Ms. Madison to sin city and maybe get her to loosen up."

"You just met the woman, and why would she go out of town with a man she just met?"

"How many women have I taken out of town, brother dear? Are you getting old or what? Women give it up on the first date."

"I have a feeling that Ms. Madison is in a class all by herself. She's nothing like those bimbos you dated in the past, and you need to recognize, or you're going to lose her."

"I just want to spend some quality time with her."

"Take it slow and not rush into anything."

"You're right, and I should listen. I just want to be with her."

"I know, and I'm sure she's thinking about you too. Tricia wouldn't give me the time of day because of her weight, but when I proposed to her in front of our family and friends, she realized that she was the woman I wanted. Women like Tricia and Madison, you have to handle as fragile, and with special care."

Toxic laughed. "Madison doesn't fall into the fragile category. She'd cut my balls off in a heartbeat and stuff them down my throat, and wouldn't blink an eye. She's a feisty woman."

"And you know this by staring at the woman."

"We did talk at McDonald's, and she probably thought I was wasting her time. I'm just for a booty call. I bet you one hundred dollars that she doesn't think I'm going to call her."

"She's a challenge, and you can handle it."

"I hope so," he said. "I'm ready to settle down with a real woman."

"I wish you the best with Ms. Madison. I can't wait to meet her."

Toxic laughed. "I'm glad you've married my handsome brother."

Tumor touched his goatee and did a twirl around the room. "I'm very handsome, and my beautiful wife tells me this all the time. Sometimes, her jealousy gets on my nerves. We went to a party, and my wife was mingling, and women threw themselves at me. When my wife walked over to me and introduced herself as my wife, you should have seen the shock on the women's faces as they stared her up and down."

"Then she went into the ladies' room and was in a stall when two women came in and started talking about me. She gave me word for word what they said."

"How in the hell would a fine man as Tumor Lyons marry a fat woman?" the first woman said. "Is he double-blind, or does he need bifocals?"

"She's not that fat, "the second woman said. "She has a big ass, and you know Tumor has always been an ass man."

"He could sleep with the bitch, and then marry someone as petite as I am. I can't believe this. I love him."

"You need to move on," the second woman said. "He's happily married with children, and he's not about to leave his wife for your whorish ass. We're good enough to sleep with, but no one wants to marry us."

"Talk and speak for yourself," the first woman stated. "I'm a good catch for a man, and I'm going to get Tumor in bed and send his wife the photos, and then she'll run like a fat rabbit. How does she think she's going to keep a man like Tumor? I bet he's cheating with a skinny woman."

"Tumor is in love, girl."

"Fuck that," the first woman said. "I love him."

"You love his name and money," the second woman said. "When was the last time you had a real job? You go from men to men as long as they're paying you money, and you give them that body of yours."

"And why are you judging me? Why should I work when men are dogs, and all they need is a sexy woman with a vagina to get it on? I am giving men exactly what they cheat on their wives with, and Tumor is no exception to the rule. He is a man, and men are dense as hell. Let me show up naked one day and show the bastard what he's been missing. I bet you he can't throw that fat cow around or pick her up."

"You are so stupid, Cat."

"You won't be saying that when I have all the money, and you'll be begging for some of it," Cat stated.

"If that day comes, I'll be happy for you,"

"Shut up, Sheila. I'm going to find me another sugar daddy until I can get Tumor on my page. I saw this old white man staring at me. He probably wants me to suck his nasty dick, and then give me plenty of money. I need to pay for this high ass condo I'm living in."

"Get a job, Cat?"

"Right," Cat said. "You're stupid as hell."

"My wife never came out of the stall, but she was distraught, Toxic, and asked me for a divorce. I told her it would never happen. I love my wife, and women like Cat and Sheila are great to sleep with, but my whoring days were over when I met my wife."

"Tricia is a fortunate woman, and please don't hurt her. I like my sister-in-law. I know you're a good man."

"I'm in love, and love conquers all."

"I'm waiting to find love."

"And her name might just be Ms. Madison."

Toxic laughed, and then he frowned. "It might be, and it might not, but I hope so. I'm tired of dealing with a woman who is out for what they can get like Cat and Sheila, for instance."

"You asked God for the right woman, and you have to believe that Ms. Madison is it. So now you need to spend your time courting her until she falls madly in love with you, and then she's putty in your hands."

Toxic smiled. "Okay!"

Madison Johnson

M onday and back to work as Madison sat in her office in her condo in Lombard, Illinois. She loved working at home and sitting in her office and working on five briefs. She was reading and researching a case, and then she would write her brief.

Madison was a great legal writer, and she had a waiting list of clients. Imagine doing something you loved doing. She remembered the times when she hated to go to work. She could not stand the prejudice people and their attitudes. Now, she loved her job and was happy as ever. She was only thirty and did not have a nine to five job. What a blessing indeed.

She focused on the case she was working on, and she could relate to it. *Jasmine Jones was suing her boss, Max Roku, for firing her from a job she had been on for fifteen years. Of course, Jasmine Jones was a full-figured woman, and she loved her curves. Max had no problem at first, but when he met other skinny women throwing themselves at the handsome, thirty-two-year-old attorney, he got tired of seeing his assistant fat ass and made a move. The bimbo he had working for him was a black female, and she was a size zero with no ass or breasts, but Max was all over her. Jasmine was furious, and she was going to make this bastard pay for firing her.*

Madison focused on the case, researching the facts. She had to make sure that Jasmine won this case. She told her boss, Fink Stick, to make sure he won this case. She used to be fat, and she could relate to Jasmine's problems. She was online, so any of her bosses would be able to IM her. Madison heard a beep on her computer screen and smiled. It was one of her boss' Fink Stick. He was a very nice white man, fifty years old, and always flirting with her. Fink had lost his wife three years ago to breast cancer, and he was not in the mood for another wife. He truly loved and missed his deceased wife. Madison missed her too. Yolanda Stick was a gorgeous former model and the love of Fink's life. When she started working for Fink three years ago, he endorsed her fat ass, and he is truly a friend and boss who had her back. She started typing to Fink on the IM app. "Hi, and how are you doing?"

"I'm good, Madison, and yourself?"

She started work at 6:00 in the morning and worked until 3:00 in the afternoon. After three, she was off the working clock. Sometimes, she worked overtime hours, but most of the time, she could clock out at 3:00.

"I'm blessed. What can I do for you?"

"You can let me take you to Las Vegas, and we can have some fun. I'm eager to visit sin city, and, of course, it's on business, and I want you to go with me. We can tackle the private plane."

Madison was stunned. "I'd love to go, Fink, but only for business."

"I'm disappointed, Madison."

"Fink, you're a great boss, but the two of us are employee and employer. I love you like a father. Please stop flirting with me. I've never been to Las Vegas, so I'd love to go with you at different hotels and business only."

"I did flirt with you when you were fat, but you ignored me too. Do not get revenge on the men who didn't like you when you were fat. I saw the inside of your personality, and knew you'd be a great asset to my private law practice."

She smiled. "I love working for you, Fink."

"I'm just teasing you, honey. I know you're going to find the man of your dreams and live happily ever after. I can see it now."

She smiled and thought about Toxic Lyons. Was he the man of her dreams? She could not stop thinking about the handsome white man, with the lovely green eyes. Mr. Lyons was attracted to her, and she was shocked. He could have any woman that he wanted, and he chose Madison Johnson. He said that she was the one.

"Are you there, Madison?"

She shook her head and focused back on her mac computer. "I'm here, and the trip is fine if it's business only. Do you ever see Rita? She's so in love with you, but men are dense as hell."

Fink laughed. "Rita, the secretary?"

"Yes, Fink, she loves you, and the two of you are close to age too. She is forty-five years old, and very attractive, and your type. Why don't you give her the time of day?"

"I never thought about Rita, but she's a very pretty woman. What's her story?"

Madison smiled. "She's divorced and has a grown daughter. When she is not working at your law firm, she's focused on her hobby which is knitting and crocheting. I brought some lovely things from her. She's a very talented woman."

"I might just give her a call," he stated.

Madison smiled again. "I think the two of you will make lovely music together." *She could see the two of them getting married and living the rest of their lives in wedding bliss.*

"You're too romantic for me, Madison. I need to find you a man."

She thought about Toxic Lyons. "Fink, do you know a Toxic Lyons."

Fink laughed. "Who does not know the Lyons, honey? He is a very rich man, and so is his family. Tumor, his brother is into real estate, and their three siblings are very successful woman. Tumor and Toxic are my clients. I handle all of their business transactions. I'm their personal attorney."

Madison had never been so stunned in her life. "Are you kidding me, Fink?"

"No. How do you know Toxic Lyons?"

"I don't really know him that well. I met him when Sylvia, Helen and I had lunch at the Lyons restaurant. Our eyes met, and the electricity was unbelievable. I've never met anyone like him before, but I'm not educated in the mechanics of men."

"Wow," Fink said. "I love that family, and Toxic is a very handsome and debonair man. He is a successful attorney and he designs buildings when he is not working in law. Are the two of you talking?"

"I don't know, Fink. He is so debonair, and I'm so new to relationships. I see Toxic with fashion models, and glamorous women. I am not his type, and I do not want to get involved with someone for sex, or just for fun. I'm a serious kind of woman, and I want a real relationship that can permanently lead to marriage and children."

"If he is attracted to you, Madison, then he's no fool. You are a gorgeous woman, fat and skinny and I told you this often. Go with the flow and see where this is going or you are going to regret it? Toxic does not play games. He is tired of the women who pretend to be in love with him for his name and money. He's got serious vibes with you."

"I'm so afraid," she cried.

"Be yourself and never be someone else. If Toxic is the man for you, then no one or anything will stop the two of you from falling in love and getting together. I'm cheering for the two of you."

Madison frowned. "I'll see, Fink. I don't know if he's going to call or not. I doubt it, so let's change the subject, but I'll keep you posted if he does call. What is happening with this Las Vegas trip and when? I'll love to go with you."

"A friend of mine, Monty Spray is in trouble," Fink cited. "He's accused of killing his girlfriend, Model, Stable Jones. I've known Monty for years, and he'd never hurt anyone."

She was stunned. "I read about the case, Fink. Stable Jones was a model and actress, and she was a bitch to most people. I read that she used and abused people and did not give a damn."

"I know, but Monty fell in love with her, and when he caught her in bed with another man, he almost lost it, but he left, running out of her condo, and a few hours later, someone stabbed her to death about fifteen times. Monty was the last person who saw her alive, and the man she was banging, but he's nowhere to be found."

"I'm very interested in going with you, and maybe Rita can join us to do some of the secretarial work, and the two of you can get acquainted. You can hire someone from a temporary agency to watch the desk until we get back."

Fink laughed. "I like you so much, Madison."

Madison laughed. "I like me now too. When are we going to sin city?"

"It's Monday now, so not until next week."

"I'm looking forward to it."

"Also, I need you to work exclusively for this law firm only. I will double your salary to make up for the other three firms, but you need to give your notice. I have plenty of work to keep you busy for the rest of your life, Madison. I really want you to go to law school, and then you can join me as one of my partners in my firm. I'd love to have you aboard."

Madison thought about law school often. "I don't know about law school yet, but I'll resign from the other jobs. I love working for you Fink, and your law firm is the most prestigious and highly recommended law firm in Chicago and the world. I'm honored to be working with you, and able to work at home."

"I had no choice, Madison. After you lost the weight none of my men employees could get any work done. With your body, hair and face, the men were having hard-ons left and right, but I do want you at the Friday's meetings."

She laughed, imagine men having hard-ons because of her now skinny ass. "I'll be there, and what's going on with Jasmine's case. I sent you her files, and I want her to win this case. Her boss is an ass."

"Let's not get personal on these cases, Madison. We are going to court in two weeks, so get me the brief today and we are going over it on Friday when you come into the office. Also, I need everything you can find on this Max Roku. I have my private investigator working on the case, but I know you can probably find more information too."

Madison reached for her yellow legal pad and wrote down Max's name to do more research on the bastard. "I'm on it Fink. Is there anything else?" *I truly love my job, and I owe it all to God.*

"Yes, I emailed you five more cases, and read them, and give me your opinion and facts on the case in your brief form. How is your Masters in paralegal science goimg?"

"Very good, Fink. I am done with Lesson 1 and waiting for lesson 2 to begin. I can't believe I'm going to get my Masters in paralegal science, having had my associate and bachelor's degree in paralegal science."

"Sounds like law school to me."

"I owe you so much for paying my tuition, Fink."

"I flirt with you, but you're like a daughter to me."

"Fink, you're only twenty-five years older than me."

"I know, but you're still a daughter to me. I love you, Madison."

She was touched by this white man's words. "I love you too."

"Now get back to work, and IM me if you have any questions."

"I will and think about Rita. Now you can look at her in a different light."

"The file folders should be coming to your home in a few minutes. Read the cases efficiently and then give me a separate brief on all five of them. I want this done as soon as possible."

"I'm on it, boss, and thanks."

"Thank you."

Madison ended the call and focused back on her notes for Jasmine Jones. This case was the most important case to her, and she was going to make sure that Fink won it. She had to fight for full-figured women, even though she was skinny now, but she still remembered the pain and suffering being fat. It was definitely a crusade for her.

The ringing of her doorbell alerted her. Madison left her office, and hurried downstairs to the door. She looked through the peep hole and smiled. It was her favorite UPS driver. She opened the door. "Hi Nate, and how are you today?"

He was speechless staring at her. Madison loved working at home, and not having to get dressed. She was wearing a polo shirt, green, and some green shorts, not too high or long, and green flat sandals. "Hello, Nate."

He cleared his throat. "I'm sorry, but you look so fine now."

"So, when you delivered packages to me before, you would drop them off, I will sign for them, and then you'd move on. Now I am fine as hell now. I can't stand men like you, Nate." *She snatched the package out of his hand, and then slammed the door. Who did he think he was? She was skinny and half naked, so Nate wanted her phone number. Men could literally kiss her skinny ass. Madison walked back to her office, and sat down, breathing like a mad woman. She took a few deep breaths, and then focused on the package. She removed five file folders, blue, green, beige, red, and orange, and glanced at each of them as she focused on not being so angry. When she got to the green one, she was stunned. What was Fink doing investigating Ice, a mob figured and the most dangerous man in the world? Was he insane? She put the other folders down on her desk, and began reading about Ice. His wife was dead, and Ice was accused of killing her after finding her in bed with another man. Was she stupid or what? You do not get caught sleeping around. She was sure her lover was dead too with all of his body parts missing. He was yet to be found, but Madison was positive the sharks had him for lunch or dinner. She shook her head as she continued to read the file. There was no way Fink could be interested in Ice and nailing him for the murder of his wife, and so many other people? This was crazy as hell.*

Madison's apple watch vibrated as she stared at it, and then smiled. It was Toxic Lyons. She was stunned as the file she was reading fell to the floor, and she just stared at the watch, vibrating his call.

Madison finally pushed the green button on the apple watch. "Hello!"

Toxic Lyons

"**H**ello, beautiful lady," Toxic smiled. "How are you doing this lovely Monday morning? I took a chance to see if you are up this early. It's only seven o'clock in the morning. I'm an early riser, and I had a feeling that you'd be one too."

Madison smiled all over herself. "I start work at 6:00 in the morning until 3:00."

"So, what's the perks of working at home?"

"Do you have time?" she laughed.

Your voice and your laughter are music to my ears."

She shook her head. "What can I do for you, Mr. Lyons?"

"I'd like to come over and bring you breakfast."

Madison was stunned. Was he for real? She could not find her voice.

"I know you don't know me, and inviting myself to your house is inappropriate, but Madison I'm not about to play games with you. I am interested in getting to know you, and I have a feeling we are on the same page. Let's start with breakfast. What are you favorites?"

"I don't eat a lot of breakfast, Toxic."

"I love the way you say my name."

She smiled. Was he for real?

"You don't have to starve yourself because you're skinny now. I am going to bring pancakes, bacon and lots of sweet tea. I will be there in twenty minutes. Please let me in."

"How do you know where I live?"

"I have skills, Ms. Madison."

She frowned. "Okay, Mr. Lyons, I will give you breakfast."

He laughed. "Thank God."

I laughed at him.

"I'll see you in twenty minutes."

"Okay," she said.

Madison ended the call and ran into her bathroom to look at herself in the mirror. Should she put on a dress or a pair of jeans? She was wearing shorts, and she didn't want to give Toxic the wrong ideal. But it was a hot day, and she was in her house. Why should she change? She did add some lipstick and blush to her lips and face, and then made sure her hair was hanging down her back instead of up in a ponytail. Madison had white girl's hair because of her father's family, of course. All she had to do was wash and blow dry, and her hair was perfect, adding rollers to it for curls. She never needed a perm. Her hair was straight as a long line in a supermarket. She had pretty, long legs now, and she was going to show them off. Madison remembered when her legs were so fat, with fat pockets, she had to hide them under long skirts. Now her legs are too skinny for heaven sakes. She shook her head as she continued to stare at herself in the mirror. Even her ass was not as huge as it used to be. At least she could look in the mirror without frowning. She avoided all mirrors when she was fat. She smiled, and then removed herself from the mirror. It was a nice warm day, so they could eat on the balcony. Madison hurried to the balcony to make sure everything was in place, and then she ran to the kitchen to get some place mats, and two glasses. Her place mats were green, as this being her favorite color. She grabbed her fabulous cleaner and began to shine the glass on the little patio table with four chairs and made sure it looked great. She was so nervous and felt the anxiety and her palms sweating. What was wrong with her? He was just a man. No, he was Toxic Lyons, and he was more than a man. Relax, girl, she told herself. He wasn't Jesus Christ, so you have nothing to worry about. She was definitely going to be herself.

Twenty minutes on the dot, her doorbell rang. Was Toxic Lyons ever late? She took a deep breath, and then hurried downstairs to the front door. Madison loved her four-bedroom condo, and the spiral stairs, which gave her exercise, running up and down the stairs. Her office, and another bedroom was on the first level, and there were two other bedrooms, including her master bedroom with a bathroom in her bedroom, and another one down the hall on the second level. There was also a bathroom downstairs on the first level. Madison had a large kitchen, with an island, she loved, and a large dining room. She also loved her balcony, especially in the summer months in Chicago. She'd sit out on the balcony and read a mystery or one of her romance novels for hours contented as ever. Her favorite authors were Marie Force, James Patterson, and the Kimani romance series from Harlequin.

Sylvia and Helen was always teasing her about having such a large condo, but it was all hers and she was blessed. Madison took another deep breath and opened the door. The sight of Toxic Lyons in black shorts, and a red polo shirt made her come in her panties. She felt the wetness overtake her. She was hot for this handsome, white man, and there was nothing she could do about it. He was fine as wine and then some.

"Hi," he smiled. "You look sexy as hell."

Madison blushed. "You don't look so bad yourself. Do you need help with the bags?"

"I got this, just show me the way."

She closed the door getting a whiff of his cologne, and it smelled good. She had a feeling that she was going to remember his cologne for the duration of her life. Get a grip, she thought to herself. You're not a teenager on your first date. "I thought we could eat on the balcony."

"Sounds like a plan to me."

Madison led Toxic to the balcony knowing he was staring at her ass as they walked to the balcony. She pushed opened the balcony door and Toxic set the many white bags of delicious food on the table.

"I see you set the table, and your place is nice."

"I'll give you the tour, but let's eat since everything smells so good."

He smiled, lighting up her world and then some.

Toxic filled their plates with two pancakes, three strips of bacon, and two toast, with a large cup of sweet tea for the two of them. They sat down across from each other. "Let's say grace," Madison cited.

Toxic grabbed her hand and held it as the electricity bombard them, but he held on tight as he closed his eyes. "Thank you, God for this meal, and the company, and let this moment last forever and ever. Amen!"

She blushed and smiled. "Amen!" *She was glad to release her hands because it felt like they were burning or something by the electricity. What was going on with her and Toxic Lyons? This has never happened to her before. Even when she lost weight, and went out with a few men, she never felt the electricity so strong before. What was literally happening to her?*

"Penny for your thoughts, pretty Madison."

Madison blushed. "This is nice."

"So eat, and don't waste my money."

She reached for the bacon and closed her eyes when she took a long bite. It had been centuries it seemed since she had bacon. She opened her eyes, and Toxic was smiling, and staring at her. "I'm sorry, but I love bacon."

"I know, which is why I bought plenty of it?"

"Thank you."

"So, tell me about yourself, Ms. Madison."

She smiled, focusing on her food. She was hungry as sin. "I'm thirty years old, a paralegal, in school for my Masters in paralegal science, and I love my job and my life now."

"This is a large size condo for one person."

"It's a four-bedroom condo, and your brother Tumor was the agent on the sale. I never met him personally, but his assistant gave me a nice deal. I always wanted a two-bedroom, but I saw this one, and it called to me. I've never regretted it."

"You're a very happy person."

"I'm blessed. I had such a depressed life, and it's good to have God in my life, and the fact that he never gave up on me. I'm eternally grateful for my blessings. I never literally have to worry about money again. It's a great feeling, Toxic. I remembered when I had no money and did not know how I was going to get to work. I had to rely on payday loans, and it was awful."

"It's great being able not to worry about money," he agreed.

"And not working at jobs you hated. I dreamed of working at home, and it took a long time, but God is good."

"You work for Fink," he stated.

"I do, and he's like a father to me."

"Fink is an old flirt."

"He is, but he knows not to flirt with me. I'm a serious free-lance paralegal, and I love my job, and wouldn't do anything to jeopardize it. Tell me about you, Mr. Lyons."

"I love when you say, Toxic,"

"Toxic," she sang.

He closed his eyes, and then opened them. "You light up my world."

Madison frowned.

"Please don't let the past dictate your life."

"That's easier said than done, Toxic. A man like you could have any woman he wants, but you're sitting here in my condo with me. If this is a dream, I never want to wake up."

"I'm honored to be sitting here with you, Ms. Madison. You can have any man you want, including Fink, and you're sitting here with the likes of me. I'm flattered."

Madison hysterically laughed.

Toxic laughed with her.

For the next hour they focused on food and talked about her job, and then they focused on everything about Toxic Lyons, and his siblings. Madison was having the time of her life.

She cleared off the table, and stared at Toxic. "Thanks for breakfast. It was very nice, and I had a great time."

"I still want that tour."

"Let's go," she cited.

After the tour, they ended up in her living room as she sat down on the sofa, and Toxic sat down next to her. His cologne was driving her insane.

"I want to kiss you so badly," he confessed.

She was nervous, but she wanted his lips on hers.

"Can I devour your lips, Ms. Madison?"

She nodded as she felt the ache between her legs. She knew her panties were soaking wet. She actually wanted to remove them with her shorts, and show him what she was working with.

But instead, he moved toward her and then their lips met, and forget about the firecrackers for the 4th of July. She was on fire as their lips played with each other, and the electricity was apparent. Finally she opened her mouth, and their tongues clicked, and then tasted each other. They both tasted like sweet tea, and it was wonderful. Toxic's tongue was literally down her throat, and she loved every minute of it.

She never wanted the kiss to stop as their tongues continued to mate.

Toxic was on fire as he tasted the sweet essence of Madison Johnson. She smelled so sweet, and he never wanted to stop kissing this gorgeous woman. Where had she been his entire life?

Madison broke the kiss as their eyes met, and she touched her lips. Toxic knew he wanted to find her bedroom and make passionate love to this woman. His penis was hard as a rock and he knew she felt it too. He did not want to rush or scare Madison off. She had a lot of deep issues to overcome. Toxic knew he had no choice.

"I should leave," he stated.

"Of course," Madison said. "Thanks again for breakfast."

"I want us to be exclusive, Madison. You're my girlfriend."

She was speechless.

"Did you hear me? You are off limits, so if the men continue to flirt with you, ignore them, or tell them that you have a boyfriend and his name is Toxic Lyons, and they will truly leave you alone. If they don't let me know and I'll take care of them. I have friends in higher places," he laughed.

She wondered as she stared at him. "Do you know Ice?'

Toxic frowned. "What?"

Madison shook her head. What was she thinking? She could not discuss her cases with this man or throw out names. She was losing her mind. There was a conflict of interest since Fink was his attorney, and she was breaching her paralegal contract. This course of action could have serious consequences for her paralegal career, and she was not about to compromise her ethics for anyone.

"What do you know about Ice?"

"I just read about him, Toxic. He is all over the news and the papers. Why are you getting so uptight about him? He's not a very nice man, and he belongs behind bars for the duration of his life."

"He needs to be dead," Toxic snapped.

Madison was stunned. "Why?"

"Please tell me that Fink isn't doing business with this man. He will cut you up and throw your body parts in the river for the sharks to eat lunch and dinner. The man is full of malice, and he'd kill his own mother. His wife is dead, and her lover is missing in action. That man is never going to be found."

How could she tell him that Fink was trying to nail him to the devil's bed? The two of them were just getting to know each other, so she had nothing to say to him. It was stupid, and if Fink found out her mistake, he'd probably fire her on the spot. What in the hell was she thinking?

"Madison, what's going on in that pretty head of yours?"

"You should leave, Toxic. Call me later. I'm still on the clock until 3:00 PM. After 3:00 PM I'm free for the rest of the day."

"You call me when you're done. You have my private cell phone number."

"I will, and thanks for coming over."

"It was my pleasure."

"Let me walk you out."

He smiled. "I like you."

Madison blushed. She loved him. Was she crazy as hell? She just met the man, and she had a feeling that Toxic was something else. How could she be in love with someone she just met? Madison knew she had read too many romance novels.

Toxic got into his car and stared at Madison's condo. Why did she bring up Ice? He had a feeling that she was up to something and it was not going to be any damn good. Ice was bad news, and he did not want Madison or any woman he loved to be tied up with the mob figure.

Did he say he was in love? *He shook his head. There was no way he was in love with Madison Johnson, a woman he just met, and did not know a damn thing about. Yes, he wanted to jump her bones, but what did love have to do with anything?*

Toxic put his key in the ignition and started his Range Rover. He had to talk to his brother and get a grip on his thoughts. Madison was intriguing and he could not wait to jump her bones, but how did he love her?

"She's the one," the voice said.

Toxic stared around the area, and waited for someone to jump out at him, but there was not any movement in his sight. He shook his head, and then mingled into traffic. This feeling has never happened to him before. Maybe he needed to leave Madison alone for a few days, and see if this feeling of something would disappear?

Toxic smiled. He would not call her for the rest of the week.

"She's the one for you," the voice said. "Don't be stupid."

Toxic hit his brakes as he almost hit the red car in front of him. The red car driver blew his horn and stuck out his middle finger at him. Toxic pulled over to the side of the road to get himself together. Who was talking to him, and just literally called him stupid? Toxic always believed in God and thanked him for the right way his life was going and called on him every day and night even when his life went to hell and back. Was God telling him that Madison Johnson was the woman for him?

He put down his head on the steering wheel and closed his eyes for a few minutes. He felt like he was literally losing his mind.

Ten minutes later he opened his eyes and knew it was safe for him to mingle into traffic. He just needed to talk to Tumor. He was in love, and he knew the feeling, and would give him some much-needed advice. But he still was not going to call Madison for a few days to see if he could get her out of his head.

"She's the one for you," the voice replied.

Toxic jumped as he turned left and was glad that no cars are in front of him, or he was literally going to have a serious accident. Apparently, Madison Johnson was the woman of his dreams, and he had to learn all about this woman. He knew he had no choice in the matter. God was talking, and God was the King!

After driving for twenty minutes, Toxic smiled. He had finally found a woman who was not after his money and his name, and he was thrilled. Madison Johnson was going to be in his life, and those were his hard facts. He laughed as he mingled into traffic.

Madison Johnson

It was now Friday and Madison had never been so angry in her life. She hadn't heard a word from Toxic, and she wanted to kick herself for trusting another man. How could he invite himself over to her house for breakfast, and not even call to follow up like he said he would? Madison could never date a man who didn't keep his word, and Toxic was just like all the other dogs of men in this world. Who was she fooling?

Again, she was in the mirror, staring at herself. She was wearing a green short maxi dress, showing her legs, and making her look sexy as hell. She was on her way to her job for the weekly Friday meeting, but she was so angry she wanted to spit on something or someone. The next time she ever laid eyes on Toxic Lyons again, he was going to meet her alto ego, Tee Tee, and when she finished verbally abusing the snake, he'd never hurt another female again.

Of course, it was her turn to call him, and she called him five times, and her calls went to voice mail. It was as if he turned off his phone or something. Was it her? Didn't he like her kisses? She knew her breath did not stink.

Madison shook her head as she left the mirror and grabbed her large tote bag. It was time to turn some heads at her law firm. She wanted to take off her underwear, but she thought that was pushing the button, and she was going to work.

She was going to prove to herself that there were other men out there who wanted her, and Toxic Lyons could kiss her skinny ass. She smiled as she put on her prescription, green tented sunglasses, and left her condo. She smiled because she was about to make some sexy waves.

Madison smiled as she walked into the law firm. "Hi Rita, and how are you doing?"

Rita was on the phone, and she hung up and stared at Madison. "Hi, girl, and what are you wearing?"

Rita was to honest. "A nice maxi dress. Is the conference room ready? I am a little late, of course, but traffic was hell. I am only five minutes late so it should not be a problem. Do you have my folder of materials for me, and stop looking at me like that?"

Rita shook her head. "Do you have on underwear under that short dress, girl?"

Madison smiled. "I do, and don't be so nasty."

"You're acting very strange Madison. What's going on with you?"

"Not a thing," Madison lied. "Did you and Fink knock boots yet?"

Rita blushed. "What are you talking about?"

"Girl, give me my folders so I can get into the conference room. I'm late, and Fink is going to kick my ass. Will you stop playing games with me? I'll talk to you after the meeting."

"You need to go home and change. You look pretty with your long ankle dresses on."

"I have legs, and it's hot, and I'm going to show it."

"Whatever girl," Rita said. "Here's your folder."

"Thank you."

Madison smiled as she walked down the hall to the large conference room, smiling as men and women looked at her. She could see the men getting hard, and she smiled to herself because she still got it. Toxic Lyons could go to hell.

She took a deep breath as she stared at the closed conference room door. This was it, and let the games begin. She pushed opened the door, and Fink was talking, but all eyes were on her, and Fink closed his mouth and then opened it in shock. Madison walked into the room, making a show of showcasing her short dress, and giving everyone in the room a glimpse of her lovely small thighs. She then found her seat next to Fink and another associate. She put her folders, and tote bag on the table, and then she crossed her legs, and all eyes were on her as her black panties made its appearance and then she smoothed out her dress. "Hi, everyone, I'm sorry for being late, but that traffic was hell on wheels. Did I miss anything?"

Silence was golden as Madison reached for her folder on her desk and opened it to the first page. She smiled to herself.

After a few minutes, Fink cleared his throat. "Janey, the secretary will read the minutes of the last meeting."

Janey began reading and Madison avoided looking at Fink. She knew she was in trouble, but all she had to do was flirt with the man, and maybe let him touch her. Was she for real? She couldn't remember the last time she had a man suck her pussy.

Madison looked us and noticed that all five men were staring at her, and Janey was staring too, and she had a frown on her face. Madison didn't give a damn. She was having the time of her life.

"Bob let's begin with you," Fink stated, staring daggers at Madison. She smiled at him. He was livid with rage, but she still did not give a damn.

Bob cleared his throat, staring at Madison's legs. "I'm working on the Abby case, and so far, it's going along as planned. We're going to trial in two weeks, and my client is innocent of hurting her best friend, who is in a coma now."

"Is the depositions done, and did the best friend complete them?" Fink asked.

"Yes, but she is very hostile, stating that Abby wanted her husband, and slept with her husband, and then when he broke it off with her, she wanted her dead. Abby is obsessed with her husband."

This is why she was glad her two best friends would never betray her in the back like that, Madison thought to herself as she uncrossed her legs, and then crossed them again showing plenty of black panties and legs.

Fink cleared his throat. "Jackson, your turn," *he snapped.*

Madison smiled.

Jackson focused on Madison and no one else. She could see the passion in his eyes. This man wanted to fuck her, and she might give him the time of day. Toxic did not want her but look at the way these five men were drooling over her, including Fink. She was going to have so much fun.

"My case is still pending on finding a witness to testify," Jackson said. "The investigator will be keeping me posted."

"Stanley?" Fink snapped.

Madison smiled.

Stanley was sweating like a water faucet. "I'm still doing discovery on my case."

"Mark?" Fink snapped.

"The trial is in its fifth week, and so far I think the jury is heading on my team," Mark said, eyeing Madison. "I'm going to win this case, and another one down the tube," he smiled.

"Foster?" Fink snapped.

"I just won my case, so I'm going on vacation for two weeks with my new bride," Foster stipulated. "We're finally taking the much-needed honeymoon that we couldn't take when we got married six months ago. I can't wait to spend some alone time with my bride."

Madison laughed. She wondered what his bride would say seeing the way he was staring at her legs, and wanting to get a glimpse of her goodies. All these men in the room would jump her bones if she gave them the chance, and she was going to find one who delivered. Today she was going to get her sex on. Toxic could go to hell.

"Madison?" Fink snapped.

Why was he so angry? Did he want to bang her ass? Maybe she would, but he was her boss and she never mixed business with pleasure. The other men in this room were attorneys, and she was their paralegals, but Fink was like a father to her. She wouldn't bother Stanley because he had a new wife, but the rest of them were going to fuck her senseless. She had the body now, and she could get any man she wanted.

"Madison?" Fink snapped again.

She focused on Fink and smiled. "My goal is to update you all on your discovery process. I'm eager to work with Fink to get Jasmine's case going. My goal is to get her a lot of money for her boss firing her because she is fat. She has plenty of meat on her bones, and you men should be grateful."

Stanley laughed. "No one wants a fat woman."

Madison saw red, and this was a forbidden subject for her.

"This is why you lost the weight," Stanley continued. "Now look at your sexy ass. If I wasn't newly married, I would be all over your ass, and then some. Look at the way you came into this meeting."

"What's wrong with my dress?" Madison asked.

"It's too short," Fink snapped. "What is wrong with you?"

"It's a hot day, and I wanted to show my legs," Madison cited.

"Hmmm," Janey snapped.

Madison focused on Janey who looked like she was ninety years old in a long black skirt, and white blouse. She looked awful and was wondering why she could not get a man. "My clothes is not up for discussion. I want Jasmine to win her case. I've been there."

"You look fine to me," Mark said. "Why don't you come to my office after this meeting, and I'll show you a good time."

"This is a place of business," Fink snapped.

Madison smiled at Mark, and then she winked. "Anyway, if anyone can help Fink with this case, it's a good thing. Jasmine has been working with this firm for fifteen years and Max Roku decided she was not pretty or sexy enough and he was sick of looking at her fat ass. He put a bimbo as his assistant, who has no breast or ass, and cannot count if you paid her. Jasmine is a competent assistant, and she's being discriminated because of her weight."

"She just needs to lose some weight," Bob stated.

Madison rolled her eyes at Bob. "And when are you going to get rid of that huge gut you have eating all those doughnuts," she snapped.

Bob stared daggers at her.

"I didn't lose my job," Bob stated.

"And neither did I," Madison said. "I was fat until last year, you bastard, and now you all want to sleep with me. I can see it in your eyes. I can remove my panties right now, and who wants to suck my cunt?"

Fink stood up so fast his chair fell to the floor. "This meeting is over, and Madison in my office right now. The rest of you get your mind out of the gutter and get back to work. I do not pay you to be fucking anyone on my time. I'm appalled at my employees."

Madison uncrossed her legs making sure everyone, including Mark get a glimpse of her goodies, and then she grabbed her possessions and followed the angry Fink to his office.

He shut the door, and then sat down behind his desk. Madison put her things on his desk, and took a chair in the front of him, and crossed her legs, showing plenty of panties and legs. "What's the problem?"

"Did Toxic dump you or something?" Fink shouted.

Madison felt the tears forming, but she was so in shocked. "Excuse me?"

"Why would you come into our meeting looking like a whore?"

"Women dress like this all the time, Fink."

"This isn't you, Madison. Even I wanted to fuck that sweet ass of yours."

Madison walked over to the door, locked it, and pulled the shades, and then she stood in front of Fink and removed her dress. Now she was in her bra and panties, and Fink was staring at her. Madison smiled because this old man was getting a hard on.

Fink continued to stare at the beauty as his body went into overdrive, and he did not need any Viagra pills. He was on fire.

Madison removed her panties and then her bra and stood naked in front of the man. "Are you going to come and get some of this Fink? I know you want me, so show me what you can do for me."

Fink stared at Madison's naked body and then he stood up and removed his clothes, and then he picked her up and carried her to his back room and shut and locked the door. He positioned her on his bed, and then he began kissing her all over, moaning all over himself and then some.

Madison was hot and on fire as Fink kissed her nipples until they were raw, and then he inserted two fingers into her pussy, and began playing with her cunt. Madison closed her eyes as her body lit up with pleasure, and then she found herself coming, as her body shook over and over with an orgasm. Madison was literally seeing stars as Fink continued to use his fingers in her pussy. When he saw that she was spent. He got up and went to the drawer for a condom, and then he added it to his hard penis, and took her from behind. Madison was shocked and on fire as he pumped her in the ass over and over and screamed out his pleasure.

The pain was killing her, but the act was exciting her too. She had never made love with anyone in the ass, and when Fink fingered fuck her again, she forgot about the pain and collapsed with two more orgasms. After she climaxed, Fink was about to come, and she covered his mouth with plenty of kisses, so he would not scream out his pleasure. They were in his secret room that she only knew about and loved.

Fink was finally spent as he groaned with pleasure. He fingered fuck her again when he found his breathing back in place, and they fucked for another hour. It was the best fucking in the world. Madison was on fire, and her body was singing from the front and then the ass. When they laid spent again, Madison took his hard penis into her mouth and she gave him more pleasure than he thought possible.

Afterwards, they stared at each other in wonder. "Wow, Fink, I didn't know you had it in you," Madison cried. "That was the best sex in the world and then some. I am spent and exhausted. You made my body tingle in all the right places and fucking me from behind was great. I want to continue to rock your world."

"This can never happen again, Madison. I'm your boss."

Madison laughed. "Are you for real? You turn me on, old man."

Fink played with her breasts as they laid on the bed still in their naked glory. "Your body is so perfect," he stated. "I love playing with your breasts and I want you again and again, Madison. What is happening to me?"

Madison laughed as he guided his fingers to her pussy and spread her legs wide. "Make me come all over the place and then some. Let my pussy juices drench your hands. I want you to suck my pussy and get all of my pussy juices, Fink."

Fink opened her legs as far apart as they would go, and then his tongue took over and Madison was screaming all over the place and then some. She closed and opened her eyes, and watched as Fink sucked her pussy, and she never thought anyone would be sucking her pussy like this. An image of Toxic entered her mind, but she shook her head as the pleasure began to take over. Fink was working her clit, and she exploded as all her pussy juices covered his face.

Fink wiped his mouth, added another condo, and entered her vagina this time, and he pumped like a wild man as he was hot and ready, and in less than five minutes he exploded inside the condom, and the two of them rocked with more orgasms, until they were exhausted.

After a few minutes Fink fell off her and Madison sat up. "I need to take a shower."

"The bathroom is ready and waiting," he whispered. "I'm exhausted."

Madison laughed. "I guess you are." *She hurried into the nice size bathroom not believing that Fink had this hidden room inside of his office. It was unbelievable. Did he bring women in here all the time, or was she the first one?*

She stepped into the shower turned it on, making sure she didn't get her hair wet, although she could since she had white women's hair, but she didn't want anyone to know what was going on behind closed doors. She found the shower gel, smelling like cherries, and washed her entire body about four times, and then got out, finding a clean towel, and drying off her body. She could not believe that she just fucked her boss. It was all Toxic's fault for dumping her for no reason. Who did he think he was? He was not the only man in this world for her.

Ten minutes later she was dressed and looking like the whore she was. The secret room was locked and hidden behind a bookcase, and Madison stood up. "What's going to happen now? Are we going to fuck from time to time?"

Fink stared at her. "I don't know, Madison. If you and Toxic get together, I cannot be sleeping with you. I do like Rita and she can never find out about this. But we can fuck until this happens."

Madison smiled. "Okay, but I don't think Toxic is the man for me. We had breakfast, and it was nice, and we kissed, and then he just did not call me anymore. I don't know what happened, and I don't want a man in my life like that."

"He's just convincing himself that he can get you out of his system, Madison. He is probably falling in love with you, and do not know how to deal with it. I know he is going to call you, so give him a chance. It's not easy meeting someone and then falling in love with them when you don't even know them. I do know the feeling."

Madison kissed Fink on the lips. "I had a great time, and you're good in bed, and you surely rocked my world, old man." *She grabbed her possessions and opened the door, making sure no one thought she was fucking her boss. She put a frown on her face and walked out the door as Rita stared daggers at her, shaking her head.*

In her car, Madison reached for her phone, and noticed that she had two missed calls. It was probably Sylvia and Helen checking up on her. She could not wait to call them and tell them that she fucked her boss. They were truly going to be shocked. She pushed the button for her voice mail and listened. "Hi Madison, this is Toxic. I know you are probably angry with me, but I had to make sure that you and I were going up the right path, and this was not a game or just lust. I do want to jump your bones, but I do not want to have sex with you right now. I just want to get to know you. This is my second call. Please call me so we can talk, Toxic."

Madison wanted to puke, and she felt like puking. She had just fucked her boss, and she had to make sure that no one found out about it, or Toxic would never be with her. What made her act like a whore and fuck her boss? She let the tears fall as she listened to both of Toxic's messages and let the tears fall. She prayed she had not made the biggest mistake of her life. She mingled into traffic as her tears blinded her.

Toxic Lyons

Toxic stared at his cell phone. He had plenty of messages, but nothing from the woman where he wanted the messages from. He was sure that Madison got his message and decided not to return his calls. It was Friday evening, and he found himself sitting at home, waiting for his cell phone to ring. What was going on with him? He never had to wait for a woman to call him.

His cell phone rang, and Toxic stared at the caller id. He frowned when he saw his sister face, Tammyann. He pushed the button. He clicked the button. "Hi sibling," he said.

"I have a feeling you were waiting for one of your ladies' friend to call. I also have Tanyann and Toniann on the phone too. I thought I should tell you before you talk about them."

"Hi brother dear," Tanyann replied.

"Hi Toxic," Toniann said.

"What do I owe the pleasure?" Toxic asked.

"We were thinking about our second born sibling," Tammyann said. "What is the most handsome brother in

74

the world doing home on a Friday night? Where are your many women?"

Toxic frowned. "I'm chilling out tonight, and is that okay with my sisters? What are the three of you up too? It's very nice that my sisters are concerned about their second born sibling."

"We spoke with Tumor, so it's now your turn," Toniann replied.

Toxic smiled. "I love you too."

"I'm coming to Chicago for a fashion show for Sylvia Fashions?" Toniann. "I know my big brother is going to let me stay at his mini mansion with the five-bedrooms. I cannot wait. It's Friday so I should be there on Sunday or Monday."

Toxic smiled thinking about Madison. "Sylvia was at the restaurant the other day with her two best friends, Helen and Madison Johnson. I met Helen a lot of times, but I was surprised to meet the lovely Madison Johnson."

"Is our brother smitten with Madison Johnson?" Tammyann asked.

"She's a gorgeous woman," Toxic pointed out.

"She's works with Fink," Tanyann replied. "He's always singing her phrases when I'm talking to him about a legal issue. I'm thinking about going to medical school, and I was using some of my money for the tuition."

"I'm so proud of you, Tammyann," Toxic said. "Mother would be so proud."

"If you need money, you have it," Tammyann stated.

"I'm all in," Toniann said. "My money is just sitting in the bank collecting interests. You need to go girl and make this happen. We're not getting any younger, thank you very much."

"I have plenty of money in the bank too," Tanyann replied. Thank you all, but I am good. I am so blessed to have the best family in the world and then some. If I run out of money, I'll be sure to give you all a call."

"So, what's going on with you and Madison Johnson," Tammyann asked? "Don't bother lying to us so get on with the truth. It's about time you settle down and make some babies."

Toxic laughed. "She's someone I met briefly, and we ate at McDonald's, and we had a great time. The next day I brought her breakfast at her condo, which is very nice, and we hit it off, but she has plenty of issues, and I did not call her for a week. I wanted to see if I could get her out of my mind."

"That's a wrong move," Toniann stated. "She's furious with you, and I'm sure she probably went out and found someone else to rock her world and then some. How could you be so stupid?"

"Ouch," Toxic snapped.

"You don't take breakfast to a woman, and then don't call her for the rest of the week," Tammyann snapped. "What in the hell were you thinking? We three need to come over there and beat your ass."

"I say," Toniann agreed.

"I had to see if she'd be on my mind after a week," Toxic replied. "I can't afford to get involved with the wrong woman. I'm sick of women throwing themselves at me."

"I'm on the internet and Madison Johnson used to be fat as hell," Tanyann said. "She's fine as hell according to her website. She's a free-lance paralegal and she's thinking about going to law school. She's also getting her masters in paralegal science."

"She's very gorgeous in person," Toxic said. "I can't get her out of my mind."

"If you don't want her, I am sure someone will," Tammyann pointed out. "Madison Johnson is the most gorgeous woman in the world and then some. Fink likes her."

Toxic frowned. "Fink is an old man."

"He's a flirt, and he's still handsome," Toniann said.

"Fink is her boss," Toxic said. "I need support."

"I'll try to talk to her when I see Sylvia," Toniann stated. "Hopefully, her friend will be around, but if not, you are on your own, brother dear. We don't know what to do with you."

"Guy needs to give you some pointers on black women," Tanyann said. "My husband knows how to rock my white world and then some. I'm having the time of my life being married. I also want to inform my siblings that I am three weeks pregnant. Guy doesn't know because he's working on his sitcom, but when he comes home, I am going to give the father my wonderful news."

"So, there's going to be a baby in our family," Toxic said. "I'm so happy for you and Guy. The two of you are going to make a pretty baby for sure. I'm going to be an uncle."

"It's very exciting news," Toniann said.

"I agree," Tanyann stated.

"What's going with you Toniann and Tammyann in the love department?"

"I'm dating but no one special," Toniann confessed.

"Me either," Tammyann said. "I'm dating."

"I'm my husband's agent, and manger so I'm pretty busy," Tanyann said. "I'm also going to be managing Jerold and Kick Jones."

"Wow," Toniann said. "I'm impressed with my sister. "They are great singers and I'm going to buy their album when it comes out. How did you manage to catch them?"

"Guy met them, and he told them about me, and the rest is history," Tanyann pointed out. "My goal is to manage four groups or more than that. Maybe no more than six or five. I don't want to overwhelm myself since I'm pregnant."

"You're a great agent," Toniann said. "I remember Sylva telling me that her friend loves to read and write books and she had a book of short stories she was working on. Forty short stories about everyday life and reality. Maybe you can manage Toxic's future wife," she laughed.

Toxic beamed. "I didn't know she wrote books."

"You need to get to know your future wife," Tammyann said.

"You three need to leave my love life alone," Toxic stated. "I don't know if Madison is ever going to speak to me again. I need to find out. I left her a message, but she didn't return it."

"You might have blown it," Tanyann said, but I am going to help you out. "I'll be calling Sylvia to see if Madison is interested in letting me read her book of short stories. If they are good, then I'm going to represent her and turn her short stories into movies."

"I need all the help I can get," Toxic stated.

"You owe me," Tanyann said. "You lived with four women so you should know how to treat a real woman.

Madison isn't like those bimbos you date. She has class, and she's intelligent, and she can hold a complete sentence."

Tammyann and Toniann laughed.

Toxic laughed too. He loved his sisters.

"When are you going to call Sylvia?" Toxic asked.

Tanyann laughed. "I guess I'll call her when the four of us get off the phone. I'm anxious to get more clients, but Toxic don't get your hopes up. I'd love to represent a writer at my agency, but if she's not a good writer, then I can't represent her because you like her. I have a reputation to uphold, thank you very much. I will read her work."

"I know the deal," Toxic said. "I appreciate any help you can give me."

"I'll text you the results," Tammyann said.

"Good luck," Toniann said. "I think Madison is an excellent writer according to Sylvia. She pointed out that Madison could write a short story in less than five minutes, an essay or a poem. She spent most of her life in the law, so this is like a hobby for her."

"Time will tell," Tammyann stated. "When are you coming back to New York?"

"I'm living in Chicago now," Toxic said. "I'll be there on business from time to time, but this is where I live. I have a mini mansion in Wheaten, Illinois. I find myself spending a lot of time at the restaurant."

"My brother has finally found the right woman," Toniann pointed out. "It's about damn time. I cannot believe the bimbos you dated. The last one, Cynthia was dumb as a cow."

Toxic laughed. "She was great in bed."

"Really?" Toniann stated. "Who could tell?"

Tammyann laughed. "Toniann you're crazy."

"That's for sure," Tanyann laughed.

"You three are crazy," Toxic laughed, but I love you."

"And we love you too," Toniann said.

"I need to get off this phone," Tammyann. "I have work to do."

"I have a fashion shoot in the morning," Tanyann stated.

"I have to be at work at seven," Tammyann said. "I'm working a double shift for another nurse, and then I'm going to have two weeks off. I do not know what I'm going to do with myself. I might be registering for medical school. I took the test, and if I pass, I am going, and if I do not pass, then it's not for me. I do want to be a doctor and have my own practice. It's a dream of mine."

"You're going to pass with flying colors," Toxic said. "Medical has been your goals since you were six years old. When you were growing up all you talked about was being a nurse, Tammyann. You have definitely made your dreams come true."

"Thank you, brother dear, "Tammyann said. "I'm very excited for this new venture in my life. Now do not tell mother about this. I don't want to get her hopes up."

"We know the drill," Toniann said.

"Good luck," Tanyann said. "I'll talk to you three later."

"Thanks for calling, and keep me posted," Toxic said.

"We know," Tanyann stated.

"I love you," Toniann stated.

"I love you," Tanyann said.

"I love you," Tammyann said.

"I love you three," Toxic said. *He disconnected the call and stared at his phone still thinking Madison was going to forgive him, but he had no call from her. He had never been so disappointed in his life. What was he thinking? The woman was fine as China and she was probably getting her groove on with plenty of men. Damn!*

Toxic continued to stare at his phone, willing it to ring, and hoping that it was Madison Johnson.

Madison Johnson

Two weeks had passed, and it was now another Monday and Madison found herself sitting in her office waiting for Jasmine to come over. She was going to take her statement and get this ball rolling. She still had not called Toxic and he was better off without her.

Madison dreamed of a man really fighting for her, and she thought maybe Toxic was the one, but she never responded to his text because she felt he deserved better. She slept with Fink, and she still hated herself for it. He was now dating Janey, so they had to forget about ever repeating their sexual games. What in the hell was she thinking going to a meeting half naked, and exposing herself to her coworkers?

Mark, Stanley, and Foster wanted to sleep with her, and she informed the three of them that she wasn't a whore, and they could kiss her skinny ass. There was no way she was going to whore around again. She slept with her boss, and she could not even face him. They did talk on the phone after their sex charade, and Madison would never forget their conversation.

Madison stared at her iPhone as she saw Fink's number and clicked the button. "Hi," she said.

"I think we need to talk about what happened in my office." Fink stated.

"Are you talking in the office, Fink?"

"Don't be stupid," he snapped. "I can't believe you and I slept together, and I never want this episode to happen again. You are like a daughter to me, Madison. I flirt with you, but the flirting is harmless. I'm dating Rita now and I really like her."

"I have no intentions of seducing you again."

"Don't you ever come to a meeting dressed like a whore again, or I'm going to fire your ass, and there's nothing you can do about it. We both made a lustful mistake, but we never talk about this, and it dies with us."

"I don't want Toxic to ever find out about us. I did not fuck by myself, Fink. Do not put the blame on me. You men act like you never seen a woman in a short dress, and in panties."

"You set out to seduce someone, and you got your wish. Do not play these games with me, Madison. You were angry with Toxic, so you had to prove something to yourself, and it was good, but I am with Rita now. I want to settle down. I'm not getting any younger, and Rita will be my wife one day."

"You didn't even know she was interested in you, Fink."

Arroz con pollo is ready! Enjoy your meal!

"Men are dense and blind, and I thank you for putting her in my path. We had dinner every day this week, and Rita is so funny, and she has a lot going on. Did you know that she has paintings in museums and galleries, and she makes money off her paintings?"

Madison was stunned. "She mentioned once that she painted, but I never thought she sold them or anything. I'm so proud of her, and glad the two of you are getting it on."

"How are you and Toxic doing?"

Madison frowned. "I think he's better off without me. If he found out about the two of us, he'd never forgive me. I cannot even forgive myself. He did text me on Friday and apologized, but I just left the situation along. I'm no good for anyone. I need to focus on my career which hasn't let me down."

"You like Toxic and he likes you. What is the problem?"

"I'm a slut."

"Have you slept with anyone else besides me?"

"No," she said.

"Then you are not a slut, Madison. You were vulnerable and you wanted someone to give you some attention, and I was the one, and I am eternally grateful. I always wondered how you would look naked after you lost eighty pounds. I'm flattered."

Madison smiled. "You still have it going on."

"I know I do, and Rita is going to have the time of her life."

"Thanks for breaking the ice, Fink. You're a great boss."

"And that's all I am too you, Madison. Your boss and friend."

"I know, and thanks again."

"If you and Toxic is meant to be, nothing or no one will stop it."

"I know, and he said the voice told him that I was the one."

"See a shrink or someone so you can get rid of the issues. Toxic is a rich and important man, and he needs a confident woman in his life with no insecurities, Madison. Women will continue to throw themselves at him, but you have to trust him, and know he's with you, and no one else. You have to portray confidence. You read enough romance novels to play the game and win."

"It's not easy having all this attention after being invisible for so long, Fink. Sometimes I wish men would leave me alone, and other times, I crave the attention. I just can't see myself with someone like Toxic Lyons. I'm not in his league."

"You're putting yourself down. Toxic isn't in your league, thank you very much. Don't let me come over there and whip that ass of yours, girl. He should be honored to be with you. Don't get cocky but play the game."

"I do understand, Fink. Thank you so much. I'm not going to call him. If I run into him again, then it's meant to be, but he has to make the next move. I'm still old-fashioned. I won't throw myself at him like these other women."

"He'll be back. Now get back to work."

"Thanks, boss."

"My pleasure, Madison."

Madison came back to the present as the doorbell rang. She was wearing a business suit as she walked to the door in professional mode. She smiled at Jasmine as she opened the door. She was definitely a plus-size woman, but she wore a blue power suit, and she was beautiful. "Hello and please come in. I thought we could sit on the balcony since it's such a cool day."

"That's fine with me," Jasmine said. "I spoke with Fink, and he's going to win this case for me. I'm excited and sad too."

"Let's go out to the balcony. Can I get you something to drink?"

"A diet soda would be nice. I'm thirsty for some reason."

"Of course, and I'll be right back. Make yourself at home."

"This is a nice place," Jasmine said.

Madison showed Jasmine to the balcony, got her seated, and then walked to the kitchen to get two diet sodas. She grabbed two glasses, and two paper towels, and then she grabbed a tray of doughnuts, and carried everything to the table.

"Thank you," Jasmine said. "I'm thirsty and those doughnuts look good."

"Please help yourself, Jasmine."

Jasmine took a long sip of her diet soda in the bottle. She did not need a glass. She then reached for a chocolate doughnut and a paper towel as she took a long bite. "This is heaven."

Madison smiled as she reached for her blue file folder that held Jasmine's paperwork and her case. "So, I'm going to ask you a series of questions."

Jasmine nodded, enjoying her doughnut. "I love to eat."

"I do know the feeling."

"But you lost the weight."

"I did," Madison pointed out.

"And does losing weight change your entire prospective on life?"

"I'm not invisible anymore."

"I don't feel invisible at all. I put myself out there, Madison. If someone put me down, I put them down back, and most of the time I ignore them. At my job, I loved it, and I had to fight with women all the time. I was not about to let anyone put me down. Fat people are in the background because we choose to be there. I lost fifty pounds once, and I thought I was the bomb and then some, but I was not. Men dated me and treated me like shit, and it did not matter that I was smaller. They still used me. I had men knocking my door to get to me, but it was a nuisance because they just wanted to get into my panties. Men that rejected me came out of the shadows to sleep with me. I let them, and then one day I fell in love with someone, and he treated me like dirt. I looked at myself in the mirror, and I said never again. I gained my weight back, and my life went on."

"I'm glad to be skinny."

Jasmine frowned, finishing off her doughnut, and wiping her face and hands on her paper towel. She found the garbage can and disposed of her waste, and then walked back to her chair and sat down. "My power to you."

Madison smiled. "Who is Max Roku? I'm taping this interview, and please consent to the taping."

"I consent, "Jasmine said.

"What size are you if you don't mind me asking?"

"I'm a size twenty."

"You look great."

Jasmine smiled. "I know and I love it. I would love to model for the plus-size woman. I am not about to lose weight again, but I'm going to maintain my size twenty. It's a dream of mine to be on the cover of Vogue as a plus size woman."

Madison smiled. "I might have a friend who can make your dreams come true. Let me talk to her first and see if this will work."

"Are you serious?"

"As a heart attack. Her name is Sylvia."

I thought Jasmine was going to faint. "She's my best friend and she was going to do a full-figure line for me to model, but since I'm not fat any longer, she's looking for another model. I'm going to give her your name and number."

Jasmine was speechless.

"Maybe I can make your dreams come true, Jasmine."

"OMG," she cried. "Sylvia is a famous fashion designer and all the celebrities wear her clothes. She lives in New York City. I cannot believe this is happening to me. I love her fashions, and I emailed her a hundred times about doing a plus-size line."

"Your dreams might be coming true. I cannot promise anything, Jasmine, but I'm going to do my best. I think everyone should make all their dreams come true. I'm living my dream."

"Thank you so much," Jasmine cried.

Madison handed her paper napkin off the table.

"I'm so emotional," Jasmine cried. "This is unbelievable."

"I know, but let's get you some money for this case, and satisfaction. Who is Max Roku?"

"A pain in my ass, but he's a litigation attorney."

"And how long have you worked for him?"

"Fifteen years."

"Were you overweight when you were hired?"

"Yes," Jasmine stated.

"What exactly is your job title?"

"Assistant to Max Roku?"

"And what are you job duties entail?"

"I type his briefs and correspondence, and run errands for him, make him coffee, pick up his cleaners, etc. I do everything and anything for the man. I make his appointments, and flight arrangements. The list is endless."

"Did Max hire you?"

"Of course. I passed his three tests with flying colors. A typing and vocabulary test. I didn't miss one answer, so he was very impressed with me."

"Did he make any references to your weight?"

Jasmine frowned. "All the time. I had a pretty face, and hair, but my body needed some work. He told me to join the gym and paid for a membership. There is a gym in the building. I went a few times but to maintain my weight, and not to lose weight. I lost a few pounds, and this was when Max complimented me. One day we were working late, and I noticed him staring at me. Before I knew it, he was kissing me, and we had sex."

Madison was stunned. "How long did it last?"

"We slept together for a few months."

"Can anyone testify to this?"

"I didn't tell anyone because Max threatened me, and I needed my job. When I gained most of my weight back, he did not want me anymore. He had women coming in and out of his office, and I knew what was going on. He had this back room in his office where he took me and other women."

Madison remembered Finks back room. What was going on with these men? "If we could prove he had sex with you, this will truly make our case. The bastard---I hate men sometimes."

Jasmine laughed. "I do know the feeling."

"So, when and how did Max Roku fire you?"

"He called me into his office and shut the door. I thought we were going to have sex, but I told myself that our sex days were over, and if he fired me on the spot, I was going to report him. He fired me and hired this black bimbo. Max likes black women."

"So, he's not prejudiced."

"Not at all."

Madison began thinking.

"I see the wheels turning in your head."

Madison laughed. "His office is in Downers Grove, Illinois."

"Correct," Jasmine stated.

"I'm going to pay your boss a visit all sexy and see how this plays out. I am a paralegal and I'm searching for a job. I'm going to have a tape recorder in my purse and nail the bastard for sexual harassment."

"I like you."

Madison smiled. "I want you to get justice. I'm not fat anymore, but I'm still going to fight for plus-size women. I had no confidence in myself when I was fat, and I wanted to die. I could not stand being around other women or anyone, and I hated mirrors. You remind me of Monique."

"She had the confidence, but Monique lost the weight."

"It was for health reasons," Madison claimed.

"Her fine husband nagged her about losing weight, and she wanted to keep him, so she did what she had to do."

"Do you think about getting married?"

Jasmine took another sip of her diet coke. "I almost got married once. His name was Tumor Lyons."

Madison had never been so stunned in her life. "Who?"

Jasmine laughed. "He's the rich Lyons, of course. He likes fat women, and when he spotted me at a restaurant, I thought I had died and gone to heaven. I was eating alone, and he walked over to my table and seduced me with his eyes, and I was memorized. I thought he just wanted to sleep with a fat woman, so I played along, but Tumor really liked big women. When I realized that he really liked me, it was too late. My insecurities were in the way of our relationship. He is married to another plus-size woman, and have children, and they are happy. I regret that moment in my life, but I come to the conclusion that Tumor wasn't my soul mate. If so, nothing could have driven us apart. It was fun for a while. He took me somewhere every weekend. I went to Las Vegas three or four times, Los Angeles, New York, Miami, Florida, and I even met his family."

"Wow," Madison cried. "I met his brother, Toxic."

"The playboy of the family."

Madison frowned.

"Toxic is representing him in this case against me."

"What? Are you kidding me?"

"Max has the best, and Toxic is the best."

"There might be a conflict of interest, Jasmine."

She frowned. "What do you mean?"

Madison wanted to puke or something. This could not be happening to her. Why didn't Fink tell her that Toxic had this case? What in the hell was going on?

"What's going on?" Jasmine asked.

"I just need to make some phone calls before I say anything."

"You have me worried."

Madison smiled. "Don't be. We're going to win this case with bells on."

"I hope so," Jasmine replied.

"What kind of work are you doing now?"

Jasmine frowned. "I'm still searching for work."

"How are you living?"

"I have savings, but it's not going to last forever. I saved $500 out of every paycheck. The law firm pays well. I just had this feeling that I needed to save money and thank God I did."

"If you can get into modeling, you'll be set for life."

Jasmine closed her eyes. "I'm going to pray about it, especially at Church. I am not in the wrong, so why should I be punished because I'm being discriminated because of my weight? It's not fair, and people like Max shouldn't get away with it."

"What do you want from this case?"

"I want monies for defamation of character and discrimination."

"How much are you seeking?"

"I'm seeking the fair amount over fifty thousand dollars."

"I'm going to get you much more than that."

"It'd be nice. I am tired of working. I just want to model and live the duration of my life in peace. I'm tired of working for someone, but if I could work with Sylvia, it's okay."

Madison smiled. They continued with more questions for another hour, and then Madison turned off the tape recorder, and had Jasmine sign papers, and then she left. Madison stared after her, and then she reached for her iPhone. What in the hell was going on?

Toxic Lyons

Toxic knew he had to get down to business, so as he sat in his office at home, he reached for his Samsung Note 10+, and dialed Fink's number. There was a way he could see Madison, and it would be business, but business could always turn into pleasure.

Toxic smiled as Janey put him right through to Fink. "Good morning, counselor," he replied.

"Toxic what's going on?" Fink asked.

"I'm taking Max Roku case, and I wanted to let you know. Who is the paralegal you have working on the case?"

Fink laughed. "You don't beat around the bush, do you?"

"I'm eager to win this case."

"Your client is a discrimination pig."

"He has a right to hire who he wants to hire, Fink."

"Jasmine worked fifteen years for this person, and she was fat when he hired her. How could you take such a case, Toxic? I'm appalled at your behavior in this matter, and

Madison is working on this case, and I know it's a conflict of interest."

"Madison and I aren't dating, so how?"

"I'm your attorney, Toxic, and you're representing the enemy."

"I want to work with Madison on this one."

"Madison is fighting for Jasmine's rights. She used to be fat, so she understands. She is so determined about this issue. I cannot have the two of you falling in love or something and compromising this case unless you can reach some kind of settlement with Mr. Roku. The man has billions, and it's not fair that my client is out of work because of him. She does not have the kind of money he has, and she hasn't found another job. She worked with him for fifteen years. Jasmine is a lovely woman, and because she has meat on her bones should not prevent her from working. She passed all the required tests when she was hired and did not miss one question. Your client is insane."

"What kind of money are we talking about Fink? I made a mistake with Madison and I want to try again with her. I know she is probably seeing someone, but I need to apologize to her. I can't stop thinking about her, Fink."

Fink smiled. "She's a very beautiful woman, Fink. I literally had to let her work at home because once she lost the weight, the men in my office act like they never seen a gorgeous woman before. She came to the meeting on Friday and she had on this very short dress and every man in the room was memorized. We actually saw her black panties."

Toxic was stunned. "Did she find someone?"

Fink frowned, thinking about himself, and the way the two of them fucked, in his private room, but he could never tell Toxic this. "I believe she did, but I don't know. I was furious with her and marched her out of the office and told her to go home and change her clothes. I believe you had something to do with that Toxic. How could you lead her on like that? Madison is very vulnerable now, and she is new in the dating game arena. She's not going to be able to trust men, and you didn't help the matter any."

"I made a mistake, Fink. Help a man out."

"You certainly did, but the only deal in this game is for your client to settle out of court. I am sure he and Jasmine slept together a few times because Max is a dog. She had lost weight at one point, and this changes everything."

"How much does your client want?"

Fink thought about the money. "Eighty thousand dollars."

Toxic laughed. "Are you insane?"

"My client has been out of work for months now, and she's still unemployed, using some of her savings which isn't much. Her rent is two thousand dollars a month, not to mention electric, phone, and the list is endless. Your client needs to watch how he treats his employees, and he cannot get away with this because someone does not look the way he wants them to look. If I have to go to court, I'm going to win this case, and it's going to cost your client more money. This case is based on his treatment of my client—"the unjust or prejudicial treatment of different categories of people or things, especially on the grounds of race, weight, age or sex" (https://www.google.com/?gws_rd=ssl#q=definition+of+discrimination

"Your client isn't going to win. She has fifteen years."

Toxic frowned. "I'll talk to my client, but forty thousand is probably his only deal."

Fink laughed. "I don't think so and let us go to court. Madison is interviewing Jasmine now, so I am sure she is going to find a lot of facts about Max Roku. He uses his power and money to intimate woman, but he has met his match with my client. Make your client settle and let's move on to more important facts."

"What can you do to get me time spent with Madison?"

"What do you want me to do, Toxic? She is like a daughter to me, and you hurt her. I don't want to see her hurt. She can have any man she wants, and she doesn't have to settle for someone who wants to play games with her."

"Fink, that's not fair. I am a rich man, and I cannot have any woman. I need to make sure that she is the one. I heard the voice, but it could be the devil too. I have never felt this way about a woman before. I needed to make sure that she was the one. If I did not think about her for the rest of the week, then I can move on, but I could not stop thinking about her. I had breakfast at her nice condo, and I felt so alive Fink. Just being around her made me feel so damn good. I cannot explain it, but I do know I have never had this feeling with all the other women I dated in my life. How can I just move on? I made a mistake, but I am trying to fix it. I text her, but she didn't text me back."

"I'm going to set up a meeting at a restaurant I owned, and instead of me being there, you will be there, and this is your chance to make it right, Toxic. If you hurt her again, I'm going to beat your ass myself."

Toxic smiled. "I'm not going to hurt her."

"I will set the meeting up for four this evening. Can you make it?"

"I'll be there with bells on. Where should I meet her at?"

"Rain Restaurant in Lombard. I will have a private table for you, and just ask for Skip and he will take care of you. Don't blow this."

"I owe you, Fink."

"Good luck. Madison is a Taurus and she's very stubborn."

"I'm a Gemini," he laughed.

"The two don't mix," Fink laughed.

"I'm going to change that fact."

"I hope so but get your client to settle. I don't want to take this to court. My other phone is ringing and it's Madison. I'm sure she has some interesting information for me."

"I'll be there at four and thanks so much."

"Again, good luck."

Fink switched to his other call and smiled. "Hi Madison, and what's up?"

Madison Johnson

M adison was livid with rage. "Fink, why didn't you tell me that Toxic was working on this case? Jasmine told me and I thought I was going to puke or something. This is definitely a conflict of interest."

Fink smiled. "I just talked to Toxic and he told me the news. I convinced her to settle out of court with his client. I need for us to meet at Rain Restaurant in Lombard at 4:00. Ask for Skip if you get there before me. I have another meeting, but it shouldn't run over."

"This is unbelievable," she snapped. "I can't get away from this man."

"Maybe God is trying to tell you something."

She shook her head. "Toxic isn't the man for me."

"Let's not go down the route of low self-esteem because you have no reason for it, Madison. Look at yourself in the mirror, and your body is to die for. I know it."

"We never speak of our encounter, Fink."

"I'm sorry," he said. "Get your confidence back."

"It's apparent that I want to win this case for Jasmine."

"And a settlement is good. Do you have some information?"

"Max slept with Jasmine a few times, especially when she lost a few pounds. When she gained the weight back, he ended their sexual pleasures. The man is a dog on four legs. I was thinking about pretending to be searching for a job, and getting his ass on tape harassing me."

"That's not a bad idea, but it'd backfire on you and me. It's called misrepresentation. You knew how Max was and you misrepresented yourself when you walked into his law firm asking for a job. We have to go by the book, Madison."

"I wanted to screw the bastard over."

"Toxic is going to convince him to settle. I said the amount should be eighty thousand, and Toxic laughed, but I'm not playing."

"I agree," Madison snapped. "He needs to pay for his crimes."

"How are you holding up?"

"I'm good, busy with work. I'm finishing up with my other clients, and they weren't happy when I resigned, and then I'm going get started on the five cases you brought to my attention. I'm curious about the file folder on Ice."

"I've been trying to get Ice for years."

"He's a very dangerous man, Fink. Ice will hurt you and all your family members including Rita. He is just not worth it. I have a feeling he is going to get his one day, and payback is a bitch. All we have to do is sit back and wait."

Fink scratched his head. "I wish I could be there."

"We all do, but I'm going to give you his file back, and you can file it under open case until the bastard pays for his crimes. I'm going to get back to work, and I'll see you at four."

"I'll be there and have a grand day."

"You do the same." *Madison clicked off the phone and then leaned back in her chair. If they could settle this case, then she did not have to worry about Toxic and his presence in her face. Fink always let her go to court with him, and she did not want to see his face in court or anywhere. She had to forget about him.*

Madison smiled as her iPhone rang, and she stared at her best friend Sylvia. She was about to call her, so they were on the same page. "Hi best friend. I was going to call you."

"We're on the same page," Sylvia said. "How are you doing?"

"I had better days. Can you get Helen on the other line?"

"I'm on," Helen said.

Madison smiled. "Hi other best friend."

"Hello Madison and how are you doing?"

"I'm doing fine hearing my best friend voices. What's up?"

"We're back in New York City and wanted to touch basis with you," Sylvia said. "What's the update on Toxic Lyons?"

Madison frowned. "I don't know, he dumped me for no reason."

"What?" Helen and Sylvia said in unison.

"He came over and we had breakfast in my condo, and he promised to call, and I waited by my cell phone for hours, and he didn't call. On Friday he left me a message apologizing, but I ignored him. I was dreaming that I could be with a man like Toxic Lyons. Who was I fooling?"

"Why didn't you text him back?" Helen shouted.

"What's the point," Madison stated.

"You don't give up on someone you like, girl," Sylvia said. "Helen and I need to come back to Chicago and give you a class in romance 101."

"I agree," Helen said.

"That ship has sailed," she cried.

"I doubt that," Sylvia stated.

"I need to ask a favor of you, Sylvia," Madison stated.

"Why are you changing the subject?"

"I can't stop thinking about Toxic if we keep talking about me. I'm sure he's not losing any sleep over me, thank you both very much. Men are breaking down their door to get to me, so when I want some sex, I will just find a man and fix my urges. I do not think I'm ever going to get seriously involved with a man. I don't need the headache."

"Isn't that why you lost the weight?" Sylvia stated.

"I lost the weight for many reasons," Madison snapped.

"You're lacking confidence," Helen pointed out.

"Sylvia, I need you to call Jasmine Guymon. She is a plus-size woman, and I think she's going to sell your line to the fullest. She is a beautiful woman, and she's only a size twenty. She has a lot of confidence in herself."

"I'm searching for the right person since you changed the game on me," Sylvia laughed. "I'll give her a call and try to meet up with her. If she could get to New York City that would be nice."

"I'm sure she'll fly there right now," Madison laughed. "It's a dream of hers."

"I'm interviewing right now, and I'll know the right person when she comes along," Sylvia said. "I can't promise you she's going to represent my line, but I'll definitely give her a chance."

"It's all I ask," Madison said. "I have a meeting at four. What's going on with the two of you?"

"I'm good," Helen said.

"My husband assured me that he's not cheating on me with George, but I don't trust him, and I saw a divorce attorney. I am going to file for divorce. I don't want to spend the rest of my life with a man on the down low who can't figure out if he wants to fuck men or women."

"I'm so sorry for you," Madison laughed.

"Don't be," Sylvia cried. "I'll survive."

"He's your husband," Helen cried.

"Okay," Sylvia said.

"Are you seeing someone else?" Madison asked.

"No," Sylvia quickly replied. "I'm too busy with my fashions to worry about a man. If I do get a divorce, I am going to take a break from men, and just do me. I'm tired."

"I do understand that logic," Helen said.

"I have my career, and the children will suffer, but my husband didn't give a damn when he was having sex with supposedly his best friend. It's going to devastate his children and me, but we have to move on."

"You're so understanding," Madison cried. "I don't even want to be bothered with a man. Romance is just words on paper, and it's not for the real world. I need to move on."

"My marriage is fine," Helen said. "Don't let Sylvia's situation taunt your future. Everyone has a purpose in life, and what's right and wrong for Sylvia has nothing to do with Madison Johnson."

"She's right," Sylvia said. "My business is mine, and since I saw my husband sleeping with George, I can't stand the sight of him. I do not even want to be in the same room with him. I told him to move out, and if he's not gone this week, then I'm going to make his life a living hell."

"Wow!" Madison cried. "I can't believe this."

"It is what it is," Sylvia said. "I had this instinct that something was going on with my husband, and I was right on the market. I thought he was cheating on me with another woman. I never thought it'd be another man, and his best friend. The bastard still denies it. I saw it with my own eyes, and I took pictures, and he refuses to admit it."

"He's a sick puppy," Helen said. "You know we're here for you."

"I know, but I'm fine," Sylvia said. "I can definitely take care of myself, and he will take care of his children. This is why women need to be independent of men because you just can't depend on them."

"That's for sure," Madison said. "I did something stupid."

"What did you do?" Sylvia asked.

"I slept with Fink," Madison cried.

Silence took over the room. It was three minutes when Madison spoke. "Hello."

"I'm in shock," Sylvia said. "I know he flirts with every woman he sees, but for you to sleep with him is bordering on craziness."

"What possessed you to sleep with your old boss?" Helen asked.

"Don't judge me," Madison cried. "I thought Toxic had dumped me because he came over to my house for breakfast, and then didn't call me for the rest of the week. I was vulnerable and I went to my Friday meeting in a green short, maxi dress, with black panties, and I made an impression. My boss was so hot he marched me into his secret room in his office, and the two of us got down and dirty. I have to say that Fink has it going on and then some with his big dick. The man has a lot of energy and he's fifty-five years old. His tongue was a lethal weapon."

"You are sick," Helen cried.

"Really?" Sylvia snapped.

"Again, ladies, don't judge me. I got sex finally, and it was damn good. Fink and I will never mention this again. I am telling you two because I love you, and you're my best friends. I know I can trust you to take this to heaven."

"My lips are sealed," Helen said. "It's too crazy for me to picture in my mind."

"Nasty," Sylvia cried.

"Actually, it was sexually satisfying," Madison sang. "I was so orgasmic satisfied I thought my body was never going to come down from the high. Never judge a book by its cover. Fink is good in bed, and now he's dating Rita so the case is closed."

"Wow!" Helen said.

"I love you both too," Madison cried. "I have to finish up a brief before my meeting at four, so I'll talk to you both tomorrow and have a blessed day. I'm going to be okay."

"We hope so," Sylvia cried. "Are you done with Fink?"

"Or any man for that matter?" Helen cited.

"Yes," Madison cried. "I'm done."

"Great," Helen said. "Keep your black panties on."

"Unless his name is Toxic Lyons," Sylvia pointed out.

"My legs are tightly closed," Madison laughed. *She ended the conference call, and smiled to herself as an image of Toxic Lyons entered her mind. Damn!*

It was five minutes to four when Madison practically ran into Rain Restaurant. She hurried to the desk because she did not want Fink chewing her out about being late again. Why couldn't she be on time? "I need to speak with Skip."

"Are you Madison Johnson?"

"I am," she smiled.

"Your table is ready and let me show you. I'm the manager."

"Thank you Skip," she said. *She followed Skip to a back table and was stunned when Toxic stood up and Skip left. Their eyes met, and Madison was speechless as she stared at the handsome man in jeans and a yellow polo shirt. She was wearing jeans and a green V-neck shirt, which showed plenty of cleavage. Her jeans were tight, and she looked damn good. She remembered when she could not even wear jeans.* "What's going on?" Madison asked.

"Please sit down," Toxic asked.

"I should leave right now," she snapped. "What's going on with Fink?"

"I asked him to set this up because you weren't answering my texts. I had to see you Madison. I miss you like crazy. I know this isn't the right thing to do, but I needed to see you."

She stared at the handsome white men, trying not to focus on his green eyes. Instead she took a seat and reached for the glass of water on the table and took a long sip.

Toxic sat down across from her. "You look so lovely."

For some reason she blushed. "So, do you."

Silence took over the room as Madison focused on her water, and Toxic continued to stare at her. Fink was unbelievable. What was he thinking arranging such a meeting?

"How are you doing?" Toxic asked.

"I'm fine and working diligently."

"Are you dating anyone?"

"That's none of your business," she snapped. "What do you want from me?"

"I want to start over with us. Are we on the same page?"

"I don't know. You didn't call me."

"I had to test myself to make sure that it wasn't lust."

"And?"

"I couldn't stop thinking about you. I do not want to play games. My name is Toxic Lyons, and it's nice meeting you."

Madison laughed. "I'm Madison Johnson, and it's nice meeting you Toxic Lyons."

He smiled. "Let's eat."

"I'm famished."

"What would you like?"

"Their fish is good. Fink took me here once for a meeting."

"What about their steaks?"

"Great choice," she said.

"Hi Toxic," a female replied as she walked up to their table.

Madison stared at the half-dressed woman. It reminded her of when she walked into the conference room with her short dress on. This woman might as well be naked.

Toxic frowned. Why? "Hello Barbara and how are you doing?"

Barbara stared at Madison up and down. "Who is this lovely woman? Is she your sister? I never did get to meet them."

"Madison Johnson, and she's my girlfriend," Toxic bragged.

Barbara was speechless.

"You have a girlfriend," Barbara snapped. "She must be good in bed."

"I think you should leave, Barbara," Toxic said.

"How can you dump me for this bitch," Barbara cried.

"I'm not a bitch," Madison snapped.

"Barbara leave, or I'm going to have you escorted out. I do own half of this restaurant, and the media will have a field day seeing an actress kicked out of a restaurant. What are you doing in Chicago?"

"Go to hell, Toxic, and burn."

Madison shook her head as she reached for her water. "I need a strong drink."

"I'm sorry," Toxic said.

"I see you broke a lot of hearts, and I don't want to be on that long list."

"Barbara is my past, and you're my future."

"I need a drink," she repeated. "A vodka tunic will do."

Toxic motioned for their waiter and ordered two drinks as their eyes met.

Toxic Lyons

❧

The drinks arrived and Toxic drained his, and he stared at Madison who did the same thing, but hers went down the wrong pipe, and she coughed a few times. What was Barbara thinking? Women were so foolish at times. Why would Barbara embarrass herself like that? "Are you okay?"

Madison grabbed her glass of water. "Vodka is strong, and I don't drink that much. Let's order and talk about the weather or something, but I do want to talk about the case I'm working on."

"Fink told me about it and I'm going to get a settlement?"

"I hope so, and why would you defend such scum of the earth?"

"Everyone is entitled to a defense," he stated.

"Max Roku discriminates against weight issues."

"He's entitled to hire anyone he wants to become his assistant."

Madison frowned. "Are you for real?"

"Yes," Toxic said.

"So, I'm sure you don't have fat or black people at your firm."

"I have both, thank you very much. Jasmine got a wonderful severance package, and a great recommendation."

Madison frowned. "Remind me never to get fat again."

"Why should my client be ridiculed because he wants a skinny assistant? It's his choice who he wants working for him."

Madison shook her head and motioned for the waiter herself. "Hi and give me another drink and make it a double this time."

The waiter smiled and left.

"Are you trying to get drunk on me?" he asked.

Madison frowned. "I just don't know why we're here."

"We have an attraction for each other, and I'm eager to see where it's going. I thought you and I were on the same page. It seems to me that you're letting everything and everyone get between us. I think you're afraid to be with me or let us flow."

"You're losing your mind." *Madison was glad when the waiter handed her another drink, her third or fourth one and she took a long sip of it. What was Fink thinking? Toxic Lyons was not the man for her. They absolutely had nothing in common.*

"The 4th of July is next week. I want you to come to a barbecue with me that my family has every year. You can get to know my family, and I can get to know you on a fun level."

Her mouth was opened-wide, and she couldn't find any words. Was he for real? She didn't want to meet his rich family. She reached for her drink, and this time she drained the glass as it hurriedly went down her throat. She wanted to scream from the strong drink, but she controlled the urge. What was so wrong with her? She was fine as hell, and she did not have to hide not being confident in herself. Why was Toxic Lyons affecting her so? "I don't think meeting your family is a toxic ideal, excuse the pun."

Toxic laughed. "I like that and why not?"

Madison shook her head. "I have plans," *she lied. All she was going to do was spend some time catching up on some romance novels, and mysteries. Maybe the latter because romance was not working for her at the moment. Her best friends were staying in New York City, and she had no plans. Madison was tired of spending the holidays alone when her friends could not get away. It'd be nice seeing how the rich celebrate the holidays.*

"My parents will be there, my three sisters, and brother, and his wife and their children. It's just family so I think you should go and let your hair down so to speak, no pun intended," *he laughed.*

Madison did not want to laugh, but he was funny. "Okay," she said. "What time should I be ready next Monday?"

Toxic could not believe that she said yes, but he was not going to do anything to change her mind. "I'll pick you up at 3:00. I'm going to introduce you as my girlfriend so don't embarrass me in front of my family."

Madison laughed. "Of course not."

They laughed, and it was music to Toxic's ear. He had a feeling his family was going to give her the third, fourth, and fifth degree, but he also had a thought and a feeling that Madison Johnson was no push over, and she was definitely going to handle his family. "Are Sylvia and Helen going to

111

be in town? They should come with you, of course. Sylvia and Helen have been to our barbecues before, with their husbands, and they had a great time. Although, I think Sylvia and her husband are having some issues which is what two people do in a marriage."

Madison stared at him. How did he know Sylvia was having problems with her husband? Was Toxic Lyons that observant? "They are staying in New York this year, so I won't get to see them. We facetime Monday morning for hours, and then we're going our separate ways."

"I'm right about Sylvia and her husband?"

She stared at him. "How did you know anything was going on between the two of them? Sylvia is a great actress."

"They would have heated conversations when they were alone, and the looks on their faces weren't happy faces. Last year her husband ended up leaving, and a few minutes later, Sylvia took an Uber home. I offered to drive her home, but she assured me that she needed to be alone."

"You're right, but I can't discuss it."

He smiled. "I don't want you to betray a friendship, and I hope everything works out. Sylvia is a fantastic woman, and she deserves the happiness that is bestowed on her."

"I agree. Did you know that Jasmine, my client, dated your brother for a while?"

Toxic was stunned. "Really? What happened?"

"She was insecure and didn't believe that a man as debonair as Tumor Lyons would be interested in her fat ass. She regretted her decision, but he's with the woman that was meant to be with him."

"Tricia is the best thing that has ever happened to my brother. I've never seen him as happy as he is now. His wife is lovely` and she's only an eighteen and she wears it well."

Madison frowned. "Remind me never to get fat."

"I don't have anything against fat women."

"Now your ass is lying," she snapped.

"I just don't think anyone should be obese. It's too many diet pills, and gyms for anyone to lose weight. Food should not be an issue. Tricia refuses to lose weight, and I just don't understand."

"And you never will," she snapped. "Where is my food?"

Toxic motioned for their waiter, and soon they were feeding their faces in silence. What in the hell was wrong with him? They were having a pleasant conversation and then he had to go and blow it. He did not like fat women, and he had to work on that. If he were going to get married, and have children, his wife would gain weight to carry the baby, but he'd make sure that she got on the gym and lost the weight. What was wrong with him? He was dating a black woman, so he was not a racist, and he should not be discriminating against weight. He looked over at Madison who was eating, but she had a frown on her face, and he had a feeling he was the problem. How in the hell was he going to turn this moment around?

It was an hour later when Madison stared at her watch. "I have to go, but thanks for the meal. I can pay for my portion, or better yet, I can pay for our dinner. Why not?"

Toxic stared at her in shock. "The meal is on the house, and please don't disrespect me, Madison. I know you are angry at me, but it's something I have to work on. I'm sorry."

"You should be," she snapped. "If your wife gets pregnant and she gains weight, are you going to divorce her if she doesn't lose the weight in a month or two? You have fucking issues,"

Now she was mad, and acting ghetto. "Don't curse at me, and show your ghetto side," he snapped. "Most men don't like fat women, and if their wives get pregnant, then they have to immediately lose the weight."

"I'm truly sorry that Tumor is a happily married man because I'd be all over him and then some. He likes thick women, and he is a man in my book, thank you very much. His wife is a very lucky woman."

Toxic was angry as hell now. "So, what's it to you? You are miss skinny Minnie, so what are you getting all bent out of shape for? You did not want to be fat which is why you lost the weight. You need to show other fat women what you did and give them the incentive to lose weight too."

"You need to kiss my ghetto black ass." *Madison grabbed her iPhone and searched for the Uber app, and then she pushed the button for a ride, putting in the restaurant's address, and then her address for her destination. This man was a pain in her ass.*

"So, I guess you are not going to join me on the 4th."

"I'll be there to see how the rest of your family thinks about black and overweight women."

"We don't have drama but fun on the 4th of July."

"Then I suggest you do not come, and I'll get there with Uber. I do not need you to pick up this ghetto ass woman, thank you very much. Again, Toxic Lyons, kiss my black, skinny ass."

Toxic was stunned as she grabbed her large tote bag and marched out of the restaurant. He watched as she stood outside, sitting on a bench, that the restaurant provided, for people that were taking the bus, or waiting for their rides. A few men tried talking to her, but she brushed them off. He could not believe this was happening to him. And the fact that she was still coming to his holiday celebration.

"Is there anything else, sir," the waiter asked.

Toxic stared at Jake, and then he reached into his pocket, and removed his wallet, taking out a clean and crisp one-hundred-dollar bill. He then grabbed another one and handed it to her. "Have a nice day, Jake."

Jake was speechless as he stared at the money. "Sir, this is too much for a tip."

Toxic laughed, and then grabbed another hundred- dollar bill. "Three hundred dollars should do it."

Jake shook his head. "Sir, I….."

Toxic interrupted him. "Take the money and stop being so crazy. You did a fabulous job here, and the manager always give me great reports on you. Also, you are going to college and raising your little brother. I believe the money will come in handy. Now take it or you're going to be in big trouble."

Jake smiled. "Thank you so much, sir."

Toxic smiled. "Stay in school, support your brother, and keep up the great work. If there is anything I can do for you, please don't hesitate to contact me. I know you won't, but …."

Jake saluted Toxic and went back to work. Toxic smiled, and then focused back on Madison. Her Uber driver was smiling all over himself as he got out the car, and literally opened the door for her. He frowned. Did she know this man?

Toxic was livid as the car pulled off, and then five minutes later he got into his car and drove home, furious as hell. He wanted to hit something he was so angry. Why did Madison Johnson infuriate him so?

Maybe he truly needed to forget about her and find a woman that just wanted to have sex with him with no commitments. Of course, he would have to pay their rent, or give them money, but it was less complicated than falling in love.

Toxic hit the steering wheel of his range rover. There was no way in hell he was in love with this woman. It was out of the question. Madison Johnson was ghetto, and he did not date ghetto women. What would his parents think? His mother was married to a black man, and his sister was married to a black man, and now he was in love with a black woman. Was it all in the family? He shook his head as he focused on his driving. Maybe she would not show up for his family barbecue and he could get on with his life. Right!

Madison Johnson

*I*t was the 4th of July, and Madison was grateful to God for seeing another holiday, and thankful that her friends were alive and well. Her parents were in heaven, and Sylvia and Helen were her only family. She turned on her desktop computer, and skyped Helen and Sylvia, and waited for them to boot up.

It was ten in Chicago, and eleven in New York City.

"Hi girl," Sylvia said. "Happy fourth."

Madison smiled. "Hi best friend."

"I'm here," Helen said.

"Hi best friends," Madison said. "What were you two doing?"

"I was making sure my husband got out of my house," Sylvia snapped. "He finally agreed to move out, and guess what?"

"What?" Madison asked.

"He's going to move in with his lover, George. The two of them are so in love, and when our divorce is final, which I filed for, by the way, he's going to marry George since it's now legal in Illinois for two men to get married. I'm livid with rage."

Madison was speechless.

"I'm so sorry," Helen cried. "I'm in pain for you."

"Me too," Madison cried. "Is there anything we can do for you?"

"I'm handling it," Sylvia cried. "I knew it was coming when I found him in bed with George, so I'm coping with it. I feel like a failure. I am wondering why my husband could not love me. Why did he need to love a man? I am fine as wine and then some. I am Hispanic for heaven sakes. I just do not get it. Our two children are gorgeous, and he has what most men crave for. I just don't get it."

"Your husband was probably gay and refused to believe it," Helen exclaimed. "He's on the down low, which most men are. I know women who are still with their men, knowing they are sleeping with them, and men too."

"That is crazy," Madison said.

"I can't condone it," Sylvia cried. "He didn't want to disrupt his family, so I had to deal with him sleeping with George, because he'd never slip his penis inside of me. Why stay with someone like that? I cannot believe this is happening to me. Sometimes, I think I am living in a lifetime movie or something. This just can't be happening to me."

"It's happening to a lot of women," Helen stipulated.

"What are your plans for today?" Sylvia stated.

"We're having another barbecue for the family," Helen said. "Joseph, Fatima and Michael are looking forward to our yearly barbecue. Joseph is in his element, and he has three brothers and they come over with their wives, and girlfriends. We do have a lot of fun. I wished you two could be here."

"Me too," Sylvia replied. "How do you maintain your marriage with Joseph? You two have been married for a very long time. Joseph is fine as wine, and he loved the women."

"Joseph cheated on me left and right, and when I threated to divorce him and take the children, he played right," Helen confessed. "This started back in elementary school when he was dating me and other girls."

"Wow," Madison added.

"Is he still cheating on you?" Sylvia asked.

"The device on his cell phone tells me no," Sylvia said. "But when or if it happens again, me and the children are divorcing his ass. Fatima is twelve, and Michael is eight, but they're aware of what's going on."

"Wow," Madison replied. "You seem to have your act together."

"I'm not searching for a disease," Helen shouted. "I let Joseph cheat on me in the past because when you love someone it's difficult to disconnect with them, but you do come to a point that you need your self-respect ladies. If he needs to spend the duration of his life cheating on me, then I do not need to be with him, and I would not put up with it. The app on his phone is undetectable, and so far, my husband is the devoted husband."

"Is putting a device on him worth it?" Sylvia asked.

"Yes and no," Helen said. "I trust my husband, but once a cheater is always a cheater in my book. I can take care of myself and my children if I need to get a divorce. Life goes on."

"What are you doing today, Madison?" Sylvia asked.

"My usual, but Toxic invited me to his parent's house for their yearly barbecue," Madison stipulated.

"Wow," Sylvia said. "Are you two dating?"

"I don't know," Madison said. "Fink set us up at Rain Restaurant, and everything was going good for a moment, but his attitude on fat women got on my last nerve. I cannot stand his views, and he had the audacity to call me ghetto when I went off on him."

"Wow," Helen said. "You're not fat so why can't you leave that issue alone?"

"I can gain the weight back, Helen. I just feel the pain that fat women go through. I want to do something about it. I want to be a crusader for fat women. Did you talk to Jasmine?"

"I did," Sylvia said. "We facetime each other, and she's perfect for my fashion line for the plus-size woman. I also need another model too. It'd be nice if you two knew others."

Madison smiled. "I do, Tumor's wife Tricia. She's an eighteen."

"Talk to her about it, and give her my number," Sylvia said. "I'm going to launch this line in September or October. I have the fashions done, and Helen is the best seamstress in the world. It'd be great to have the models in line."

"How many do you have now?" Madison asked.

"I have three now," Sylvia pointed out. "With your two, that will be five and that's enough. I want to promote these five women and my fashions all at the same time. I have a feeling this line is going to sell out more than my slim lines. I have maxi dresses galore, and shapewear that will work."

"I'm so proud of you," Madison said.

"I am too," Helen stated.

"I'm proud of myself," Sylvia said. "I don't have to focus so much on the end of my marriage, and more on my career which so far, has never let me down. I am having the time of my life with this line. My agent is impressed, and my fashion associates. We are on the map, and with the plus-size line, we are going to stay on the map. Maybe next year, I am going to try and have a reality-based competition for the plus-size woman. I am in negotiations with the NOW network. I want it to be on Penny's network."

"Are you serious?" Madison asked.

"As a heart attack," Sylvia said. "Penny Jake got in touch with my agent to pitch the ideal to her, and she praised me all over the place and then some. She's a plus-size woman, and she wants to see fashions for the bigger woman as for the skinner woman."

"Wow," Helen said.

"Way to go," Madison said.

"I can't believe it either," Sylvia exclaimed. "When my agent, Carolyn called me and told me the news that Penny Jake was interested in working with me on a reality competition I thought I was going to pea in my panties or something."

"Things do happen for a reason," Helen stated.

"That's for sure," Sylvia said. "This couldn't come at a good time for me. I also have Danny trying to talk to me. He is so in love with me, but he knows I'm married, and he's so in tuned into me, but he's not going after a married woman.

I respect him for that. He doesn't know anything about my filing for divorce, so Danny is genuine."

"What?" Madison cried. "Why are you just mentioning it to us?"

"Really?" Helen snapped. "The three of us are keeping secrets. It drives me crazy most of the time. I know we have our own lives, and sometimes we want to handle our own problems, but what are best friends for? We need the support of each other."

"You're so right," Sylvia said. "This is why I brought up Danny. He is a very handsome white man, and into me. He is respectful, and I like that about him. I might give him the time of day if he is still available. I don't know."

"White is the thing for us," Madison pointed out.

"I'll stick to my black husband," Helen exclaimed.

Madison and Sylvia laughed.

"What does Danny do?" Helen asked.

"He's an internal medicine doctor," Sylvia stated. "I wasn't feeling well, and thought I was pregnant, and my doctor wasn't available, so I saw him. I was not, thank, God. I don't want any children by my almost ex-husband."

"We're glad about that," Helen said. "I can't imagine the pain that children see their parents breaking up, not to mention the fact that my father likes men. I still can't understand it, and I'm an adult."

"I'm grateful for no children. Something told me not to have any with this snake of a husband." Sylvia said. "Something told me not have three, and I'm glad I listened to my instincts. This is so much harder when children are in the picture."

So true," Madison said.

"Are you going to join Toxic and his family?" Sylvia asked. "I had so much fun when I went over there. His sisters, Tammyann, Tanyann and Toniann are hilarious, and his mother is funny as hell."

Madison laughed. "I've heard, but I just don't know. Toxic believes I am not going to come. I should go and show out my ghetto said, since I am so ghetto according to the likes of Toxic Lyons. I can't even stand his last name."

"The two of you are a cat and dog?" Helen said.

"Jelly and peanut butter," Sylvia said. "When together, the two match perfectly."

Madison and Helen laughed.

"I'm supposed to be over there at three, so I'm going," Madison said.

"What are you going to wear?" Sylvia asked.

"Should I go over there looking like a whore?" Madison laughed.

"Absolutely not," Sylvia shouted.

"I agree," Helen said.

"Why not?" Madison asked.

"You know that's not you, Madison," Sylvia pointed out. "Stop trying to be something you're not. You want Toxic to see the ghetto side of you so you can turn him off. Stop being afraid of finding love and going with it. You should be a pro with reading all those romance novels."

"Toxic is a good guy," Helen recited.

"And you're not getting any younger?" Sylvia said. "Get married and have some babies at thirty, or at least when you're thirty-one. With the right kind of man, you two can be a power couple."

Madison didn't want to be a power couple with Toxic or did she? They would have some gorgeous babies with his green eyes. She shook her head. "Ladies, what should I wear?"

"What about the flora-print maxi dress," Sylvia pointed out. "Now that's a gorgeous long dress, and it's perfect for a barbecue."

"I do like the dress," Madison said. "It'd be perfect for the barbecue. I am going to wear it, and my lilac sandals to match. This is going to work, and thanks so much. I forgot about that dress."

"You bought it when you went to Macy's to shop for the new Madison Johnson," Helen said.

"I bought a lot of clothes, ladies," Madison said. "I remember almost maxing out my credit card. My bill was over eight hundred dollars, but it was worth it. I lost weight, and now I'm a size six. I love the way the maxi dress bounces with me. This will definitely be the perfect dress for Toxic's family."

"And wear your long and pretty hair down," Helen said. "When Toxic sees you he's going to get a hard-on right in front of his family and then some. I wished I could be a fly on the wall."

Madison laughed.

"Are you going to drive?" Sylvia asked.

"No," Madison stated. "I'm going with Uber."

"I think you should drive," Sylvia said.

"I sold my car last year, ladies," Madison pointed out. "You two forget that two years ago, I almost died from a horrific car accident because some woman decided it was more important to text and drive than wait until she got out of the car. I was in a coma for a month, and then my legs would not work. I can't believe the woman is dead, but it's her own fault."

"How cold-blooded," Helen snapped.

"I'm not cold-blooded at all," Madison snapped. "Why did she think it was okay to text and drive? She could have killed me with her. I'm sorry that she died, but it was a lesson to her and others."

"I wonder about you sometimes," Sylvia said.

"I'm good," Madison said. "I just don't drive, and if Toxic or any man have a problem with it, then I'm glad God invented Uber. I have regular drivers now since I take Uber all the time."

"Are they flirting with you now?" Helen asked.

"They are, but I reject them so fast, it's funny," Madison said. "This one driver would speak to me, and then he ignored me. When I lost the weight, he was all over me, and I told him off. My Taurus the bull came out."

"You need a shrink," Helen said. "You can't blame men who don't want a fat woman. You're out there rejecting men because they didn't talk to you when you were fat."

"They didn't see the inner core of me," Madison shouted. "I'm the same person without the big stomach, thighs, and arms. I'm going to wear this dress with my arms out, and I don't have to cover them up. It's a nice feeling."

"Stop punishing men because you liked to eat," Helen said.

Madison rolled her eyes, staring at the two of them. "Just fuck off," she stated. "I'm the way I am and that's not going to change. I resent men who only see the outside of you. I have a problem with Toxic relating to this issue. He hates fat women."

"He has fat women and black women working in his law firm," Sylvia said.

"I don't give a damn," Madison snapped. "He doesn't like fat women."

"This chick will never change her views," Helen said. "I need to shower and change and get ready for a house full of people. I hope you two have fun and forget about your problems for the moment. Today is Independence Day."

"I have work to finish up," Sylvia said. "I'll be working and eating barbecue. I did manage to order me some to have for today, and a nice bottle of wine. I did the same thing last year; my husband was working, but he was spending his time with his lover, George. I still can't believe my marriage has ended because my husband is in love with a man."

"I'm so sorry for you," Helen cried.

"Me too," Madison cried.

Sylvia let the tears fall. "I feel like such a failure. Wasn't I enough for him? I sucked his dick and had sex with him from behind. I did all the kinky things he wanted me to do."

"He's gay and it has nothing to do with you," Helen cried.

"She's right," Madison pointed out.

"I know," Sylvia said. "It's going to take some time for me to come to terms that I'm going to be single again. Girls, I like having a man in my life. I need a man. I don't like being alone."

"Then when you are ready call Danny," Helen said.

Sylvia smiled. "I'm going to call him sooner than you think."

"Be careful," Madison pointed out. "You don't want to use Danny when you know he has feelings for you. Make sure you have some for him because this can get dangerous."

"She's right," Helen declared. "I saw a lifetime movie once when the main character got a divorce from her husband because he was cheating on her, and her best friend, a man--was in love with her, and she was so vulnerable that she started dating him. It turned out that her husband never cheated on her, but the best friend paid someone to ruin her marriage, and she found this out. Her husband forgave her, and they got back together, but the best friend went on a rampage and tried killing her husband, and then he took her hostage, and was going to kill her and himself."

"What a movie," Sylvia said.

"It's so true in this world today," Madison said.

"I'm just going to mourn for a while, and then have some sex," Sylvia said. "If it's with Danny, then he's the one—if not there are plenty of men out there. I'm still fine as wine."

"Yes, you are," Helen said. "I love you both."

"We love you too," Madison said.

"I conquer," Sylvia said. "Madison have fun."

"I will try," Madison said. *She ended the skype with her two best friends and hurried to her bedroom, and to her walk-in closet to find the flora maxi dress. She grabbed it from the back of the closet and hurried to her full-length mirror, putting the dress in front of her. Yes, this dress is going to be perfect.*

Madison smiled because she was going to try and have a good time despite Toxic and his views on fat women.

She smiled as she hurried into the bathroom to get ready.

Toxic Lyons

Toxic walked into his parent's house Maggie and James Lyons. Of course, Toxic smiled as he smelled barbecue and then more barbecue. He closed the door and hurried into the kitchen where he found his mother. "Hi my lovely mother."

She smiled at her second son. "How are you doing? I see you don't have anyone with you."

"Mother, I just got here."

"And you should have a lovely woman on your arm."

"I'm starving," Toxic said, changing the subject.

"Your name agrees with you," she snapped. "Where is your date?"

"I have someone, and we had a fight, so I don't know if she's coming or not, mother. I really like her, but her issues are getting on my last nerve. She used to be fat, and she's a crusader for the fat women out there."

"I see," his mother said, stirring something in a pot.

"What are you making?" he asked.

"My famous macaroni and cheese. What is her name?"

"Madison Johnson," he declared.

"And what does she do?"

Toxic sat down at the kitchen table, staring at the bowl of rolls. "Mother, can I just have one roll?"

"Boy, is your hands clean?"

"Yes, mother." *He reached for the roll and took a long bite. It was delicious as he tasted the butter.* "She's a paralegal."

"You two have a lot in common," she started.

"She's beautiful and black, mother."

"Okay, it runs in the family."

"Where is father?"

"He's in the basement with Tumor."

"Is Tricia and the kids here?"

"They will be coming soon. Tricia is visiting her family. They live in Michigan and will be going back home soon. I just love my daughter-in-law and my two grandchildren."

Toxic stared at his mother.

"What's on your mind, son?"

He smiled because he could never fool his mother. "Do you think that Tricia should go on a diet or something? She is a gorgeous woman and she doesn't have to be fat. I just don't see how someone could let food take over their lives."

His mother put a lid on her pot and turned the fire down and then she sat down across from her son and gave him her full attention. "I think this has something to do with Debbie Jones."

Toxic was stunned. He had not thought about her in years. She was this very fat girl in his third-grade class, who made it her mission to pick on him because she had a crush on him. She beat him up a few times and made him be her boyfriend. She even kissed him and tried making out with him, but he would not let her, and then she beat him again. Toxic hated Debbie Jones. She was a white girl, and a bully.

"I don't even remember her?"

"You hated her, Toxic and you faked being sick so many times so you wouldn't have to go to school, I finally caught on to your plan. I made you confront her, and the two of you fought, and she never bothered you again."

"Whatever happened to her?"

"She's on a wrestling team now, and she's the reigning champion."

Toxic laughed. "Is she still fat?"

"She's still big, but she has more muscles than fat."

"Wow," Toxic laughed.

His mother laughed with him. "Honey, Tumor always liked women with meat on their bones. When he dated in high school the girls, he brought home were big girls, and I am not talking about their height. He is so in love with Tricia you should see the two of them together or in a room. I go over there to babysit my grandchildren James and I so, they can have some alone time. They're so in love with each other."

"Wow," Toxic said. "I never seen them like that."

"Today you will see a real marriage, besides me and James, and get some pointers in how to treat this new woman in your life. You should be picking her up, son."

"She's taking Uber," he snapped.

She laughed. "I think you might have met your match, and I can't wait to meet her. So far, she sounds like a nice person. I love her name by the way, Madison. It's going to be okay and stop hating."

"I love you, mother."

She smiled. "I love you very much, son."

"What's going on here?" Tumor asked, walking into the room with his father, James.

Toxic stared at his brother and father. "Just a mother moment."

Tumor sat down next to his brother as his father embraced his wife. "I want you to be nice to Tricia, Toxic. She does not believe that you like her. I hope she's not right about that."

Toxic frowned. "I have a problem with her weight, but I'm working on it."

Tumor frowned. "Why?"

"Debbie Jones," his mother added.

"It's a long story," Toxic said. "I have a date coming, if she does decide to show up so everything will be okay. I love my sister-in-law, and you have nothing to fret about, older brother."

"You two behave," his father said. "I'm on call at the hospital, and I'm praying I don't have to leave. I don't want to leave your mother dealing with the two of you in a fight."

His father and mother the doctors, Toxic thought to himself. He could not get any luckier to have the best parents in the world, not to mention his siblings, which got on his last nerves most of the time.

"My brother needs to talk with my wife," Tumor stated. "I have no beef with him."

"Good," James said, kissing his wife.

Toxic loved the affection between his white mother and black father. He could not believe that he had interracial parents, and it was hell growing up, but their love conquered all, and he wanted to be in a relationship like his parents. Was Madison the one for him? He shook his head. Absolutely not!

A few minutes later, Tricia walked in with her two children. She looked gorgeous in her long blue maxi dress with sandals to match. She was a full-figured woman, but she wore it well. My sister-in-law did not have a stomach, Toxic thought to himself. She had an ass, and this attracted his brother, and he could not blame him. She was gorgeous. "Hi Tricia, Edward and Molly."

Tricia frowned as she walked into the living room and spotting only Toxic sitting on the sofa. "Hi Toxic and where is everyone?"

"Outside," Toxic said. "I want to talk to you."

Tricia stared at him. "Edward and Molly go and find your grandparents. I will be out there in a few minutes. Your father should be out there too." *She sat down on the sofa across from Toxic, waiting for the children to leave. When they were gone, she focused back on her brother-in-law.* "What can I do for you?"

He could not blame Tricia for her attitude. He did not once welcome her into the family and convince Tumor not to marry her. What in the hell was wrong with him? His brother was very happy with his wife, and he had reason to judge. "You look beautiful, Tricia."

She shrugged her shoulders at him. "Okay."

"I know you don't like me, and I can't blame you."

Tricia laughed. "You think! I guess I am not skinny enough for your liking. The fact that you begged my husband not to marry me is something I have forgiven, but I'm never going to forget, Toxic."

"I'm so sorry about that," he reasoned. "I hate myself for hurting you on your wedding day. If I could take that day back, I would Tricia. My brother is very happy and you're the reason and his children."

"You think!" she snapped.

"I have serious problems with fat women, and my mother pointed out the reason why. Debbie Jones in elementary school bullied me, and made me be her boyfriend, and everything imaginable. I am so sorry for disliking you. I really like you Tricia. You are the perfect woman for my brother. I've never seen him so happy with you, and it has been six years."

She frowned. "I don't know what to say to you, Toxic."

"Can you just try to forgive me?"

"I'm working on it, but it's going to take months."

"I'm so sorry."

She smiled. "You do look sincere."

"I am. Anything I can do to make it up, I will."

"I'll think of something, and you're going to pay, brother-in-law. I love your brother more than my own life, I'd die for him, and you'll never understand until you fall in love with your soul mate. I did not think he cared that much for me, but only wanted me for a booty call. I almost lost him, and you did not help the situation, I might add. Your brother always dated heavy women. It doesn't mean something is wrong with him."

"I understand now," he said.

"Do you because your wife is going to get fat having babies, and you can't stop loving her because she's pregnant with your child. Have you heard of unconditional love? If your wife got sick and she had cancer, would you abandon her? If she got some disease and it made her fat, would you divorce her? If so, Toxic you need to stay single for the duration of your life, and make sure you protect yourself with plenty of condoms when you're sleeping around."

Toxic stared at the floor.

"I didn't think Tumor was the man for me, and I tested him so much that he told me no more games, or I was going to lose him. He passed the test with flying colors," she laughed. "I remember testing him with my cousin, Jamie. Now she is a beauty and I hooked Tumor up with her, and they hit it off, but when she tried seducing him, he rejected her. I was stunned because no one could reject my cousin, Jamie. He did not speak to me for weeks, and I thought I had lost him. Spending two weeks away from Tumor made me realize that he is the man for me, and I was miserable as hell. Do you understand where I am going with this? If you cannot love someone for themselves, you do not need to be with them. Where is the current woman in your life?"

Toxic stared at her. "I don't know, but her name is Madison Johnson."

"I've heard her name before."

"She's Sylvia's best friend."

"Yes, Sylvia talked about her all the time, and Helen too."

"I really like her, but she used to be fat, and she doesn't like my views on fat women. We fought the last time we were together, and I do not really know if she is going to show up or not, Tricia. I know I can't stop thinking about her, and I want to get to know her."

"Then you need to talk to someone about your views, or you're going to be a very lonely man, Toxic, and that'd be a shame since you're handsome, but Tumor is more handsome, of course," she laughed.

Toxic laughed with her. "Maybe I do need to see someone."

"Yes, you do," she shouted. "You have to get over what this Debbie Jones did to you? It was traumatic and it's affecting your adult life. If you want Madison, you need to do the work."

"My brother is a very lucky man."

"Yes, he is," Tricia laughed. "I'm on the news and I've been there for ten years. I am not about to get fired for a younger or smaller woman. My fans love me, and I let big women know that they do not have to hide in the house. I used to be one of those. I did not think I was ever going to find a man. I went on diet, lost weight, and then gained it back. I came to the conclusion--when I almost died that I am a plus-size woman, and this is my destiny. I believe this is why---Luther Vandross died because he kept going up and down and it wasn't good for his health."

Toxic nodded.

"I'm healthy as a skinny woman, believe it or not. Tumor and I run together most mornings, but my schedule is crazy. I maintain this weight, and I make sure I do not gain any more weight. I was bigger when I had his children, but a size eighteen or sometimes twenty is my ideal weight, and I make sure I do not go over. I ran a marathon last year, and won, Toxic, or didn't you hear about it?"

"Tumor shows me the trophy when I'm at your house."

"I love my husband," she smiled. *She stood up.* "Now I'm going to go and find my lovely husband and spent some time with him because we don't get this opportunity."

Toxic stood up. "Can I have a hug?"

Tricia stared at him. "I guess so."

They embraced, and Toxic felt so much better. "I do love you."

"Back at you," Tricia said. "I can't wait to meet Madison."

Toxic frowned, staring at his watch. "It's almost three and I don't see her. I might have blown it big time, and it would be all my fault. I'm never going to learn in this lifetime."

"I hope you do learn from your mistakes, Toxic, and if she's worth it, then you're not going to give up on her. If Tumor gave up on me, then you and I would not be having this conversation. Be a little bit more open about fat women. God didn't make everyone skin and bones."

"Thank you."

Tricia smiled, and then she pushed opened the door to go outside. Toxic stared after her, glad he made peace with his sister-in-law. He just prayed he did not blow it with Madison.

Finally, it was three, and Toxic frowned. Madison was not coming, and he wanted to weep, a damn grown man, but he still was not going to give up on her.

The doorbell rang, and Toxic froze.

Madison Johnson

·❁·

Madison could not believe she was standing at Toxic's parent's house. Now they were living in a mansion. This house took up the entire block, and there were no other buildings in sight. She could not believe the enormous size of this house. She ran the doorbell and waited in anticipation of seeing Toxic again, and the rest of his family. She was early, but he said be there at three, and she was here, sitting in her car for ten minutes.

Madison had arrived at 2:30, bent on changing her mind, but she stayed in her car and waited. She watched as a woman with two kids walked in, and she was gorgeous and a plus-size woman. Why was she meeting these fat women when she was now skinny? Was there a purpose?

The outside was modern and beautiful. The door opened as Madison stared at Toxic who was in another polo shirt, and shorts. He looked good to eat. "Hello," she said, breaking the ice.

"You look so gorgeous," he stared. "Hi."

"This place is to die for," she exclaimed.

"Come in so I can give you're a tour. I'm glad you showed up."

Madison smiled. "Me too." *She walked in, and her mouth was wide-open as she stared. This place was out of this world and then some.*

"As you see this place looks over Lake Toe, and it's the most beautiful sight in the world, and then some. I come here often just to sit and stare at the lake for hours. I think great thoughts then."

"I can imagine," she pointed out. "I love it."

Toxic smiled. "This is really a spectacular landscape."

"I agree," she cried.

"The property also has a private dock used just for boating."

"Wow," Madison stated.

"You can sit outside in the evenings and enjoy the sunset when it's not raining," he pointed out. "I do it often, but I have my own mini mansion now. It's not as elegant as this one, but it's next to it."

Madison blushed. "It's so beautiful. Can I take a picture?"

"Of course," Toxic laughed.

Madison grabbed her iPhone in her hand and took several pictures of the spectacular view. This was living in heaven and then some.

"This is the living room," Toxic pointed out.

Madison was speechless as she took more pictures.

"This is the spiral staircase," Toxic stated.

Madison thought she was going to faint. "Are you kidding me? It's made of glass, and it's something I've never seen before. It's fantastic," she cried.

Toxic laughed.

"This is the boardroom where meetings are held with the family and for business purposes," Toxic explained. "My parents will be opening up their own medical practices next year, and I'm so proud of the two doctors in my family."

Madison shook her head in wonderment. This moment was so unbelievable to her, and she did not almost come. She sat in the Uber car for hours, and luckily, she had someone who knew her because they were going to get a big sum of money for just sitting in the car with her. Madison continued to follow him around this mansion.

"This is the indoor swimming pool and sauna and spa."

"Wow," Madison cried.

"You're welcome to come here anytime and use it."

"Are you serious or crazy?"

"I'm dead serious, Madison."

Their eyes met for two seconds, and then Madison stared at her cell phone.

Toxic cleared his throat. "Let's continue the tour."

"I'm right behind you," she said.

"The sauna room also consists of fitted closets that lead to three bedrooms, including a master bedroom, each with their own bathroom."

"Lovely," she cried.

"Here's the basement, garage, and another conference room."

Madison continued to take pictures with her iPhone. She was intrigued.

"These are the elevators, which makes it much easier to get around."

"Your parents are very modern."

"Yes, my interracial parents."

"It seems to run in your family."

"Yes, it does," he laughed.

The rest of the house was dynamite, and Madison had so many pictures she could not wait to show Helen and Sylvia, but they had been here before. Why didn't they tell her about this place? She was going to get them for leaving out minor details.

"Everyone should be in the large living room."

Madison took a deep breath.

"You look lovely, and everyone will like you."

"Let's get this done," she said.

"Follow me."

Madison was nervous as hell as they walked into the living room. She stared at the many faces as conversation stopped when she and Toxic walked into the room. They were the center of attention for the moment.

"Everyone," Toxic spoke, this is Madison Johnson. "Madison, this is my parents Maggie and James; my three sisters, Tammyann, Tanyann and Toniann, my brother, Tumor and his wife, Tricia, and over in the corner, at their two children, Edward and Michael. Tanyann's husband, Guy Rough isn't here because he's shooting a movie."

"It's nice to meet you all," Madison said.

"She's very lovely, son," his mother stated.

Madison blushed.

"Come and have a seat next to me," his mother said. "I want you to call me Maggie for the moment, and when you two get serious, then you can call me mom," she laughed.

Madison wanted the floor to open-up and swallow her whole.

"Mother, really," Toxic said.

Madison sat down in the chair next to his mother, who was petite and very lovely, looking very young. She had to have had her children young. She did not look over fifty.

"How old are you, Madison?" Tammyann asked.

"I'm thirty," Madison said.

"And you're a paralegal," Toniann stated.

"I am," Madison said.

"Would you like something to drink?" Tumor asked.

He was very handsome for an older brother, looking just like Toxic. The two of them could pass for twins if they stood next to each other. "I'm kind of thirsty," Madison replied.

"Get her some wine," Tanyann said.

"Anything is fine," Madison stated.

"I'll get her a rum and coke," Toxic said, leaving the room, and walking over to a bar in the corner.

Madison smiled.

"We love Sylvia," Tanyann said. "I'm modeling for her."

"She's one of my best friends," Madison pointed out.

"We love Helen too," Maggie said.

"Are your parents alive?" James asked.

"They're in heaven," Madison said.

"We're sorry," Maggie said. "Do you have siblings?"

"I'm an only child," Madison stated.

"Well we can be your family," Tricia said.

"Thank you," Madison said. "I don't know if Toxic and I will have a long-lasting relationship. We're different than night and day, and I didn't want the family to think otherwise."

"I like her," Tammyann said. "Our brother doesn't bring most women around his family, so there's something different about you, and you're lovely as sin, so I can see the attraction my brother has for you."

"I do see it too," Toniann stated.

"We all see it," Tumor pointed out.

Madison blushed, and was thrilled when Toxic handed her a tall glass of rum and coke. She took a very long sip.

"I heard that you write short stories," Tammyann pointed out.

Madison was stunned that she dropped the glass, and it splashed on Maggie and everyone close to her, not to mention the black carpeting on the floor. Madison wanted to die. "I'm so sorry," she cried. "I should leave." *She stood up.*

"Don't be silly," Maggie said. "I am going to get this up and Toxic will get you another drink. You sit back down and do not dare leave or think about going anywhere. I know we are overwhelming you, and I am sorry about that. Once you get to know us, you'll be more comfortable around us."

Madison nodded as Toxic stared at her, and then he took her glass off the floor, and walked back over to the bar to get her another glass and refreshed her rum and coke.

Madison wanted to run and hide. What in the hell was wrong with her? She had class, and it was time to act like it. She did not want to embarrass herself or Toxic. How was he feeling?

The electricity bombarded her when Toxic handed her another drink, and she thought she was going to drop this one, but she controlled herself, and took another long sip.

"I'm sorry about mentioning the short stories," Tanyann stated. "Sylvia is always talking about her best friends, and she mentioned that you wrote some very creative short stories. I would like to read them and publish them for you. I am an agent for my husband, and many other celebrities. We can talk about it after the holidays, that is if you want your short stories published. Some writers write for themselves."

Madison was stunned. "I never thought about having them published, but I'll definitely talk to you about them. I'm just surprised, and Sylvia never told me that she mentioned this to anyone."

"Don't beat her up," Tanyann said. "If you have talent, then I'm going to open up your world. She mentioned that you had a book of short stories about forty of them."

"I have sixty of them," Madison bragged.

Tanyann laughed. "I'm very impressed."

Madison laughed. "I wrote them in a journal and Sylvia and Helen caught me one day and began reading them, and they were impressed too. I was going to self-publish them one day, but my paralegal work took up most of my time."

"God works in mysterious ways," Maggie said, walking back into the room. "Dinner is ready so let's all go into the ballroom and pig out on food. I have a buffet of everything known to man," she laughed.

Everyone laughed.

It was two hours later when Toxic and Madison sat on the porch and stared at the gorgeous water. Madison was full as hell and knew she would not be able to eat for three days.

"Penny for your thoughts," Toxic said.

"Your family is so wonderful," she cried. "It's been a very long time since I was in a family. Sylvia and Helen are my family, but it's not the same. You have your siblings, and your parents, and it's a very nice feeling. I miss my parents, who died in a car accident. They died together which gave me closure, but I miss them."

"I'm sorry," he cried. "You smell so good."

"So do you," she cried.

Their eyes met, and then as Toxic moved closer to Madison their lips met. Madison felt the electricity and the dynamite in her body, and she thought she was going to explode, as she explored Toxic's tongue, tasting like wine and some of the food he had. Their lips played with each other, and then their tongues began the kissing dance.

Madison was on fire, and she thought she was going to explode. She had never felt this way when she kissed, and she remembered kissing Fink, but it was nothing like this. Why did she bring him up? Toxic could never find out about her and Fink.

Toxic had his hands all over her body and Madison wanted him like she had never wanted a man before.

"I want you now," Toxic said.

She felt his manhood on her thighs, and she wanted him too.

"We can go to my room which is away from everyone," he said. "Madison, I need you right here and right now. Look at me. I know this isn't appropriate, but I want you naked."

Madison stared at him. "Let's go."

They were on the elevator in minutes, and when they reached his room, the two tore off their clothes, and stared at their naked bodies. Madison was stunned at the way his dick stared at her, ready for some action.

Toxic picked Madison up, and carried her to his queen size bed, and began kissing her lips, and then playing with her nipples as he sucked both of her breasts.

Madison moaned out her pleasure as the electricity bombarded her with sensations. She felt herself about to have an orgasm and he was only touching her breast. Then Toxic moved down to her stomach, which was finally flat and her belly button. When he opened her legs and stuck his fingers into her wet cove, she screamed out his name as more pleasure took over her body.

Madison was ready and her body shook with a powerful orgasm, as she cried out his name. She was on fire as Toxic opened a drawer and took out a condom and placed it on his large and ready penis and he quickly entered her because he was ready and on fire. He thrust into her, and Madison screamed out because it was not the same with Fink. This was not just about sex but making love. Their bodies rocked as the two was in sync with each other and they both exploded together as their mouths kissed, and the thrills of sensations took over their bodies. It was five minutes before they came down to earth.

"Wow!" Toxic stated.

"I know," Madison said. "I never thought this would happen so soon."

"It's okay," Toxic said. "I wanted this and so did you."

She blushed. "It was wonderful."

"Yes, it was, and I want you again."

Their lips met again, and the two made love until they fell asleep from exhaustion and this is how they spent the rest of the 4th missing the fireworks but making fireworks of their own.

Toxic Lyons

---

*I*t was morning as Toxic opened his eyes and smiled as he stared at the sleeping beauty sleeping next to him. They were both naked, and Toxic could not stop the smiling.

Madison looked so happy and peaceful as she slept. They made love for hours, and it was kinky as sin, but it was perfect. Toxic could not get enough of her gorgeous body.

He stared at her long hair covering her face, and he pushed the hair out of her face, but he did not dare wake her up. They had truly missed the fireworks, and he knew his family was thinking the worse of him, but he was not going to apologize for being with Madison. He was in love with her, and he was going to confess his love when she woke up.

He covered her body with the sheet and blanket, and then he quietly eased out of the bed, and walked his naked body to the bathroom and closed the door. He was going to take a shower and get dressed and go and find some breakfast. It was seven o'clock in the morning and a Tuesday morning. Madison was going to be livid and blame herself for being a tramp in heat.

He had no intentions of letting her put a damper on their lovely night. It was the best lovemaking in the world, and the best way to spend the 4ᵗʰ of July.

The smell of bacon and eggs opened Madison's eyes as she focused and then stared around the room. She also noticed that it was very light outside. She covered her mouth in shock as she sat up in bed, noticing that she was naked.

The memories of making passionate love to Toxic brought a smile to her face, and then she frowned. What was his family thinking? She searched around the room for her tote bag, finding it on the nightstand and reaching for it. She sighed, as she covered her mouth again. It was almost eight in the morning. She missed work, and what would Fink think. She never missed work.

She was about to get up when Toxic walked into the room with the most beautiful tray you could imagine. The tray had flowers of all colors in a vase, and then she noticed the plate full of bacon, toast, and scrambled eggs. She felt her stomach protest in anticipation, and she was famished. She covered her naked body with the sheet and stared at the handsome, white man. Madison could not get over his cuteness.

Toxic stared at the beauty. He was so blessed to have Madison Johnson in his life. He was in love with her, and that was the bottom line. "Good morning," he smiled.

Madison blushed, but she loved his smile. "Good morning, and you made me miss work," she pouted.

"I called Fink, and he said take the day off."

Madison eyes grew wide. "You called my boss."

"Yes, Fink is my attorney, so I had his number."

Madison covered her face. "You didn't tell him that we…"

Toxic laughed. "Of course not, Madison, it's none of his business what you and I do. I just said that you got drunk, and he was all for you having a personal life."

"Wow!"

"Now sit back against the headboard, and eat," he insisted. "I want to watch my naked beauty feed her face. I ate earlier, and it's such a pleasure waking up with you Madison. I'm in love with you."

Madison was flabbergasted this time. "What?"

"I know we just met, but I knew there was something special about you, and I did hear the voice. I am in love with Madison Johnson, and I will tell it to the world and then some. I would not hold back. I'm in love with Madison Johnson."

Madison took the tray and sat it on her lap, and then she stared at it, and then Toxic. Was she in love with him? Did she even know what love was? Should she say the same thing to him? Relationships were so damn difficult, which is why most people did not want to be bothered. She was so conflicted.

Toxic sat down on the bed next to her as it sagged with his weight. "Honey, I love you, and I know you like me a little, or we wouldn't be having this conversation. It's okay if you don't return my feelings. I want you to say the words when you mean them, and not because I am saying them to you. I love you, and when the time is right you and I will be getting married. I am not about to waste another minute without you in my life. Now eat."

She picked up a slip of bacon, and gladly added it to her mouth. She closed her eyes as she sampled the taste. She loved bacon.

Toxic laughed.

Madison opened her mouth. She was so embarrassed. "I'm sorry."

"Its okay, Madison. I know you love bacon which is why I made it for you. Enjoy your breakfast and sweet tea."

"I can't remember the last time I got breakfast in bed."

"I'm glad to hear that."

"I don't know what to say, Toxic."

"Don't say anything negative. You and I will pursue our relationship. Maybe we're not on the same page. Do you want to have a relationship with me, Madison Johnson? I don't want to assume anything."

Madison took a long sip of her sweet tea, then ate the rest of her bacon and eggs, chewing and laughing at the same time. After drowning her food in sweet tea, she stared into his green eyes. "Yes, I do want a relationship with you, Toxic, but I'm a….."

Toxic covered her mouth with his hands. "That's all I want to hear, Madison. If we want this to work we can't let negative influence come between us or negative people. Let's spend the rest of the day together, and matter of fact, let's spend the week together at my condo."

Madison was stunned.

"You work at home, and then you can talk to Tanyann about getting some of your short stories together and making one of your dreams come true, Madison. Life is short, and Tanyann is the best agent in the world. She is going to make you a famous author and then some. I'd love to read some of your stories but give them to Tanyann first."

"I don't know, Toxic."

He frowned. "Do you ever do anything without thinking? It's not going to kill you to spend time with me and be in my space. It gives me the opportunity to get to know you."

"I never lived with a man before."

"I've never lived with a woman before so we can learn together."

Madison frowned. "I find that hard to believe."

"Trust is also a factor in a relationship, Madison," he snapped.

"So now you're angry. I won't be dictated by a man."

"What?" he exclaimed.

"You heard me, Toxic. I know you are rich and use to getting everything you want, and then some, but I am not the one. I don't consider myself a passive woman by any means."

Toxic laughed. "Are you trying to ruin this moment."

Was he correct? "I'm afraid."

"So am I, but this gives us a chance to get to know each other, and I want to know all about you. I want to come home from work, and you are right here waiting for me, not with my slippers and the newspaper. I know you're independent, and I love your independence, but let a man be a man too."

Madison shook her head, taking the last sip of her sweet tea, and then she put down the glass. "I should wash the dishes and clean up since you cooked."

Toxic laughed. "Now you are sounding like a wife, but I have Mae who comes in and clean for me. It gives her a job to take care of me, and it also gives her something to do."

"You're a very nice man."

Toxic found himself blushing. "I'm not just rich and selfish."

Madison smiled.

"So, are you going to agree to stay here for a week? We can do the mansion if you are more comfortable with this format. We each have our own floor, so you are safe with me on the 4th floor. No one can just walk on this floor. They have to call up, and then I have to let them in."

"This place is magnificent, but what will your parents say?"

"I'm a grown man, and it doesn't matter what they say. When I explain to them that you're the woman I'm going to marry, they will move on. My parents have their own lives, and they let us make our own mistakes, and fall into it. I'm blessed to be in a family that is wonderful."

She smiled. "I had great parents too."

"But no siblings," he stated.

She shook her head. "Sylvia and Helen are my sisters, and people are brought into your life for many reasons. Anyway, we can stay here for the time being and get to know each other before we get to the condo stage."

Toxic laughed and then he removed the tray and placed Madison in his lap, and then kissed her face. "Thank you so much."

Madison laughed. "Wow!"

"I love you," he cried. "I'm so happy."

Madison smiled again. "Why don't you show my naked ass how happy you are, Toxic Lyons?"

"I like my aggressive girlfriend."

"You're my boyfriend?" she laughed.

"Yes, I am, so keep the men away."

Madison frowned, thinking about Fink. Should she tell him the truth? She did not want any lies between the two of them. What would he say? They were not dating at the time, so who she slept with was her business? Should she confess?

"What's going on in that pretty head of yours? Do you need to confess something to me, Madison?"

"How did you know?"

"I'm so connected to you in so many ways. I just cannot explain it. If you feel that this confession will give us the closure we need to begin this new relationship, please confess your sins."

"I don't think you're going to like this one."

Toxic kissed her lips, tasting her tongue. She smelled like sweet tea, bacon and eggs, and he loved the scent of her. "I need to hear it since you brought it up. You can't go back now."

"Fink and I slept together once."

Toxic jumped up so fast, Madison held onto the bed before she fell to the floor. She was naked, and she stared at the shock on Toxic's face. Did she just make the biggest mistake of her life?

Toxic never in his life expected Madison to confess the truth about Fink. Fink was like a father to her, and he was his family attorney. How could she sleep with an employee? He could not move as he stared at her, angry as hell.

Madison Johnson

ow could she be so stupid? "I guess I should leave?"
"I think you should," he snapped. "How could you?"

"It just happened that one time, Toxic. It was my business."

"Why did you have to tell me?"

"I didn't want the secret to come out, and they do."

"I can't deal with this."

"And all the women you slept with in the past, is the past, Toxic. Fink and I made a mistake, and it's never going to happen again. He is dating Rita, our secretary, and he is very happy with her. Please do not confront him. I am being honest with you, and this is the payment I'm getting for telling the truth. I can't win for losing," she snapped, shaking her head.

"He's like a father to me," Toxic snapped.

"But he is not your father, but your attorney and he's only fifty-five years old. He's not that old, and he's..."

"Don't you dare tell me he's good in bed," Toxic snapped. "Are you fucking crazy?"

Madison saw stars now, and stood up in all her naked glory, not caring about not having on any clothes. She put her hand on her hips. "Who are you to call me crazy? I am going to get dressed and get the hell out of here. Toxic Lyons, you can kiss my skinny black ass." *Madison grabbed her clothes off the floor, and chair, and then headed to the bathroom, slamming the door behind her. She had never been so furious in her life. The bastard slept with a lot of women, but he had the nerve or the audacity to get angry with her because she had men. Who did he think he was?*

She took a couple of deep breaths, and then pulled the purple shower curtains back which were very pretty --as she stared at them. Was Toxic's favorite color, purple? It did not matter now because he hated her. She hit her forehead. Why did she tell him the truth? She could have carried the secret to her grave, for heaven sakes.

Madison stared at herself in the mirror. She was falling in love with Toxic Lyons, and now the relationship was over before it even got started. She turned on the water in the shower and stepped into it. She had the kind of hair that could get wet, and still work with a blow dryer. She had white women's hair, of course. She let the warm water flow down her body thinking about the lovemaking she shared with Toxic, and feeling the sexual vibes heat up especially between her legs. Madison had this urge to stick her two fingers inside of her wet cove of pleasure and excite her clit by the memories of their shared lovemaking, but she was furious and the feeling went away.

As the water cleansed her soul, she wanted to puke. How could someone claim to be in love with you, and the minute something happens, they want to run and hide? So Toxic Lyons was going through the motions. He was not in love with her. Love does not run away but stay to handle it. He did not love her after all.

The tears fell, and Madison could kick herself for being such a cry baby. She regretted sleeping with her boss, but the deed was done, and she was hot and on fire, and needed someone to put her fire out. Fink was the one, and it was good, but she did not want or love him. It was just sex, and men do it all the time, so when a woman does it, they cannot take it.

She hysterically wept as the tears fell like rain, mingling into the water from the shower. She grabbed the shower gel sitting on the tub, and a sponge, and began cleaning her body. It was probably Toxic's sponge, but she did not care. It was time for her to get the hell away from such a spoiled brat. He was probably gone from the mansion and went to his condo. She had the memories to last her lifetime, and sometimes, the memories were all you could have in this life. Why in the hell did Toxic come into her life? What was his purpose if he was not going to stick around? She wept for five more minutes, and then she ceased the tears, washed her face, and finished up with her shower. Another five more minutes, and she turned off the water, and then found a clean towel in the handy basket and cleaned herself off. She also found lotion and covered her entire body in it. The lotion smelled like cherries. This mansion was equipped with everything, but this was Toxic floor, of course. She wondered how many women got to take a shower in his bathroom and use his shower gel.

She shook herself from the stupid thoughts, and then added her dirty clothes to her body. She had no choice in the matter.

She'd call Uber and then go home, and forget she ever met Toxic Lyons. Madison had a feeling that she'd never forget the handsome, white man. Sometimes, she could kick her ass for leveling with the man. What was wrong with her?

Madison stared at herself in the mirror one last time, and then she opened the bathroom door and walked back into the bedroom. She stopped in her tracks, staring at Toxic still sitting on the bed. She was stunned. Why was he still sitting there? Their eyes met, but Madison wasn't going to say anything. She had said enough to last her a lifetime, and then some.

Ten minutes passed, so Madison took the bait. "I'm going to wait outside on the bench for my Uber. Thanks for a wonderful 4th of July, and it was nice. But remember, don't tell someone you love them, and when they say or do something you don't like, then you're done with them. Do you know the meaning of love, Toxic Lyons? Your spoiled ass probably don't," she snapped. "When you claim to love someone, you work out your problems with them, instead of dismissing them like a little kid. You don't love me after all. I'd define the word before I throw it out to another woman."

"Sit down," he stated.

She stared at him.

"Can you please sit down for a minute?"

Madison didn't want to sit down, but she sat across from him on the bed. "What do you want Toxic? I can't be with someone who runs at the drop of a hat. I'm so confused, and this is new to me, but I've read enough romance to know what love is."

"I'm sorry," he said. "I was just angry, and you couldn't blame me. I never thought you'd confess that you slept with my attorney. I was stunned beyond comprehension."

"We weren't happy about it, but it just happened," she cried.

"And only once," he asked.

Madison rolled her eyes at him. "You and I weren't dating, Toxic, but it only happened once. "I told you he's dating Rita now. I have no plans but to work for my boss, and not sleep with him ever again. It was only sex. What you and I shared was making love."

"I do love you, and this is why I'm going to forgive you," he confessed.

Madison laughed. "Oh really?"

"I do know what love is, and this is why I'm still here. We are going to go to your place and get you whatever you need to spend the rest of the week with me, so you will be going home next Tuesday. This is like an apartment so you'll have everything at your beck and call, and my housekeeper will work for you, and my cook makes dinner. All you have to do is look pretty."

Madison laughed. "I do have a job."

Toxic smiled. "I know this."

"What about the case, it's a conflict of interest?"

"Let's get a settlement, and I'll be talking to Max to make that happen. If he wants to go to trial, then he's going to need another attorney. I'll excuse myself from this case."

"That was easy," Madison laughed.

Toxic laughed. "I'm ready when you are."

"I love your jeans and polo shirts."

"I love that maxi dress, and you?"

"I like you too."

"That's something," he cried.

Madison laughed, getting her tote bag. "Let's go. I don't know how this is going to work, you and I in the same space for an entire week. I'm new to this, so don't hate me."

"We're going to try and I'm going to be at work too."

"I need to sign in and check some work myself. I do need my laptop."

"I'm ready to go to your condo." *He grabbed his keys and phone.*

Madison stared around his place. "I've never seen an apartment in one room. You have everything on this floor, and the bedrooms upstairs. I feel like I'm in a condo instead of a room on a floor in a mansion."

Toxic laughed as he walked to the door. "My parents are very modern, and I lent my architectural skills also. I love being here when I'm not at the condo. I spent most of my time here because the place is private and inviting. I can go a week and not run into anyone. I spend all my time on my floor, but when I want to visit my other siblings, I leave, but they have their own places too."

"I don't think I'd ever move from here," she cried.

"You do want your own space from time to time. It's called independence."

Madison smiled as she walked to the door and opened it. "Let's get this show on the road."

"Sounds like a plan to me."

They got into the elevator and Toxic pushed the button for the lobby. He smiled at the most beautiful woman in the world.

Madison smiled at Toxic, the most beautiful man in the world. She was the luckiest woman in the world, but was she?

Toxic Lyons

T oxic was sitting in his office waiting for his client Max
Gent to meet him so they could discuss the case. He
was hoping that Max would agree to a settlement for Jasmine
and they could move on, but Max was a bastard.

As he stared out the window, he relieved the moment he
spent with Madison, dropping her back off at the mansion,
and showing her the office, where he left her turning on her
laptop and getting ready to go to work. We had to work, of
course, but he couldn't wait to get home and find her there.
She had packed up, almost her entire, house.

Toxic smiled as the beep entered his office. He reached
for his phone. "Yes, Mable, his legal secretary."

"Mr. Gent is here," Mable said.

"Show him in."

"Okay!"

*The door opened and the tall, and handsome white man
walked into the office as if he were the king or something. He
had a chip on his shoulder, or something.*

"Hi, Max, and please have a seat. Do you want something to eat?"

"No, but why couldn't you come to my office. I'm a very busy man."

Toxic opened his file on his desk and stared at it. "I thought we could reach some kind of settlement before we have to waste tax payer's money for a trial. Jasmine is entire to money since she has been off from work for months now."

"The fat bitch needs to lose some weight."

"But you slept with the fat bitch."

"I'm a man," he laughed, touching his goatee.

Toxic shook his head. Max was a son of a bitch. "She worked at the firm for fifteen years. It's not fair that you fire her because she's not skinny as the other whores you employ. This is a place of business, not a club house for your whores."

Max frowned. "Whose side are you on?"

"The side of justice. Just give her a certain amount, and then we can close this case."

"How much does the fat bitch want?"

Toxic winced. This was a cold-blooded turkey. "Eighty thousand dollars."

Max laughed. "I definitely need a new attorney."

"You can afford this amount and then some."

"I'm not paying a fat bitch my money because she lets food take over her life. I urged her constantly to lose weight. I have a gym at the firm so she can work out. She refused."

"How many times did you sleep with her?"

"I don't remember, once."

"Was it only once because Jasmine stated that you slept with her four times?"

Max frowned. "Who would sleep with a fat bitch that many times?"

Toxic stared at him, and then he took out a photo and pushed it over to him. "Who is this person? They look like they are about ten or eleven years old."

Max frowned again. "Where did you get this?"

"I have my ways when I'm representing a client. That picture is you, and you were a chubby little boy, so this is why you hate fat people. You were bullied until you lost the weight. How dare you ridicule other fat women? You should know better."

"How dare you?" he shouted. "I don't pay you for getting into my personal business. I will give the bitch thirty thousand and this case is closed for the duration. Make her sign something stating she will never contact me again."

Toxic shook his head. "We're going to court, and I have to remove myself and suggest one of my associates to handle your case. I'm in a conflict with the opposing counsel."

"This is some bullshit," Max snapped.

"You can go to court, and the opposing counsel is going to ask you why you slept with a fat woman four times if you despise anyone fat? Do you want to humiliate your reputation in court? The media is going to ridicule you."

"I knew hiring that fat bitch was going to be a problem for me."

"I think you like fat women, so stop playacting with me. I know your game, so you protest too much, thank you very much. I want you to consider eighty thousand and we can close this case."

Max was livid with rage. "Okay," he snapped.

Toxic smiled and pushed over the papers. "I need you to sign and then give me the check for Jasmine, and my fees, thank you very much. This case is null and void, and it was great doing business with you."

"This case is costing me a fortune," Max snapped, signing the papers. *He handed the papers back to Toxic.*

Toxic looked over the signatures, and then handed him his copy. "Our business is done."

Max frowned. "I need another favor."

Toxic frowned. "What?"

Max stood up and began pacing the office. "I used to date a woman name Linda Price, and we were dating for five months, and then she caught me with another woman, and broke off our relationship. I really liked her because she was the only woman, I dated for five months. I don't know why I cheated on her? I guess I wanted to end the relationship because she was getting to close. I really love Linda."

Toxic stared at her. "I read that she was murdered last week."

"She was and the prosecutor is bent on putting the blame on me."

"Did you have anything to do with her murder? Don't lie to me."

"Of course not," he stated, still pacing the office. "I loved her."

"Someone shot her five times in the chest. It's a crime of passion."

"I had nothing to do with it, but I don't want to go to prison for a crime I didn't commit. I think someone is framing me. I have a lot of enemies."

"You don't think." *Toxic grabbed his yellow legal pad and began writing.* "You never learn, Max. You think your shit don't stink. You need to find one woman, and settle down. It might make your life a lot happier, thank you very much."

"Linda would have been the one. I missed her so much, and if she was with me, someone wouldn't have killed her. I know she was upset about something, but she would not discuss it with me. I had a feeling that she broke up with me to save my life. I think she was being blackmailed or something. I don't know the trouble she found herself in."

"Someone hated her and made sure she was dead on impact. Do you know if she had enemies?"

Max shook his head. "Linda was beautiful and kind. I miss her, and I blame myself. If she was with me, she might still be alive. I don't know how I'm going to live without her."

"I'm sorry for your pain." *Toxic thought about Madison. He could be a crazy if he couldn't be with her. He loved her.*

"Can you take this case?"

"I'll talk to the prosecutor and see if you're a suspect. Alice is a decent prosecutor, and she doesn't prosecute unless she has evidence. I suggest you not leave town. I'll get back to you on this. Stop being so cocky Max and live in the real world. You're no better than anyone because you have money."

"I know the drill," Max said. *He took out his briefcase, and opened it, putting in his copies of the agreement to pay Jasmine, and then he took out his checkbook and made out two checks, one for Jasmine and the other for legal services and past legal services.* "I think this should cover Jasmine's case ending, and the new case."

Toxic stared at the check with all the zeros. He smiled. "I'll take a retainer, but you might not be arrested."

"I just have this feeling," Max stated. "My sins are catching up with me."

"You might be right about that. I will talk to Alice and keep you posted. Again, I'm sorry about Linda. Life is too short, and we can't waste time, Max like we have all the time in the world. You have to take happiness when you can."

Max stood up and shook Toxic's hand. "I will take heed now. I do understand the way life gets in the way of true happiness. I need to go to Church. I have a lot to be grateful for, and it's time I get my life in order."

"Good luck," Toxic cited.

Max smiled and left his office.

Toxic stared after him, and then he reached for the telephone to dial Alice's number. He might as well get this over with. It was ten minutes before Alice Spent came on the line.

"Mr. Lyons, what can I do for you?" Alice said.

"And good morning to you too," he laughed.

"What do you want Toxic?"

"Who do you have in custody for Linda Jones murder?"

"I see Max hired you, the bastard?" she shouted.

Toxic was beginning to smell a rat. "Is he a suspect, or you're just a woman scorned?"

"What?" she exclaimed. "I beg your pardon."

Toxic laughed. "Did you sleep with Max?"

"That's none of your damn business."

"We slept together a few times, so you do get around, Alice. Don't play these games with me. I need to know if my client is a suspect. If not, don't waste time trying to pin this

165

Carol Ann Culbert Johnson

murder on him. My client loved her, and he'd never hurt or kill her."

"I hate you, Toxic Lyons," she snapped. "Are you busy?"

"For what?"

"I'm in the mood for you to suck my pussy."

Toxic shook his head. "You don't waste time, Alice, but I'm off the market, and my girlfriend Madison would have a problem with me sucking that gorgeous pussy of yours."

"What?" she shrieked. "I can't believe Toxic Lyons has a girlfriend. Does she know what she's getting into? You're not married, Toxic, and I love the way you get my clit all worked up, and then you give me multiple orgasms."

Toxic smiled. "I'm sorry, but I won't be sucking your pussy any longer. My girlfriend's pussy will be the only one I'm sucking for now and the duration of my life. Now let's get back to business."

"Max isn't going to go down for this murder. I have a person of interest, and she's going down for the murder. It seems that Linda was sleeping with men and women, and the woman she was with fell in love with her, but she broke off their relationship when she got involved with Max."

"So she shot Linda five times in the chest. She was angry as hell."

"She did, and tried killing herself, but, of course, she didn't succeed. I'm going to get her to confess, and this case is closed. But if you and your girlfriend don't work out, you still have my number in your big black book," she laughed.

"That book is burned," he laughed. "Thanks, Alice, and it's nice talking to you. I'll give Max the news so he can get on with his life."

Alice sighed. "Have a nice life, Toxic. You're going to break every women in this city heart, and then some. I do want you to find someone and be happy. I'm going to miss your tongue."

Toxic laughed, and ended the call. He wanted to suck Madison's pussy, and he was going to make sure that he go off early. He was glad he didn't have to represent Max. He found Max's cell phone number, and text him a message. "Alice has a suspect, and it was a woman, so you're off the hook. Linda was sleeping with men and women, and it was the death of her. I'm sorry man. I'll return the retainer."

Five minutes later he got a text from Max. "I can't believe she was sleeping with Shelby. I remember seeing her a lot of times and wondered why she was hanging around all the time. Linda assured me that Shelby was her best friend. Thanks and keep the retainer. You're the best and then some."

Toxic smiled as he put down his cell phone. Life was just grand.

Madison Johnson

As Madison stared around her she couldn't believe that she was sitting in a mansion, and on the 4th floor. She moved in her things and everything fit right in. She wanted to scream as she sat in Toxic's office and sat at his masculine desk. He was clean, and there wasn't a pencil out of place. He gave her a drawer to use, and she was making herself at home.

Once her laptop booted up, she quickly skyped Sylvia and Helen, hoping they'd be available. She couldn't wait to show them where she was, and give them the excited news.

First, Sylvia connected, and then three minutes later Helen connect. Madison smiled at the two of them. "Hello, ladies."

"Where are you?" Helen asked.

"She's at the mansion," Sylvia said. "She's also in Toxic's room. I know that mansion left and right and everyone's rooms. I've been there so much, I probably have my own room," she laughed.

"What are you doing there?" Helen asked.

"I spent the 4th of July with Toxic and his family, and I'm living with him for a week at the mansion," Madison exclaimed. "I know this is a shock to my two best friends, but I can't believe I'm here. I'm sitting in his office working, and Toxic is at work."

"Wow," Sylvia said. "Are you two dating?"

"He told me that he loves me," Madison cried. "Toxic Lyons is in love with me. Can you two believe it? I'm falling in love with him too, but I'm not going to say the three words until I'm sure he's the man I want to spend the rest of my life with him. I'm getting to know him and he's definitely a neat freak."

Sylvia laughed. "Yes, he is, and then some."

"We're so happy for you," Helen cried. "You deserve some happiness."

"I'm very happy for the moment," Madison cried.

"Don't blow this opportunity," Sylvia said. "I know you."

"She's right," Helen said. "Let Toxic Lyons love you the way a man loves a woman. You're the luckiest woman in the world. Do you know how many women want him?"

"I do," Madison said. "I told him about Fink."

"You did what?" Helen snapped.

"I didn't want any secrets to come out," Madison confessed. "I had to be honest with him, and now he knows and I can put that secret behind me, and get on with my life."

"Did you think that Toxic would leave?" Helen stated.

Madison frowned. "He was angry and I thought he'd leave, but when I came out the bathroom he was sitting on the bed, and we worked it out. He loves me, and sometimes, love conquers all."

"Most of the time," Sylvia cried.

Madison frowned again. "How are you doing?"

"I'm good," Sylvia cried. "My husband is with his lover, and he doesn't give a damn about me and my feelings. He is a pain in my ass. I was pregnant twice but had two miscarriages."

"We remember," Helen said. "Do you need me to come over?"

"I'm so busy, I don't have time to think about my failed marriage," Sylvia cried. "The bastard apologized to me, and explained that he thought he could get married and forget about being gay, but it was in his DNA and he's very happy with George. He still loves me, but he doesn't love me the way a man loves a woman. I wanted to kill him with my bare hands. He wasted all these years of my life being on the down low. I hate him."

Silence was evident as Helen and Madison let Sylvia vent her frustration. Madison couldn't comprehend the pain that her best friend was going through. She just had to be there for her.

"I always suspected something was going on between my husband and his best friend, George," Sylvia continued. "I used to watch the way they touched each other, or the way they looked at each other, but I ignored the warning signs. I didn't want to think that my husband was gay. That he wanted to make love to a man, and not his wife."

"I'm so sorry," Madison cried.

"Me too," Helen stated.

"When my husband wanted to make love to me always from behind," Sylvia cried. "I knew something was wrong. I have this gay fashion designer working for me, Toby, and he's always talking about his sex life with his married, partner, Hayes. The two of them would take turns sticking it in the back and make love all day and night. Now I do understand the game."

"Wow," Madison said.

"I went to a bar last night and stayed there until the wee hours of the morning," Sylvia confessed. "I had about five drinks, and then I met this white man, and he and I went to a hotel, and he fucked me all over the place. I made sure he took me from behind because I wanted to see how it felt to fuck from the back with a man. It was nice, and this white man knew how to fuck. I had multiple orgasms with him, and when he sucked my pussy, I screamed so loud he had to cover my mouth with his hand. We did some kinky stuff like handcuffs, and whips. I had the time of my life," she laughed. "I'm a very attractive woman and my husband could go to hell and back."

Silence took over.

"I have his number, and he has mine, and he called me this morning, and we're going to hook up later on tonight at his place. I'm going to fuck until I can't get enough."

"Are you insane?" Helen shouted. "The man could have been a serial killer.

"What were you thinking?" Madison shouted.

Sylvia laughed. "You two are silly. I'm safe and sound, and I had my registered gun in my purse, thank you both very much. I'm not stupid. There were a lot of men trying to fuck me, but I spotted Jake, who just stared at me. I had a feeling that he was going to be a constant in my life."

"We need his number," Helen said.

"We do," Madison pointed, out. "We also need his address."

Sylvia laughed again. "I do know the drill. I'll text the information to the both of you, and then you two can leave me alone. I'm fucking and it's nice to be appreciated. My husband wanted a man, but there are men who wants me. It feels good, and until you experience being married and having your husband leave you for another man, you two will never understand my plight."

"Just be careful," Helen stated.

"And safe," Madison pointed out.

"I'm going to be fine," Sylvia laughed. "Jake is tall, and has blue eyes, and he's rich. He owns hotels and restaurants, and New York City, thank you all very much. His last name is Jake Page."

"Are you freaking kidding me?" Helen exclaimed. "He's a billionaire and then some."

"I've even heard of him," Madison cried.

"I did well," Sylvia sang. "I sucked his dick, and had him literally screaming out my name. The man was hot for me, and then some, and I was truly hot for him. I'm going to spend a lot of time with him."

"I hope it works out," Madison said. "I love you."

"I do too," Helen said. "I love you."

"I love you both too," Sylvia cried. "I have to get back to work and then get ready for my date later. I'll text you both the info, and don't text me back. I'll be safe. He has a mini mansion, and he also has a little boy at the age of five. I'm going to meet his son, so this might work out."

"You're vulnerable," Helen pointed out. "Why are you meeting his son so soon? You just met the man. Have you lost your mind?"

"I'm just having fun for the moment, so don't you two sweat about me. I'm not about to fall in love or get serious about anyone. I have learned my lesson with my husband, thank you both very much. I'm just having fun, and I need to go. I'll talk to you both later."

"Keep me posted," Madison said. "I'm in the windy city and you two are in the big apple. I want to know how everything went with meeting his son. I hope you have a great time."

"I will," Sylvia said. "There are other men in the sea. I love you both, and good-bye."

"Good-bye," Helen said.

"Bye, you two," Madison said. *She ended the call and sat her iPhone on the desk. What was Sylvia thinking getting involved with a man so soon? She wasn't thinking, and she couldn't do anything about it, but support Sylvia. She had to put herself in her shoes to understand the plight.*

She heard a buzz, and then froze. Dammit, who could that be? She didn't want Toxic's family to know that she had moved in or something. She would just pretend that Toxic isn't here. She focused on her computer, looking at her short stories. She wanted to get the first three chapters ready for Tanyann and prayed that she was going to make her writing dreams come true. It had been a long dream of hers after becoming a paralegal.

The buzz sounded again, and Madison stood up. Whoever was ringing it was not going away. Toxic showed her what to do if someone buzzed the floor, and he assured her that no one would be bothering her, but apparently, he did not know his own family. She went to the elevator and pushed the intercom. "Hello."

"Hi, Madison, it's Tanyann. Can I come up?"

So apparently, she talked to her brother. Madison pushed the button and waited by the elevator for Tanyann to make her appearance. The doors opened and she smiled at the pretty petite white woman. She was wearing a blue V-neck top with blue shorts and blue accessories and she reminded her of Jennifer Anniston, the actress. "Hi."

"I spoke with Toxic and he told me you'd be here."

"I was working on my short story collection."

"I'm here to take a few short stories home to read."

"Please come in and have a seat in the living room. Can I get you something to drink or eat? I think Amy made some sandwiches or something. I'm working in the office."

"We can go in there," Tanyann said. "My brother is definitely in love."

"Why do you say that?"

"There's no woman ever been in his space like this."

Madison smiled. "So, he says."

"But you're not convinced," Tanyann pointed out.

They reached the office, and Tanyann took a seat on the sofa, as Madison sat down at the desk housing her laptop computer and printer. "I read romance, but it's different when reality comes along. I have feelings for your brother, and I think about him when I'm not with him, so something is going on. I'm eager to find out."

"As long as you don't hurt him, or you'll have to answer to me, and this has nothing to do with business. If I like your short stories and want to represent you, I'll be your agent regardless of your relationship with my brother. I got so thirsty. I'd love a diet coke."

Madison stood up. "I'll be right back." She was nervous as hell. This was Toxic floor, and she was still getting used to the fact that she was here in this mansion with a white man. She opened the refrigerator and took out two bottles of diet coke and headed back to the office. "Did you want a glass?"

Tanyann shook her head. "The bottle is fine." She opened the bottle and took a long sip. "That is good, so let's see these short stories. Guy and I are going to Jamaica for a three weeks, and work won't be on my mind. My husband works all the time, so this is going to be a long time coming."

"Your husband is fine, and I love his sitcom."

Tanyann smiled, taking another sip of her soda.

Madison opened the bottle of diet soda and took a long sip. She remembered when she was fat that she had to stop drinking diet soda, but she was going to have one this time. She was never going to get fat again.

"My husband is black, of course," Tanyann said.

Madison blushed.

"I'm white and he's black," Tanyann spoke. "It's a problem with most people in this racist world, but Guy and I don't give a damn. I love him, and he loves and adores me, and that's the bottom line. I don't give a damn what color he is. My mother is married to a black man, and now my brother is about to be married to a black woman, so it does run in the family."

Madison almost choked on her diet soda, as she sat it down. "Toxic and I are getting to know each other. We haven't discussed marriage."

Tanyann laughed. "Again, I know my brother and he doesn't make this kind of commitment. You're in his space while he's at work. Stop denying what's going on and live with it. I'm thrilled for Toxic. The women he has met are bimbos and you're different. I like you, and Toniann and Tammyann likes you too. I'm sure Tumor does too so welcome to the family."

Madison frowned. "We have to wait and see."

"Let me see some short stories as she stared at her apple watch. I have time to read a few of them and make a decision, so I suggest you give me the ones that you know works for me."

Madison reached for a green file folder, and smiled at the three stories she chose, and then pushed the folder over to her. Tanyann grabbed it, and then took off her shoes, and put her legs up on the sofa, and relaxed. She got into her reading and she was in agent mode, so Madison knew she had to wait with baited breath, and not bothered her.

Madison clicked on the email from Fink, and began reading. "Good morning, Madison. Jasmine has won her case, and she's going to get more money than she thought possible. I spoke with Toxic and he was so nasty with me, or cold for that matter. Did you say something to him?"

"I told him," Madison typed.

"Are you crazy?" Fink typed.

"I didn't want to begin our relationship with lies. He was angry at first, and basically told me to get out, but when he decided to deal with it because he loves me. It's out and over with."

"I don't want him to hate me, Madison."

"He's angry now, but this will pass," Madison typed.

"You could have carried this secret to your grave," Fink typed.

"No I couldn't," Madison typed. "Can we change the subject?"

"I guess so," he typed. "I'm emailing you five other cases, so get the brief done. I can't believe you were off work yesterday because it's not like you. I know it's time for you to get into a relationship, but don't neglect your independence. Toxic is a wonderful man, but you need to finish up your degree and still become a paralegal. Do you know how many secretaries and paralegals have come through my office, and quit when they got married?"

Madison laughed to herself. "I'm not going to quit my job and be a slave for Toxic or any man," she typed. "I'm still going to school and I might have an agent on my short stories. Toxic will enhance my life, and not hurt it."

"As long as you stay true to yourself," Fink typed.

"I will, and you have nothing to fear. I'll get on the other assignments and have everything done soon. Thanks for being my boss and friend. I won't tell another soul. Sylvia and Helen knows, and Toxic and that's it."

"What?" he typed. "You might as well call a reporter and put it on the news and in the papers, thank you very much. What were you thinking, Madison? If Janey finds out about this, our relationship is over," he typed.

"She's not going to find out," Madison typed. "My lips are seal."

"Hmm…" he typed.

"I promise Fink, and I'll talk to you later."

"Okay, Madison."

She smiled as she focused on Tanyann who was into her stories, and Madison didn't know if that was good or bad. She didn't have a frown on her face, so maybe she liked her short stories. If not, she couldn't worry about it. Tanyann was just one person, and if she couldn't find a traditional publisher, then she'd publish her work on amazon. Her short stories were going to be read one way or another.

It was after thirty minutes when Tanyann looked up and smiled.

Madison stared at her.…

Toxic Lyons

~~~~~~

*T*oxic *couldn't finish any work thinking about Madison at his apartment, and he wanted to be with her for some reason. He left work early surprising everyone, hurrying home to his girlfriend. He never thought that'd happen, but Toxic Lyons had a girlfriend, and her name was Madison Johnson.*

He laughed as he hurried into his range rover and headed to the mansion. The two of them were going to have dinner. Did Madison cook? He didn't want her slaving over a hot stove, so he waited for the light to turn red so he could stop his car and grab his cell phone. The light turned red, and he reached for his cell phone and programed Amy's number on his car to prevent him from talking on the phone. He listened to the cell phone and waited for it to connect as he mingled back into traffic.

"This is Amy."

"Hi, Amy, how is everything going?"

"If you're checking up on the lovely Madison; she's doing great. Right now she's visiting with Ms. Tanyann and the two of them are in the office. I asked them if they wanted anything, and they just drank a few diet cokes."

Toxic smiled. "Why don't you fix some dinner for the three of us? Madison likes pork chops, and rice. Do you think you can handle that? I don't want to put you out, of course."

"I'm all for it," Amy said. "I like Madison."

Toxic smiled again. "I like her too, and thanks Amy. How is the schooling going?"

"It's going wonderful," she exclaimed. "I can't believe I'm in nursing school and going to make my nursing dreams come true. I've dreamed of being a nurse for so long, and now that my three children are grown, it's time for me to make my dreams come true."

"As long as you stay in school, and Tammyann knows all about nursing, so seek her out if you need help in anything. Amy, you and your husband, and children are family to us."

"Thank you so much, Mr. Toxic and I'll get to the dinner."

"Thanks." *He disconnected the call and smiled. He was going to have a great day. He smiled as his cell phone rang, and he pushed the button on his car to activate his phone. He smiled when he saw his brother's picture come up.* "Tumor, what's going on with you? I still think of Cancer every time I say your name. I know you had a difficult time in elementary and high school, but it's so funny to me."

"I'm not smiling," Tumor stated. "How are you doing?"

"I'm sure you heard that Madison is staying with me, so let's not beat around the bush. This family couldn't keep out of each other's business is they were paid to do it."

Tumor laughed. "You never have a woman in your apartment at the mansion. I don't know about your condo, but not at the mansion. I like Madison and she's the perfect woman for you."

"I'm glad I have your approval," he sarcastically replied. "Is that all you call me for? How is Tricia and the children?"

"Everyone is happy, and we're just glad you finally found a woman to rock your world, and float your boat. Don't do anything to mess this up, Toxic. I know how you can be."

Toxic thought about the fact that Madison slept with his attorney. He spoke with Fink earlier and he was very chilly with his attorney. The fact that he had his hands all over Madison's body made him want to punk or something. His attorney had his dick inside of Madison made him want to hurt him, but he shook it off. "Don't order the wedding cake just yet. I have feelings for Madison, and I even love her, so we're going to try and work on this relationship. I'm not wasting another minute."

"I'm happy for you, brother," Tumor replied. "I love being married. Tricia is my soul mate in this life, and I hope and pray that Madison is your soul mate. How is work going?"

"I settled a case, and now Max might be accused of murdering his former girlfriend, but I spoke with Alice, and he's not a suspect. His girlfriend was sleeping with men and women."

"Wow," Tumor said. "So who murdered the girlfriend?"

"The woman," Toxic stated.

"A lifetime movie, and then some."

"Tell me about it. Men are on the down low and women are going with men and women. I don't know where this world is coming too, but the world is going down the toilet in a basket."

Tumor laughed. "What?"

Toxic laughed. "I don't even know what I just said."

"My brother is so in love he can't think straight."

"Maybe and maybe not," he cautioned. "Okay, I'm in love and her name is Madison Johnson. Tumor, I'm in love with this woman, and I don't even know her. What's wrong with me?"

"Get to know her, and by having her in your space is going to break the ice between the two of you. I really hopes it works out. We need to take your ass off the market for sure."

Toxic laughed. "I'm off the market for now."

"Support each other, if you don't agree or not. Tricia wants to model now, and I don't think it's a great ideal, but Sylvia is bent on having this plus-size line, and she wants Tricia to model for her."

"Your wife is gorgeous, and she'd make a fabulous model."

"Thanks for not the support," Tumor said. "My wife needs to be at home with me and the children. She's going to be flying back and forth to New York City, and the children and I will suffer."

"You have to let your wife, fly, Tumor."

"My wife never has to work. Why does she need to model?"

"Why are you into real estate?"

"I love my job, and I make enough money to take care of me and my family. Tricia doesn't have to work, and she's driving me crazy. I could kill Sylvia for even thinking about Tricia as one of the models."

"Are you serious?"

"Of course, I am. I don't want my wife working. We fought over this all last week, and I thought this week she'd forget about it, but she wants to model. What am I going to do?"

"Let her model and do her thang. She gave you three gorgeous children, and now it's her time to shine. I don't expect Madison to give up her career for me. She's a paralegal and about to become a published writer if Tanyann has anything to say about it. My sister is the best agent in Chicago and New York, and Madison's dreams are about to come true. I'm not going to block her success."

"You and I disagree on this issue. I told Tricia when we met that I wanted my wife to stay at home with the children and take care of me, and she agreed. Now she's all into modeling and doesn't give a damn about my thoughts."

"Are you dictating to her?"

"I'm the man of this family," he shouted.

"Keep with that attitude, and you're going to be a very lonely man, Tumor."

"Where is the support?"

"We disagree to disagree."

"Thanks for nothing, brother."

"I can't support you on this, but I suggest you listen to your wife and see her side of the issue, and stop thinking about your needs. Tricia isn't going to go off and make a career into modeling, and forget about her husband and children. Stop being so insecure."

"I don't like this," he snapped.

"Compromise and let her shine."

"Whatever," Tumor snapped. "I'm done with this topic of conversation."

Toxic shook his head. "Don't say I didn't warn you about your attitude. A woman doesn't like being dictated to because they will do the opposite."

"I'll talk to you later."

The call disconnected and Toxic smiled to himself. If Tumor did not listen to his wife, he was going to be in divorce court. Tricia was strong and beautiful, and she had a mind of her own. She loved Tumor, but she also love being independence, and if she wanted to model, then Tumor or no one was going to stop her. Toxic prayed that their marriage stood the test of time. Did he want to marry anyone?

As he turned left, he wondered....

Madison Johnson

Tanyann smiled at Madison. "Girl, you have a gift, and welcome to my world."

Madison was stunned. "Are you serious?"

"I love your short stories, and I read three of them, but they kept me on the edge of my seat. I am going to make you a writer, girl. Now get all the stories together, and then I'm going to assign you to an editor. Her name is Beverly Bonds, and she's the best editor in the world. She's going to go through your entire book of short stories, and edit, and then we're going from there. I'm going to put your book of short stories on the map."

Madison felt the tears forming. "Are you sure?"

"You do believe in your writing, Madison? I don't have time for insecure writers. Do you want to take this ride with me?"

"Of course," Madison cried. "It's a dream."

"Then focus on getting those short stories out for me, and begin on book 2. We don't have time to waste, and life is just too short. Let's get the ball rolling, and everything is going to work out just fine." *Tanyann stood up, yawning.* "I need to take a nap or something, so excuse me."

"What is my next step?"

"Get the rest of the book of short stories together, and then email them to the address I'm going to text you when I get home. Beverly Bonds is the editor, and she's going to edit your book. I'm going to have my secretary draw up a contract for our connection, and when I present your book to traditional publishers, you're going to get a check. It's just like in the movies and television."

"Thank you so much," Madison cried. *She let the tears fall.*

Tanyann smiled, and then she embraced Madison. "It's going to be wonderful doing business with you, and your gift. Some of the twists and turns on your stories surprised the hell out of me and I like a good twist as most readers. I want to think this is how the story ends, but then I find out that I'm completely wrong. I'll show myself out and talk to you soon. When you email Beverly, send me an email also."

"Thank you," Madison cried as she walked Tanyann to the elevator and pushed the button for the elevator to open.

"Thank you," Tanyann yawned. "Dammit, I do have to get some sleep. I'm yawning all over the place and then some. Why am I so tired lately? I've been so fatigue and just wanting to sleep and eat."

Madison smiled. "Are you pregnant?"

Tanyann's eyes opened wide. "What?"

"It sounds like a pregnancy to me."

"I don't think so, but the last time Guy and I were together we had made love the entire two days because he's busy and so am I. We didn't use a condom at every turn. My God, I might be pregnant. I need to buy one of those tests. Thanks, Madison."

"Good luck."

Tanyann yawned again, covering her mouth as the elevator doors opened. "Thank you."

Madison smiled as the doors closed and she walked back to her apartment and shut the door. Tanyann might be pregnant, and wow, she thought to herself. She headed back to her office with a smile on her face. I am going to become a writer. Madison did a dance around the apartment. "Thank you God for making all my dreams come true. Not only do I have a man, but I'm about to embark on another career for myself. I'm blessed."

Madison was busy working on her short stories when she heard the elevator. She stared at her apple watch. It was three in the evening, and she had been working diligently. She smiled as she waited for Toxic to find her. She knew it was him.

He didn't disappoint as he walked into the office, and their eyes met. "This is what I like to see when I come home from work," Toxic stated.

Madison laughed. "And what do you want to see, Mr. Lyons?"

"My lovely girlfriend waiting for me."

Madison smiled. "Mr. Lyons you got your wish because here I am."

Toxic grabbed Madison and embraced her. She loved the gorgeous scent of him, and his fabulous cologne. She closed her eyes as their lips met, and then their tongues did a dance of their own. She was truly falling for this white man.

The kiss ended as Toxic held her tight. "I want to make love to you right here and now. My body is on fire, and you light up my world and then some. What's happening to me?"

Madison took his hand, and smiled. "Let's go to the bedroom and find out."

They met on the bed in five seconds or less, and clothes went flying everywhere as their bodies touched and then the moans entered the silence. Madison was on fire as Toxic kissed her entire body, and when his tongue went down to her pleasure palace, she screamed out his name. She was so wet, and her pussy juices were flowing like a water faucet. She was on fire, and in another minute she was going to explode. Just one touch from Toxic and her body was spending out of control.

Her body shook, and then she laid spent. Toxic was ready as he added a condom to his large shaft, and Madison felt a little scared because he was so big, but he was gentle as he kissed her all over, and then eased inside of her, and Madison didn't feel any pain but pleasure as their bodies rocked back and forth. The noise they made as their bodies thrust gave Madison another orgasm, and five minutes later Toxic exploded inside the condom. They lay spent for a few minutes, as their bodies came back to life.

Madison knew she was in love with Toxic Lyons. "I love you," she cried.

"I love you too." *Their lips met again, and their bodies made love for another hour. The two of them were on fire.*

After another hour, they laid spent from more lovemaking. "Will you marry me?" Toxic asked.

Madison grasp as she stared at Toxic....

Toxic Lyons

Toxic was on pins and needles as he waited for Madison's answer. He proposed to her and there was no going back now. He stared at the ceiling and not her face. What was he thinking?

He stared at the lovely woman. "Are you going to answer me, or leave me rejected?"

"I don't know what to say, Toxic."

"Yes, Toxic Lyons, I will marry you."

Madison stared at him. "Where did this come from?"

"We love each other, so what is the problem? When two people love other, then it's time to take the relationship to the next level, Madison. I don't have to tell you this. You read romance novels, so you should be an expert in the field of romance."

Madison smiled. "My romance novels don't compare to real life."

"Then why do you read them?" *Toxic massaged her back, and Madison closed her eyes. Her back was her sensitive area. She opened her eyes, staring at the handsome man.*

"You know how to get a woman," she laughed.

"I'm beginning to know you, and now I know your back is your most sensitive area. But let's get back to the subject. I know you're the woman for me, so let's get married next month. I'm sure Sylvia and Helen will plan it."

"You're freaking serious," she cried.

"I love you, and I don't want to waste another minute. I like having you here in my space like this. I like coming home to someone every day for the rest of my life. Someone I know that loves me for me, and not my money."

Madison smiled, sitting up in bed, and staring at Toxic. "I have my own money, and I'm not about to quit my job. I'm finishing up my Masters in paralegal science, and I was thinking about going to law school, but that's not an option anymore for me. I want to spend the other half of my life writing my short stories and getting them published. Your sister, Tanyann loves my writing, and she's going to put me on the map."

Toxic smiled. "I had a serious discussion with Tumor, and he's upset because now his wife, Tricia, wants to model, and she's already doing the weekend news on channel 7. He wants her to stay at home and take care of him and their children. If she could get pregnant again, Tumor would be so happy."

Madison frowned. "Tricia is an independent woman. I watch the news just to see her, and she has a way of turning negative news into something more positive. She has the nicest smile, and she's a lovely woman. There's no way she's going to sit at home and have babies. Did Tumor realize this when he married her? This is why couples rush to get married, and they don't have a clue about each other."

Toxic sat up in bed also, staring at her naked breasts, and all he wanted to go was suck them, and then take her back to bed. But right now, he was getting angrier because Madison was going to turn down his proposal, and then their relationship would have to end. He wasn't about to just date a woman for the rest of his life. He was now ready to settle down, and if Madison didn't want to take this ride with him, then he had no reason to continue being with her.

"You're thinking too much," she cried, touching his face. "Toxic I want you to be sure about us. Why can't be just date for the rest of this year, and then get married next year? We have five more months to get to know each other, and by this time we'll both be ready to tie the knot."

Toxic shook his head. "You want to marry me in August, or our relationship is over. I'm not about to waste any more time with an insecure woman, Madison. I want you and we love each other. Maybe you're just saying the words, but not feeling them."

"Are you crazy, Toxic?" she snapped.

"I'm dead serious," he said. *He stood up and searched for his underwear. He found it on the floor and stepped into them.*

"Where are you going?" she cried.

"I'm going to the guest room or something so you can think about your actions. I suggest you think real long and hard because you're not going to get another chance again."

Madison frowned, staring at his hard dick, as he stepped into his underwear, and then his shirt and jeans.

"Are you going to run when you don't get your way?"

"No, I'm just giving you space. You don't have to leave."

Madison laughed. "I'm not about to leave after I practically cleaned out my house. I don't want you threatening me again, Toxic. You can't always have your way about things, which is going to be a problem in our relationship and a marriage. I love you, but compromise is the key. What kind of woman would I be just marrying you when I don't even know you? Why can't you see my side of it? Let's get married in January, Toxic. We only have five more months. We can get engaged as of today. It's the right thing to do. When I get married, I'm not getting married again."

Toxic knew Madison made complete sense, but the rejection was difficult for him. He just needed a moment, and he left the room. "I'll be in the office getting some work done."

Madison stared after him, fighting the tears. She got back into bed and spread the blanket over her naked body. Toxic was stubborn as five mules, but she prayed he agreed to her terms, and security would have to remove her. She smiled because she wasn't going anywhere. She closed her eyes because she was exhausted mentally and physically, and all she wanted to do was sleep and forget about the stress for the moment.

Toxic sat in his office and stared at his dark desktop computer. He didn't even want to turn on his laptop. He pushed the power button and waited for it to boot up. What woman didn't want to marry him? Madison was crazy as hell. He didn't have to take his rejection. The computer was on as he stared at his home screen. Dammit, what was wrong with her? Maybe Madison needed to see someone about her insecurities. She was slim, and she still lived in the world of fat people. He nodded his head.

What was he going to do about Madison Johnson?

He stared at his computer screen for another twenty minutes and then he reached for his Samsung cell phone and pushed button #1 for his mother's number. She'd give him some good advice.

"Hi, Toxic, and how are you?" his mother spoke.

Toxic smiled. He urged his mother to get a Samsung Note 4 because she was always keeping notes, and now she could do it on her phone. She was definitely up with the technology. "Hi mother."

"What's going on?"

"What were you doing mother?"

"Just paying some bills, son. What's going on?"

"Nothing," he lied.

His mother laughed. "Don't lie to me. Talk to me."

"I asked Madison to marry me today."

"Wow," his mother cried.

"Was I rushing it?"

"I don't know son. What did she say?"

"She didn't say yes."

"Madison is a very sensible woman, son. What did she say?"

"She wants to get engaged and then maybe get married in January."

"I like her son, and she's right. Start off the first of the year with a new marriage, Go buy her the most beautiful ring, and be sensible about this. She's not going anywhere, and she will have your ring on her finger. You don't have to rush her. I hope you didn't give her an ultimatum?"

Toxic frowned.

"Son, what's wrong with you? Is Madison still here?"

"She's not leaving after she brought her things over to stay for a week."

"I'd give her a room if you do something as stupid. I find fault with some of my parenting skills. You four did not want for anything, and I gave you everything you wanted and needed. I spoiled all four of you. Everything isn't given to you on a silver platter when others are concerned. You need to stop thinking that you're the king and everyone has to bow down to you. If Madison is the love of your life, then you need to honor her, and wait. Patience is the key."

Toxic frowned. "Madison is so unpredictable. I'm afraid she's going to run from our relationship and then I'm never going to find her again. She has fat issues."

"I'll talk to her and convince her to talk to my shrink."

"Mother you don't need a shrink," he laughed.

"I do, honey and I'm still seeing her. When I married your father, my entire family disowned me. I have two other siblings, and my family doesn't know them. I almost gave up on your father, but we're happy, and have four children to show for it. You and Tanyann might not have the pain as much as James and I did. Times have changed, but racist is still a part of the new world. Talking to someone about past issues will save a lot of pain in the marriage."

"Are you and James okay?"

"Of course, son. I'll call Madison in a few hours."

Toxic smiled, covering his face. "Thanks mother. I love you so much."

"And I love you son, and when you feel like this come to me so I can talk you down before you make a mistake. Madison loves you, but she is no pushover. You need to watch your back because you have met your match with her."

Toxic laughed. "I guess I have mother. I'll talk to you later."

"Okay, son, and have a blessed day."

"You do the same."

Toxic ended the call and smiled. His mother would make everything okay. She did when he was a child, and she will do the same thing as an adult. He clicked on a file folder on his desktop and got into his work. Everything was peachy, he thought to himself.

Madison Johnson

T he ringing of Madison's cell phone opened her eyes, and she focused as she sat up in bed, and reached for it. She was still exhausted for some reason. She stared at the unknown number, and pushed the button. "Hello," she whispered.

"I'm sorry, honey for waking you up. Please go back to sleep."

Madison sat up in bed. "Mrs. Lyons, how are you? It's okay."

"Are you sure, honey? I can call you back later. You sound so tried or just frustrated with my son. I know he's a mess and then some. I used to whip his ass the most because he was so stubborn."

Madison laughed, wiping the sleep out of her eyes, as she yawned. She put Mrs. Lyons on the speaker on her iPhone. "I'm exhausted and frustrated Mrs. Lyons."

"Please call me Maggie, honey."

"Yes, Maggie," she laughed. "I'm in love with your son, and I'm not leaving. He's stubborn, but so am I. Madison Johnson invented the word," she laughed.

"I like your laughter, and I'm glad you're not running off."

"Your son runs off when he's not getting his way like a little kid or something. I'm learning his ways so far, and it's frustrating, but I'm not going anywhere. I love the pain, and did he tell you to talk to me?"

"My son comes to me when he knows he made a mistake, but don't blame him for me calling you. He's trying to make amends. I think the engagement is a nice ideal, and don't let him pressure you. January is a blessing to get married with the New Year and a new marriage. Are Sylvia and Helen going to plan it? If not, I'll be glad to do it."

Madison smiled. "I'll see if they are. I will be honored. I don't think I want anything fancy. I just want to marry your son and try to live happily ever after. I never thought I'd find a man, but I knew I had to lose weight to make it happen. I thought I could meet someone unconditional, but not in this world. I lost the weight, and men came from all sides of the world. I didn't date that much searching for someone who is unconditional, and I believe your son fits my description."

"I hope so, Madison," she cried. "I spoiled my children a lot, and I'm glad they didn't grow up like that. Tammyann is a nurse, and she loves her job, and helping others; Toniann models, and she's always helping other young women to follow in her footsteps; Tanyann is an agent, and she's assisting others also; Tumor loves selling houses, but he's also working with Toxic to build condos for lower income people to live in the luxury without spending so much for rent."

"I never knew this," Madison cried. "Toxic didn't mention it to him."

"They put it on the backburner, but it's something they need to focus on after clearing their schedules. My children are the essence of us, and we're so proud of them. I want Toniann, Tammyann, and Toxic to find the love of their lives, and get married. Toxic is next, and then two more to go."

Madison laughed. "Love is in the air."

"You two are going to be okay, and love is moving all over the place. Just be patient, compromise, and love each other. If there's love, then you two can conquer anything."

Madison sighed. "I hope so, but I'm going to fight."

"And you should because Toxic is worth it."

"Thank you so much for taking the time to call me. I didn't know if your family would welcome me or not. I don't want to rush into anything because I'm not a gold-digger. I have my own money and my goals. I just want our relationship to work because I'm never getting married again."

"I said the same thing with I married James."

"I can't imagine the pain you went through. How did you meet James?"

"I was at the library doing some research and all the tables were taken, but James had an empty table. I asked him if I could sit down, and he stared at me like I was crazy. Prejudice and racism was all over the place and then some. So I sat down and our eyes met for some reason, and then I got into my research and ignored him. Of course, I kept staring at him, and there was just something about James that brought me to his table, and we exchanged numbers, and he called before I got home."

"We talked for hours, and secretly saw each other, but someone saw us together after five months and told my parents, and they forbid me to see James. I pretended to stop seeing him for a while. I thought it was the best. Madison I couldn't stop thinking about James, and I was miserable without him. I thought my mother would understand, but she was angry and a bitch, excuse my language. I had no one to talk too. My brother and sister were negative."

"Wow," Madison cried.

"I thought the love of my life was gone. After I graduated college I ran into James again at the college. He was there at the graduation with a friend. We embraced, and the magic was still there. We exchanged numbers and met for dinner, and the rest is history as they say. We made love for hours that same night, and we were engaged in our minds. I knew that James was the man for me. This black man was the love of my life so many years later. We secretly got married and I told my family and they disowned me. James' family ignored me, and we only had each other. It was most difficult, Madison. James had to hide out most of the time. We sat in restaurants, and they refused to serve us. We ate at home most of the time."

"As the years happened, it got a little better, but James and I fought, but we never gave up on each other. We broke up a few times, but we always found each other. We had love, and that's the most powerful force in the world."

"A love story in the making."

"Our children suffered, and the pain was unbearable, but God was there for us and he gave my family strength. Tumor was born, and he was the second man of the family. He fought like hell to survive, and when his other siblings came along, he was fighting their battles too. Then Toxic and Tumor fought the battles. Love conquers all, and if you have love, then you can survive anything and everyone."

"Wow," Madison cried. "I'm so glad you and James fought the racism, and won."

Maggie laughed. "It wasn't easy, honey, but again, as long as you and Toxic love each other the world is your oyster and then some. Thanks for listening to me, and be patient with Toxic. He's used to getting his way, and now he has met his match."

"I love him, and patience is my middle name."

Maggie laughed. "I'll talk to you soon, honey."

"Real soon, Maggie, and thanks."

"It was a pleasure."

Madison disconnected the call, and then left the bedroom to go into the adjourning bathroom. She took care of her business, and then turned on the shower. She needed to cleanse herself, and then get back into bed and sleep for the rest of the day. She was exhausted, and didn't want to deal with Toxic unless he abide by her rules. She laughed to herself as the water hit her body and she enjoyed the ride.

After cleansing her body with cherry shower gel, she stepped out of the tub, toweled herself dry, and then added cherry lotion to her body, especially between her sore vagina.

She added the green robe to her body and then she tied it, and hurried back into bed and immediately closed her eyes. She was literally mentally and physically exhausted, and right now all she wanted to do was sleep for the rest of the day.

Madison sat up and reached for her iPhone, turning the button to mute. No one was going to disturb her sleep this time, and that included Toxic Lyons. She rolled her eyes, and in five minutes she was sound asleep thinking about marrying Toxic Lyons with a smile on her face. She was in heaven and then some as she peacefully slept.

Toxic Lyons

―――――――⋇⋇⋇―――――――

Of course, Toxic had to apologize so he walked into his bedroom and stared at Madison. She was sleeping like a baby and she had a smile on her face. He didn't want to wake her up. He sat down on the bed, next to her, and touched her wet hair. She showered because her long, pretty hair was wet and spread all over the pillow and getting the pillow wet. She was the most beautiful woman in the world, and she was lucky to be in his life. When she woke up they would go ring shopping, and the engagement was on.

He just had to be patient for the marriage. Toxic removed his pants and shirts and got into the bed naked. He snuggled up to Madison as she smiled and moved closer to him. Her booty was sitting on his hard penis, and he wanted to stick it inside of her, and make love to her, but he didn't want to wake her up, so he counted to ten, and moved his penis away from her hot booty and closed his eyes. He was going to try and get some sleep.

<center>~~~~~~~~~~~~~~~~</center>

When Toxic opened his eyes, he was surprised to see Madison staring at him. He smiled. "Hi."

"Hello," Madison said.

"What time is it?"

"About six in the evening on this Tuesday."

Toxic wiped his eyes. "I'm exhausted."

"I was too, and I had a nice talk with your mother."

"I'm sorry."

Madison shook her head. "She was very nice, and I admire her so much. She lost her family when she dated James, but the love sustained their relationship. I want us to be like that, Toxic. I want our love for each other to matter, and keep us fighting for each other and fighting together."

"I love you," he cried.

"Can we get married in January?"

Toxic frowned. "I guess so."

"Then propose to me again."

"What?"

"Toxic get out of this bed, and on your knees. You didn't give me a proper proposal in the first place. Who proposes to the love of their life in the bed?" *She hit his chest.* "Get up!"

Toxic stared at this beautiful black woman as he rubbed the sleep out of his eyes, and then he yawned. "Do I have to do it right now?"

"Yes," she cried.

"Madison, I don't have the ring."

"We can take care of that in the morning, or do you have a jewelry store in this mansion of yours?" she laughed.

Toxic laughed. "I have someone who will come to me."

"Wow, the rich is something else."

"We have our moments, thank you very much."

"Get up, Toxic."

"Okay," he shouted. *Toxic got out of the bed in his birthday suit, and walked over to the other side of the bed and stared at Madison. He got down on one knee and took her left hand.* "I love you, and will you marry me?"

"You do get right the point, Toxic. Can you be a little more romantic with your words? Most men take the woman they're about to marry out to dinner, or write it in the sky or something."

Toxic stared at her. "My knee is hurting."

Madison shook her head. "I'm waiting."

Toxic closed his eyes and then opened them. "Madison Johnson, and what is your middle name by the way?"

"Tiffany," she stated.

"Madison Tiffany Johnson will you do the honors of becoming my wife for the duration of our lives on this earth. I love you, and I adore you, and I want to spend the rest of my life with you."

Madison covered her mouth as she let the tears fall. "I will do the honors of marrying you, Toxic. Now what is your middle name?"

Toxic laughed. "I don't want to mention it."

"I can't marry a man that I don't know his middle name."

Toxic rolled his eyes at Madison. "My middle name is Marble."

Madison burst out laughing. "Are you serious?"

"I told you that I didn't want to mention it."

Madison laughed again, and the she stared at him, trying to stop the laughter. "Toxic Marble Lyons I will marry you."

Toxic got up off his knee and sat down on the bed. "Thank you. I'll call the jeweler over tomorrow and you can pick out the ring. Why don't you check out the internet and see which ones appeal to you, and Michael can match your taste."

"Marble is your middle name. What in the world?"

"I don't tell people my middle name, Madison, so keep this to yourself, please. My mother had a sick sense of humor or something. I have to deal with my first name, and my middle name is just as crazy."

Madison embraced him as the electricity bombard her with sensations. "Do you feel that?" she asked.

Toxic shook his head. "I'm about to explode."

Madison broke the embrace, staring at him in shock. "What kind of electricity do we generate? I don't know if that's good or bad."

"I think its God letting us know to get our act together, especially me, of course. You and I are destined, and he's just letting us know the facts. We have to get this right."

Madison rolled her eyes. "I don't have any problems with getting it right. If you're stop running away and dictating to me, then everything will be perfect or near it. I'm not the spoiled brat here. I had to fight for everything I have now, and no one put a spoon in my mouth."

"Do you resent me for being rich?"

Madison stared at his green eyes. "I guess I envy you, Toxic, but it's not the end of the world. I had times when I had no money and I couldn't eat. I had to call off from work because there was no one to help me."

Toxic shook his head. "You had Sylvia and Helen."

"I did, but I also had my Taurus pride, and I didn't tell them I was suffering. They found out by accident when I was supposed to be at work and was at home. I paid them both back in spades."

"Pride will ruin a relationship and friendship."

"It almost did with Sylvia and Helen. I had to suffer without any money or let them know when I needed them. It was very difficult for me to get on the phone and ask Helen or Sylvia for anything. They asked me for things, so it kind of broke the ice for me. I had a feeling that they didn't need anything from me, but they wanted me to feel at ease. I love the two of them so much. Sylvia still gets on my nerves most of the time, but I love them."

"And they love you too."

"I'm famished. What should we do?"

"Do you want to go out and have a proper dinner so we can celebrate our engagement?"

"I'm still exhausted. Can we order out and relax on the beach or something? I don't know why I'm so tired, and I'm not pregnant."

Toxic opened his eyes wide, playing with her wet hair. "Are you sure?"

"Positive," she said. "I want to get to know my handsome fiancé first."

"I love the sound of fiancé," he laughed.

"I can't wait to get the ring on. I'm going to check out some rings and you can order our food. I have a taste for chicken. I wished you had a McDonalds in this mansion."

Toxic smiled to himself, thinking about making that happen for his wife-to-be. "I can go out and get us some McDonalds."

She stared at him. "Honey, you're a Lyon, and why would you eat McDonalds? You dine on lobster and crab. I don't want you to change your life for me, Toxic. I want us to be able to enhance each other."

"I love McDonalds, which is why the restaurant has one, so I'm going to run over there, and get us some fish fillets, and the works. I'm also going to call Michael so he can be here first thing in the morning I want our engagement to be real."

Madison laughed. "I can't believe I'm going to be engaged to Toxic Marble Lyons."

Toxic frowned. "Did I tell you about that?"

"Can I call you Marble instead of Toxic?"

Toxic stood up, and then he hit her ass.

"Ouch!" Madison cried, massaging her ass. "What was that for?"

"Never call me Marble again."

Madison laughed as she stood up. "I'll be in the office."

"Okay, Toxic stared. *He stared after Madison in her green robe, and her ass. She was one fine woman. He then hurried into the bathroom to shower and get dressed. He had to run to McDonalds for his fiancé. He liked the sound of that.*

Ten minutes later, Toxic was walking to his car when he stopped dead in his tracks. He could not believe it as he stared at the woman literally sitting on his car. What in the hell was she doing here, and she didn't look like the old Michelle anymore.

"Hi Toxic, and you haven't changed a bit."

He was stunned because this woman was a size two or zero. "Michelle, what are you doing here? And what did you do to yourself? The last time I saw you, you were a size eighteen."

"I'm fine as wine now, and I'm back in Chicago."

He frowned. "Why are you here?"

"I thought you'd be glad to see me, Toxic. We dated for four years, and even though, you didn't like my weight, you still dated me. We had some dynamite sex, and I kept you coming back to my fat ass. I had the gastric surgery and now I'm the woman you begged me to be. We don't have to fight anymore and can get our relationship back."

Toxic was speechless. Michelle Fost was wearing a very short blue dress, with high heel sandals, almost five inches, and plenty of cleavage. This woman was fine as wine and then some. Toxic thought he was in love with Michelle, but she was too fat, and he didn't introduce her to any of his family members. He wanted and begged her to lose the weight.

"I kept up with you, Tox over the years, and I'm so happy you didn't get married, so we still have a chance. I still love you and now we can get married and live happily ever after."

Toxic shook his head. "Our relationship ended when you refused to do the gastric surgery. It's been years now, and I'm about to become engage. I have moved on with my life. *He wasn't about to lead this woman on.*

Her smiled faded as she walked over to him. Toxic smelled her white diamond perfume from Elizabeth Taylor. "Are you freaking kidding me? I did all of this for you, and this is the thanks I get. How dare you find another woman?"

"Our relationship was over a long time ago, Michelle. I'm sorry, but I'm about to get married, and she's the love of my life. I hope you move on and find the man that's your destiny."

Michelle laughed. "Are you freaking killing me? I lost weight for you because you nagged me at every turn about my weight. How dare you move on to someone else?"

Toxic was getting tired of this situation. He moved closer to Michelle. "Leave me alone and move on."

"You bastard!" she cried. "I dream of surprising you like this and making our dreams come true. I've practically starved myself to be with you. I can't believe this is happening."

Toxic reached for his cell phone and pushed #2 for security. Less than five minutes a security guard rounded the corner and stopped in front of Toxic. "Mr. Lyons, what can I do for you?"

"You can show this woman off this property and make sure she never comes back."

The security guard grabbed his phone out of his back pocket, and snapped Michelle's picture three or four times, and then he clicked a button on his cell phone and put it back into his pocket. "Her picture will be added to the security system, and if she comes anywhere near this building an alarm will go off."

"You bastard!" Michelle cried. "I love you."

"I'm sorry, Michelle, but the feelings aren't reciprocated."

"You'll pay for this," she cried. "I'm going to make your life a living hell."

The security guard grabbed her arm.

"Get your freaking hands off me," she snapped. *She was trying to break from the security guard, but he had a strong grip on her arm.*

Toxic shook his head as he watched, Bill, their head security guard practically carry Michelle off the property. Now he had to explain this situation to Madison because he had a feeling that this wouldn't be the last time he saw Michelle again.

He waited a few minutes and then he pushed the button on his keys and got into his car. He looked left and right making sure Michelle wasn't hiding somewhere waiting to leap out at him. He drove to Lyon's Restaurant. His restaurant was opened twenty-four hours, so anyone can have McDonalds, or a decent meal whenever their hearts content.

Toxic smiled as he walked back into the mansion, and his office. Madison was deep into her work as she stared at her computer. She didn't even see that he was standing there. "I'm back."

Madison turned her head and smiled. "I'm famished."

"What were you so focused on?"

Madison laughed. "My short stories. I had one come to me so I was getting it typed up before I forget the plot. I do have to admit that the plot has a mind of its own sometimes. Where is the McDonalds? I don't smell it."

"I put everything on the balcony so after you."

Madison smiled, as she stood up hurrying to the balcony. She stared at the McDonald sitting on the table and sniffed for the smell. "This is heaven," she cried. *She took a seat.*

Toxic sat down across from her.

"Let's say our verse," Madison replied. *Their hands met, and they broke apart for a minute because the electric current was so mind-boggling.* "Let's try this again," she laughed.

Toxic laughed as their hands met, and the electricity wasn't playing. "Let's just hurry up. I'll say it." *"Dear God thank you for this food Madison and I are about to eat, and thank you for bringing us together. Amen!"*

Madison laughed. "Amen!"

She reached for her fish fillet and take a long bite, and then she stared at Toxic. "What's wrong?"

He was stunned as he stared at her. How did she know that something was wrong? Madison was really his soul mate. "I don't want to spoil this moment."

"Out with it," Madison snapped. *She took a long sip of her sweet tea, and then added fries to her mouth, full of ketchup. She then focused on Toxic.* "I'm not going to like this so go on."

He frowned. He might as well get this over with so they could deal with it. "I was leaving to go McDonalds when an old-girlfriend was sitting on my car. Her name is Michelle Fost."

Madison continued to eat her fries with ketchup, and silence was golden.

"You say I don't like fat women, but that's not true," Toxic continued. I dated Michelle for four years, and she was a size eighteen. I was very attracted to her, and I wanted to see what my brother, Tumor, saw in big women. Michelle wore it well, and she was so beautiful that you mostly focused on her face. Anyway, I was exercising with her, and I made sure she ate all the right foods. I tried being with her, but she wasn't interested in losing the weight. She would sneak and eat doughnuts, ice cream, and plenty of candy, and she ate fast food before she came home. I ended the relationship."

"Did you love her?" Madison asked.

"No! I never felt this way about a woman as I feel about you. I don't have the butterflies or the ringing in the ears, and I don't have the electricity. It was mostly sex, and just fun."

"So, you dated this woman for four years, and you didn't have any feelings for her. I don't understand the logic in that."

"Michelle is one of those fun girls. She wears her plus-size very well, and she manages to get a lot of men in her bed, and this is also why I ended the relationship. She wanted me to sleep with her, and let other men sleep with her, like an open relationship. She has a tone body, so she wasn't that fat, but men flocked to her big ass, and she had a big ass."

Madison lost her appetite as she played with her fries.

"She's a size two now, and she thought we could get our relationship back on the right track after all these years. I don't know what this chick is thinking. My family didn't like her, and I can see why. I just had security throw her off the property and she can't come back."

Madison shook her head. "She's not going to go away, Toxic."

"I don't want her, and I never told her to come back to me after she lost the weight. The woman is sick in the brain. How does she think that I didn't date thinking she was going to lose the weight and I'd open my arms and welcome her back?" *Toxic laughed, reaching for his fish fillet and taking three bites, and then washing it down with his sweet tea.*

Madison stared at him. "This Michelle is going to be a problem."

"And security will be alerted, and if she comes back to the mansion, a flash and alarm will go off, and security will come and get her. I have a security station on the premises and they work in shifts twenty-four hours. You have nothing to fear."

"This is a lifetime movie," she snapped. "How did she lose the weight?"

"Gastro surgery."

"I understand. I had this feeling that I wasn't going to wake up. I am learning a lot about the man I'm about to marry. Why didn't you tell me about dating a fat woman?"

Toxic shook his head. "I never thought about Michelle again."

"It's so easy for men to forget about a woman, but a woman never forgets about a man, who cheats on them, or dump them for another woman. It's difficult for us to move on. I'm putting myself in Michelle's shoes, and she pictured the two of you together after she lost the weight. This is what kept her going, Toxic. She's a woman scorned, and I just might pay the price. I've seen enough of these kind of scenarios in movies, on television, and in books. Most of the time it doesn't turn out right."

"I'm going to protect you with my life. I'll hire a bodyguard."

Madison laughed. "I know this is movie, but you might not have no choice. You need to hire someone to watch her, and make sure she moves on with her life. I hate this."

"I'm sorry my past is affecting our future."

"You men are so dense," she cried. "You have to be careful when you play with women's lives. I'd be angry as hell if I was in Michelle's shoes. We can't turn our feelings on and off."

"I never promised Michelle that if she lost the weight, we'd be together. We spent four years of our lives together, and she was fat all four years. Michelle is an attorney, so she's always working, and I was working. So we hardly had any time together, and she spent most of her time in Atlanta, working on cases, which is her hometown."

"How did you end the relationship?"

"I told her that I wouldn't be sharing my woman with another man. I haven't heard from her or seen her in all these years. I was stunned to see her sitting on my car, and I recognize her face, but not her body. She's skins and bones."

"Which is what the men like on women," she frowned.

"Did my mother tell you about the shrink she's seeing? I think you should see one too. You still have these insecurities about fat women. I don't want this still going on after we get married."

"Don't turn this around on me, Marble."

Toxic frowned. "How dare you?" he snapped.

"I'm sorry," Madison cried. "I'm so angry with you."

"So, use my middle name to hurt me. You know I can't stand that name."

"I'm sorry, but what are we going to do about this situation? I'm not crazy by the way, and I don't need a shrink, thank you very much. I'm just tired of the problems."

"Then you're in the wrong world because the world is tarnished left and right and there will be negative vibes shooting all over us, but we have to maintain our positive attitudes."

"Your food is getting cold."

Toxic bit into his fish fillet, and didn't say another word until he was done, as he finished off his fries, and then washed everything down with his sweet tea. "That was fresh and delicious," he said.

Madison laughed despite her anger. "I can't believe the man I love likes McDonalds. I know the two of us are meant to be together. I can't imagine anyone loving the restaurant I loved since I was a little girl."

"Destiny is for us. Are we going to let Michelle ruin our relationship? She knows I'm going to talk to you about it, and this is for you to get angry and run off or something."

"I'm cool with your past, Toxic as long as she stays the hell away from me and you. I'm not about to fight her over a man. Hopefully, she got the message that you have moved on."

"I'm going to call my friend on the police department, Detective Keys Wayne, and he'll keep me posted on Michelle. She did say that she was living in Chicago."

Madison frowned. "Wonderful!" *She finished off the rest of her fish fillet, and then she drained her sweet tea, and ate the last of her fries.* "Do you want to make love so we can exercise the fattening food off?"

Toxic laughed. "Are you kidding me?"

"Did I stutter?" she laughed.

"Let me clean off the table, and I'll meet you in our bedroom."

Madison smiled. "I love to see a man cleaning."

"I'm a neat freak, but I'm working on it."

"I'll see you in the bedroom."

Toxic stared after her, and then he began cleaning off the table on the balcony. Sometimes, it's best to tell the truth and get it over with. He had to make some calls, and then join the love of his life in the bedroom. The two of them are going to make love for the duration.

———

Two hours later, Toxic was still glowing in the after mass of their lovemaking. Madison had put it on him, and he let her do all the work. His penis was still feeling the sensations as her mouth went to work on pleasing him, and having him scream out her name over and over.

He sucked her pussy and had her screaming out his name, and they mated as he thrust inside of her until they both climaxed again. His body was still on fire as Madison slept like a baby. He couldn't sleep for thinking about Michelle and the trouble she was going to cause.

He slipped gently out of the bed, and hurried to his office. He dialed the detective's number, and waited for him to pick up. Toxic had his private cell phone number. It was almost ten o'clock at night, but the detective was a night owl.

"Toxic Lyons, what a nice surprise."

Toxic laughed. "I'm taking it you're up and about."

"You know it, and my schedule. How is the family?"

"Everyone is good. How is your wife and kids?"

"Fine. What's going on?"

"I hate to bother you, but I need information on Michelle Fost."

"What did she do now?"

Toxic was stunned. "What do you mean?"

"Her name is familiar because she's been reported to the police about ten times."

"Are you serious?"

"Yes, mostly women reporting her about their husbands or men."

"I can't believe this."

"She's bad news, and I'm sorry you're mixed up with her."

"I dated her four years ago, now she's back, skinny and wants me."

"I'd keep an eye on her. She spent time in jail for a few days because she beat up a man's wife. Michelle is bad news, and now she is skinny now. I told her to get back her life, and finish being a great attorney. She's not even practicing law."

"What is she doing now?"

"Dating men and acting like a whore. She dated Fink and he put a restraining order on her."

"Are you serious?" *Toxic stood up and paced his office. Why was this happening to him when he was trying to do the right thing and get on with his life? I don't want anything to happen to Madison, my family and me.*

"Toxic, I will handle it for you, but you should take out a restraining order on her. The woman is aching to start trouble, and she's a woman scorned. She stalked a married man and his family for months, until they had to literally move from Chicago."

"I can't believe this."

"She's a maniac."

"Do whatever you can do and keep me posted."

"I want to lock her up and throw away the key, but she always manages to get out of a legal situation. She's a wonderful attorney, but she's wasting it on getting involved with married men."

"She's a skinny mini, and now she can have any man she wants and then some."

"I guess so," he laughed. "She's finer now, but I liked her when she was fat because she had plenty of meat on her bones."

"I can't believe Fink slept with her."

"Fink is a very handsome man, and women throw themselves at him. The two of them were working on a case together, and she seduced him, and Fink is a man, of course."

"How long did this go on?"

"A few weeks until the case settled, and I remember Fink calling me because Michelle had gotten possessive, and she wouldn't leave him alone. You can't hook up with a woman like Michelle."

"It's too late for that."

"She has to be stopped, and if she doesn't someone is going to kill her ass."

"I don't want any parts of that crime, or being accused of it. I just want Michelle to find another man to stalk, and leave me and my family alone."

"We have to be careful who we date for sure."

"She didn't seem like she was a nut."

"I know, but she is, thank you very much. Her file is getting larger by the minute. Men need to stop sleeping with her."

Toxic laughed. "Are you for real?"

"I'm happily married."

"But you're not dead or blind. She was fine when she was fat, and now she's more finer, but skins and bones to me. I'm so used to her fat ass. I had my security throw her off the premises, and her photo has been taken. If she comes onto the property security will get her. I don't think she's that stupid, but she's not playing with a full deck."

"Let's keep in touch on this matter."

"Thanks so much, detective. Let's have dinner with your wife, and you two can meet Madison. She's the apple of my life, and we're about to get engaged, and married in January."

"Toxic Lyons is finally off the market."

"Yes, he is," Toxic laughed. "I have never known love like this before."

"Sounds like a song," the detective laughed. "I can't wait to meet her."

"I'll find out when my wife is available and give you a call."

"So far, you're on the right page consulting with her instead of making plans without her consent. I think you're going to make a wonderful husband," he laughed.

Toxic laughed with him. "I have plenty of examples in my family."

"Great, be safe, and have a blessed day."

"You do the same, and thanks for listening."

"I love you and your family."

"Me too." *Toxic ended the call and hurried back into his bedroom. Madison was still sleeping like a baby. He smiled as he got back into bed, and snuggled up with her, and she didn't once wake up. Toxic closed his eyes and prayed like he never prayed before.*

Madison Johnson

Two weeks had passed, and Madison found herself still living in Toxic's mansion. She loved it here, but this time she was wearing her engagement ring. It was the most beautiful ring in the universe, as she stared down at it.

Madison was sitting in the living room. It was ten o'clock in the morning, and she was working on files for Fink. She just couldn't stop staring at her ring. A Cartier Carat Columbia Emerald diamond ring in green. She couldn't stop staring at the green sensation. When she saw the price tag she almost puked on herself. What was Toxic thinking? She tried getting him to get something cheaper, but he laughed at her, and then he frowned. There was no way he was taking the ring back, and Madison had to be very careful. She remembered the shock looks on their faces when she skyped them. She flashback to their conversation on Skype.

Madison turned on her computer and began typing as she skyped for Helen and Sylvia. After a few minutes the two checked in.

"Hi," Sylvia said.

"Hello," Helen responded.

"Hi," Madison smiled. "You two are gorgeous woman."

"What's going on with you?" Helen stated.

"I have something to show you both," Madison cried.

"We're waiting," Sylvia said.

"Bam," she cried, showing her ring to Sylvia and then Helen.

Sylvia grasped and Helen screamed.

Madison laughed.

"That is a Cartier ring," Sylvia stated.

"My goodness," Helen stated.

"I'm engaged, and marriage will be in January," Madison exclaimed. "Toxic wants to get married yesterday, but it's not happening right now. I want to be sure he's the one because this is my only marriage."

"Wow," Sylvia stated. "I saw Toxic all the time and witnessed the women he dated from left to right, and the gold-diggers thinking that they were entitled to his money and his name. It got on my nerves. Now he's with a woman I love and trust."

"I agree," Helen stated. "Sylvia said it."

Madison smiled. "He's a pain in my ass always wanting me to condone to his thinking and wishes, and not compromising without me defining why he should. I thought getting married in January was too soon for us, but it's better than next month."

"You did the right thing," Helen said. "I love this ring."

"It costs a fortune, but Toxic doesn't give a damn."

"When you have billions it doesn't matter," Sylvia pointed out. "The Lyons invested in me when I was just starting out. I have my fashion house because of them. I owe them."

"I didn't know this," Madison declared.

"Still keeping secrets," Helen shouted. "What is wrong with the two of you and our friendship?"

"Let's not go there," Sylvia yelled. "I forgot."

Helen rolled her eyes. "Sure you did."

"I don't think we have to tell each other everything," Sylvia said.

"And why not?" Helen asked.

"Do you tell us every damn thing, Helen?" Sylvia declared.

"I think I do," Helen said.

"You think, but you don't know," Madison declared.

"Let's just be more honest with each other," Helen said.

"Which is what I'm doing now," Madison pointed out. "I want you two to plan my wedding, but Maggie is eager to do it. What do you think? I don't want anything fancy and going to Las Vegas and then having a reception would be nice."

"The wheels are turning in my head," Helen said. "Let's plan a Las Vegas wedding and reception right there in sin city. It'd be different, and a way to start off the New Year."

"I like it," Sylvia said. "I love Las Vegas."

"I have to talk to Toxic about it, but I don't think he's going to object. You two plan it, and I'll let Maggie know, and maybe you two can give her some responsibility so she'd feel like she had something to do with her son's day."

Sylvia laughed. "You're going to make a great daughter-in-law."

"Yes she is," Helen said.

Madison laughed out loud. "I like my mother-in-law, and most people can't stand their in-laws, thank you both, very much. I can't stop staring at this ring. I can't wait to see the wedding band."

"Toxic has excellent taste," Sylvia said.

"What is the date in January?" Helen asked.

"I want to do, January first," Madison stated. "I just want to begin marriage with a new year, and a new beginning. Can you find a chapel and get the ball rolling?"

"I have some contacts," Sylvia said. "And Helen and I will plan everything. I could let Maggie handle the flowers and the catering."

"That would be nice," Madison confessed. "I'm the happiest woman in the world. I remember feeling so lonely for a man's touch. I'd read romance novels, and actually feel the man is making love to me, instead of the heroine in the novel. I touched myself all the time, and the hero was making love to me."

"Wow," Helen stated. "I had no ideal."

Madison frowned. "It's something you can't share with your best friends."

"But you just did," Sylvia said. "Do you think about seeing someone?"

Madison frowned again. "You and Toxic think I'm crazy or something."

"No," Helen pointed out. "You have insecurities about your weight, and now it's time to put that issue to bed."

"I agree," Sylvia said. "I'm going to talk to someone."

"Are you freaking serious?" Madison asked, staring at her.

"I am," Sylvia said. "I'm getting a divorce, and I don't want this to affect the rest of my life with other men."

"But you're sleeping around?" Helen stated.

Sylvia rolled her eyes at Helen. Madison smiled at the two of them. "I'm vulnerable and wants a man to appreciate me," Sylvia replied. "But my husband is leaving me for another man, and it's most difficult. I still love him, and I don't want his soul to go to hell. He's sinning in every capacity with a man."

"Love is the most powerful force in the world," Madison stated. "Can you imagine the era that James and Maggie went through with their interracial love story? The two of them are together today because of it."

"Love stinks," Sylvia said. "I'm going to fuck and have fun."

"Yes, you do need to see a shrink," Helen pointed out.

"Fuck you, Helen," Sylvia stated.

"You two need to tone it down," Madison snapped.

"I don't want to be judge," Sylvia shouted. "You need to be in my situation and understand that it's no fun when your husband is cheating on you, but it's devastating when he's cheating on you with another man. I feel less of a woman, and so I had to go out there and prove that I'm still a fine Hispanic woman, and men still want me."

"And how does it make you feel?" Helen said. "Maybe like a slut."

"We all can't have the perfect marriage, Helen," Sylvia snapped.

"My marriage isn't perfect," Helen said. "Do you comprehend how many times my husband cheated on me? I lost count, and he could still be doing it, but I don't have any proof, and he's being videotaped, left and right. This time I'm going to divorce his ass."

Madison shook her head. "I don't know if I need to get married."

"If you're lucky enough to find the man of your soul, then do it," Sylvia said. "Don't let my marriage ruin yours. I think you and Toxic are perfect for each other, and will have a great marriage. Besides, Helen is still married."

"I'm getting married," Madison replied. "I don't know why things happen, but in your case, Sylvia, your husband was probably gay when he was a child. I don't think you just become an adult, and say I'm gay and I like men."

"You could be right about that," Sylvia agreed. "I couldn't understand why my husband was so close to George. I know he's his best friend, but the two of them went on vacation together, and they spent a lot of time together. I didn't even know that George was gay. He had a wife and children, and my husband didn't see the need to let me know. When George got a divorce, my husband explained it to me that his wife cheated on him. He lied to me so many times."

"I'm sorry," Madison cried.

"Me too," Helen cried.

"I always wondered why he insisted on using condoms. This is why we never had any children. I was pregnant once or twice, but we were in the heat of the moment. I think he was trying to prove to himself that he loved women, and he didn't want to be gay. I just don't know," she cried.

"I didn't bring up the pain," Madison said.

"Don't be silly," Sylvia cried. "It's going to take me a very long time to get over my marriage, but I'm moving on. I'm going out with Danny later on tonight. He kept asking, and I finally told him yes. I'm going to be a player."

"Wow," Helen said. "Use a condom."

"I have plenty," Sylvia said. "I asked Danny did he like fucking men, and he thought I was losing my mind or something. I asked him if he was on the down low. I had no intentions of wasting time with another gay man."

"You are crazy," Madison said.

Sylvia laughed. "I know, but the pain is just too much."

"We're here for you," Helen said.

"Just a computer away," Madison laughed.

Sylvia, Helen and Madison laughed.

"I'll talk to you soon, and keep me posted," Madison said. "I'm going to let Toxic know about the wedding plans, and one of you call Maggie and let her assist. I can't wait until January."

"I'm going to design our dresses," Sylvia said. "I do need to know the kind of dress you want so take a look right now because I'm going to get so busy, I'm not going to have time. I have assistants, but I want to make this dress personal."

Madison smiled. "Let me look now."

"Okay," Sylvia said.

"I like this style," Madison stated. "It's a cap sleeved crepe sheath, and if you can make it in green, that would be perfect. I love the back yoke, and waistband since I can now have a waste," she laughed.

Helen and Sylvia laughed.

"I also like the simple veil," Madison cried. "This is perfect for one."

"It didn't take you a long time to decide," Helen said. It'd probably take me hours, and it did, thank you both very much."

"I dreamed of getting married," Madison confessed. "I had the perfect wedding dress in my head and my mind. This is the one in a lighter shade of green. I love it."

"You have it," Sylvia said. "It's elegant and simple."

"Exactly," Madison stated.

"Let me find a style I like," Helen said. "We have to wear shades of green."

"Perfect," Madison cried. "I can't believe I'm getting married, or discussing marriage for myself. I read so many romance novels, dreaming of the day it was going to happen to me. I kept dreaming even when I was a fat cow."

"Dreams do come true," Sylvia stated. "Let me see what style I'm going to wear."

Silence took over as the three surfed the internet trying to find the styles that appealed to them.

"I want you two wearing the same dress in different shades of green," Madison cried. "Sylvia will you be able to pull this off? I know I'm asking a lot, but it's my preference."

"Of course," Sylvia said. "I'm good."

Madison and Helen laughed.

"I don't know if you two should wear long or short?" Madison stated.

"Let's just look for both," Sylvia said.

"This long sleeveless stretch satin dress is nice in Clover and mint. One of you can wear clover and the other mint."

"I'll wear the mint," Helen said. "I like it."

"I like it too," Sylvia said. "I'll get started on our dresses ASAP. This works."

Madison smiled. "That was easy."

"Not if you've been dreaming about this moment for most of your life," Helen pointed out. "I'll get the accessories to match our dresses."

"Sounds good," Sylvia said. "If we can get the shoes to match the clover and mint that would be perfect, and I know the best shoe designer in the world. I'm going to give him a call today. I know he can do it. I need to get a pattern started so he'll have something to work with."

"I can't believe this is actually happening," Madison cried.

"This isn't a dream," Helen stipulated.

"Do we need to pinch you?" Sylvia laughed. "Toxic is a wonderful man."

"Yes, he is," Madison cried.

"I'm going to go and get started on Las Vegas," Helen said. "You know its New Year's so most of their hotels is going to be booked, but I'm sure I can use the Lyons hotel in Las Vegas."

"I forgot about that," Madison cried. "They have a hotel and restaurant in Las Vegas, and we need to book it for January 1st, but it might be already booked."

"I don't think it'd be a problem," Helen said. "I know people."

"Okay," Madison said. "I love you both, and thanks so much for being my best friends."

"We love you too," Helen cried.

"Back at ya," Sylvia said.

Madison disconnected skype, and then she let the tears fall. She was getting married, and to the most handsome, white man, ever born. How could this have happened to her? Maybe reading all those romance novels has finally paid off.

Madison let the tears fall as she stared at the dresses she and the girls chose. Madison knew she was going to be a gorgeous bride, and Toxic was going to be a handsome man. She was marrying a white man with green eyes. God was good to her, and in her corner. She smiled as she continued to stare at the computer blinded by tears of joy.

Toxic Lyons

········· ❧❀❧ ·········

I t was now August, and everything between him and
Madison was coming along. She had literally moved into
his mansion, and he loved her, and everything about it. He
was sitting in his office, staring at the many file folders on
his desk. He had to focus on work, or he was going to lose
plenty of clients. He had one coming to his office in five
minutes, and he had to focus on the file. A client was suing
a woman for assault. *Toxic laughed. Why was this even put on
his desk? He read the file and then laughed, and then shook his
head. Was this for real?*

*Ten minutes later his secretary opened the door, and his
client, Justin Barnes walked in. Mr. Barnes was tall, black, and
very handsome. He was also a rich man because of his highly
successful movies. Toxic was pleased he sought out his firm. He
stood up and shook Mr. Barnes hands as his secretary closed the
door.* "Mr. Barnes, have a seat, and it's an honor to meet you
in person. I love your black movies."

Justin Barnes sat down in a chair across from him. "That is a compliment coming from a white man, and thank you so very much. Your name speaks volumes and I need to get rid of a spitfire."

Toxic nodded his head. "Tell me the problem."

"Her name is Michelle Fost, and she's a pain in my ass."

Toxic thought he was going to puke all over himself. This couldn't be happening to him. He was speechless as he continued to listen to Justin Barnes. Was he ever going to get rid of this woman?

"We met at a party and she seduced me, and I ran with it," Justin continued. "Michelle had an ass on her, but she was just a lot of fun. I didn't want to marry her or anything, but she thought she was going to be the one."

Toxic shook his head.

"When I ended the relationship, she assaulted me and I still have the bruises to show for it."

"How long ago was this?"

"About six months ago."

Toxic was stunned. "She's fine as wine, and great in bed, but the chick is possessive. We slept together, but I sleep with a lot of women. I am not about to marry anyone. I'm thirty-seven years old, but I haven't met the woman with the butterflies or ringing in my ears, yet. Michelle isn't the one."

Toxic smiled. He had the ringing and the butterflies, and her name was Madison Johnson. He frowned and focused back on Mr. Barnes. "What do you want me to do?"

"I want the bitch to go to jail or just leave me the hell alone."

"Did you try a restraining order?"

"I did, but she managed to turn up at all my parties, but she also kept her distance. Michelle is a smart attorney. She reminds me of the scheming and sick woman on that Tyler Perry show. I think her name is Veronica. Michelle is clever just like her, and the two of them could be related."

Toxic smiled. "I know the show, and you're right. I had a relationship with her, and I don't know if this is appropriate. It might be a conflict of interest. I do want to get rid of the bitch."

"Are you serious?" Justin asked.

"Michelle gets around. When I dated her she was a size eighteen."

Justin laughed. "She actually showed me pictures of herself when she was fat. I loved that big ass of hers, and glad she still has it. Michelle has it going on, but there's something frightening about her."

"I do know the feeling, and I'd love to nail her, but I don't think going to prison is the answer for her. How did she assault you?"

"She attacked me with a knife. Do you see the scar on the left side of my face? It's a permanent mark because she was trying to ruin my pretty face. She also tried stabbing me, but she beat me up pretty bad with a vase in my house, and I have the proof. My housekeeper found me passed out, and I almost died. The woman is dangerous, and she needs to be locked up. Are you insane?"

Toxic was stunned as he wrote on his yellow legal pad. Michelle Fost was a dangerous woman.

"I see her all the time, and someone is calling me and hanging up. She also wanted me to put her in one of my movies. I did, and it's coming out in September. She's a great actress."

"Are you kidding me? I didn't know she could act."

"Michelle is full of surprises," Justin stated.

"Wow!"

"I want her to pay for assaulting me. She's going to hurt someone or possibly kill them if someone don't take her out first. I'm sure Michelle has a lot of enemies."

"She has been to jail before because she had an affair with a married man and beat up the wife. Jail isn't something she's not used too. I can forbid her from ever coming to Los Angeles again."

"Man, she needs to be locked up. Have you seen her?"

Toxic stared at his legal pad. "I have, and she wants up to renew our relationship that we had for four years. It's over, but I have a feeling she's going to be a pain in my ass."

Justin shook his head. "Then you know she needs to be locked up. I have photos here that will show you how I looked before the bruises and after. I can't get rid of this scar on my face. I'm just afraid she's going to kill me or something."

He had a point about Michelle. She was evil. "Where is she now?"

"In Los Angeles, but we're doing a movie out here."

"What do you mean?"

"She has a contract to do five movies with me, and it's time for this one that's being shot here in Chicago. I'm sure she's staying at a fancy hotel, but I can't breach the contract."

"I don't think you need to be suing her until this movie is over, and she does three more movies. How are you working with her if you have a restraining order?"

"It's null and void because of the contract she has. Do you know Benny Listen?"

"He's the famous attorney for the celebrities."

"Now he's Michelle's attorney, and he never loses a case."

"I bet the two of them are fucking?"

"I'm sure of it," Justin barked. "She's a barracuda."

"And she's very dangerous."

"And she is going to ruin my career, reputation, and life if we don't do something about her. I can't deal with her right now. I'm a successful black producer, and the world is looking for something to bring me down. Michelle Fost is going to give them the dynamite to ruin me."

He was so right about that. "I'll give you one of my associates, but I'll be diligently working with her to give him all the rope he needs to hang the bitch. Leslie Ranks is the second best in my law firm. She's twenty-nine years old, very young, but she has won five out of five cases for me."

Justin nodded. "She's very young, but you know your stuff, and she can get this bitch, then I'm all for it. Is she black or white? I'm not color blind, but I just need to know because my life is on the line."

Toxic smiled. "Leslie is black, very attractive, reminding me of a taller Regina Hall, and she's great at her job. She only missed five questions on the bar exam, and she's a pro."

"Is she married or single?"

"She's single, and her career is her life, which is why she's my second in command. I'm going to bring her in here and you'll see for yourself." *Toxic reached for his desk phone, and pushed a button for his secretary, Jan. He immediately heard her voice.* "Yes, Mr. Lyons." *She never called him by his first name.* "Jan, I need you to see if Leslie is available and send her into my office."

"So noted, Mr. Lyons."

Toxic shook his head and hung up the phone. "I can't believe I can't get rid of this woman. I saw her last month, and I had to get security to throw her out. She is a bitch in heels, and now that she lost the weight, she's eager to find a sugar daddy and get on sex on."

Justin smiled. "The girl is as kinky as hell in the bedroom. Did she ride the broom with you?"

Toxic laughed. "That and among other things. I thought she only did that with me. I see she's a whore in heat."

"Yes, she is, but I have climaxes all over the place with Michelle."

"She's a pro in the bed, but her mental capabilities is what we have to worry about. I don't trust her, and she doesn't like rejection well. She's a woman scorned, so we have to get her away from us."

"I agree, never thinking that Michelle Fost got around."

Toxic frowned. "She's a slut, tramp and whore in my opinion."

"And we slept with the slut, tramp and whore."

"It's a mistake, you and I are regretting at the moment."

"What is our next step?"

"I'm going to talk to her attorney and see if some kind of settlement can be reached. Instead of going to prison, we can ban her from Chicago and Los Angeles. I'm sure she's going to go along with this deal."

Justin shook his head. "I just don't trust the bitch."

The door opened and a gorgeous black woman walked into the room with a smile on her face. She was wearing a black pencil skirt, with a white blouse, and high heel black pumps, and her legs never quit, Toxic thought to himself. He smiled at her. "Hi Leslie, and thanks for joining me."

Leslie smiled, but her eyes were on Justin. "Hi."

Toxic smiled. "Justin this is Leslie, and Leslie this is Justin, you know, the producer of fast grossing movies."

Justin stood up, taking Leslie's hand, and the electricity was so electric, they broke apart quickly, and Toxic laughed to himself because he remembered the same feeling as the two of them just stared at each other, forgetting that he was in the room. He waited a few minutes to see if they would acknowledge him, but the two ignored him. After a few minutes he cleared his throat. "Hi."

They then noticed him and laugh. "Do you two need a room?"

"Of course not," Leslie laughed. "I'm sorry."

"It's okay," Justin whispered. "I feel the vibes."

"I do too," Leslie said. "This has never happened to be me before."

"I do know the feeling," Toxic explained. "Madison, my fiance and I felt the ringing and the bells, not to mention the electricity the first moment we met in Lyons' Restaurant. We'll be getting married in January of next year."

"Congratulations," Leslie said, taking a seat next to Justin. "I'm glad you finally found the woman of your dreams, and I know she has to be special, and not about the money or the fame."

Toxic smiled. "Yes, and yes," he declared.

"Are you dating or married?" Justin asked. "I don't see a ring on those lovely and soft hands of yours."

Justin was flirting with his co-worker, Toxic said to himself. There was a match made in heaven right in his office. He couldn't wait to share this romantic moment with Madison. She was more romantic than he was, and he had to work on that fact.

"I'm single and free," Leslie flirted. "I loved the last movie you did, and I'm so glad a black man is winning awards for his talent. Not only are you giving black actors a voice, you hire all minorities in your movies. I can't believe I'm sitting next to you."

"Where have you been all my life?" Justin flirted.

"Right here waiting for you," Leslie flirted.

Their eyes met, and Toxic wanted to excuse himself from the room, but business was business and after business, the two of them could flirt later. "Leslie, I need you to take some notes. I see you have your pen and yellow legal pad."

Leslie stopped staring at Justin, and focused on her pad, and pen. "I'm ready, boss, and what's going on?"

Toxic related the situation and when he was done, Leslie was frowning.

"What is the problem Leslie?" Toxic asked.

"Michelle Fost is a thorn in my side."

Justin and Toxic exchanged glances. "Why?" Toxic asked.

"Remember that last case I won," Leslie asked, staring at Toxic.

"I do, and what about it," Toxic said.

"I had a client's wife who had a beef with Michelle Fost. She slept with her husband, and gave her a sexual transmitted disease, and she wanted to sue the bitch who he slept with and the suspect was Michelle Fost."

"I'll be damn," Justin shouted.

"I can't believe you dated that bitch," Leslie said.

"We all dated the bitch," Toxic confessed.

Leslie stared at Toxic and then Justin. "Men are dogs. That bitch is a dangerous woman. I hope you two were tested for HIV, and all sexual diseases."

"I went out with her for six months," Justin confessed.

"You still need to be tested, you dirty dog. You men are dumb as hell. Even when the bitch was fat, men ran to her as if she had some kind of spell on them. What is the attraction to Michelle Fost?"

"She's a smart, and gorgeous woman, and she has an ass on her that just won't quit," Justin pointed out. "My penis went into overdrive at the sight of her. She took Seduction 101, and all men were at her mercy."

Leslie shook her head. "So, you want to sue the bitch for?"

"Assault," Justin explained. "She put this scar on the left side of my face, and then she beat me with a vase, almost killing me in the process. I was in the hospital for almost a month, and I thought I was going to die."

Leslie shook her head as she wrote on her legal pad, staring at the other long scar on the side of his face. "It makes you look sexy."

Justin smiled. "Thank you."

"I'm going to be sick," Toxic blurted out.

"Shut up," Leslie said. "Michelle is fucking the best attorney in this universe, so I'm sure this case is worth it. I do win all my cases, but Michelle is an attorney herself, and she knows the legal eagle of the law."

"I want to ban her from Chicago and Los Angeles," Justin said.

"Is that all?" Leslie stated. "Are you in love with someone else now, and Michelle is in the way of your new relationship?"

"I am," Justin confessed, and her name is Leslie."

Leslie blushed. "I don't think you're ready for all of this."

Toxic laughed.

"Maybe you're not ready for all of this," Justin laughed.

Their eyes met, and it was five minutes and silence still took over the room. Toxic never felt so much sexual tension in a room, other than with Madison, but this was bordering on the ridiculous. The two just met each other, and it was hot as hell in here.

"I suggest you talk to her attorney?" Toxic stated, breaking the ice in the room. "His name is Benny Listen. Getting her out of this city and Los Angeles will give the two of us a break from her. If she dares to come back, then she will be arrested on the spot without any explanations and taken to jail until a Judge can be reached."

Leslie shook her head. "That might just work because she's banned from Las Vegas for the moment. Benny couldn't do anything for her because she was caught on an iPhone recording of fighting with two women."

Justin smiled. "Whatever you can do for me, and then please let's have dinner and discuss you and me getting to know each other. I'm not about to waste time since there's something going on between the two of us. Are you willing to see where the fireworks are headed?"

Leslie stared at the handsome, successful black man. She had given up on finding the man of her romantic dreams, waiting for the butterflies and the ringing, and she had both because the bells were still ringing in her ears, and the butterflies were sitting in the middle of her stomach, ignoring the hell out of her. This man lived in Los Angeles, and she resided in Chicago. Was it a waste of time to give him the time of day? She was speechless for the moment.

Toxic and Justin exchanged glances, staring at Leslie.

"I'll have dinner with you, Mr. Barnes, and maybe we need to exercise the lust that's implanted in our system for the moment."

Justin was stunned.

Toxic was speechless.

"I'm not a slut," Leslie stated, but there's something happening and my panties are wet as sin, and I want to take off my clothes, and get naked with you. I'm hot and on fire."

"I believe this meeting is over," Toxic said. "You two get out of here, and fulfill your lustful duties at a hotel, and not compromise this case, or Michelle is going to win. Talk to Benny Listen before you two get sexual satisfied."

"I guess I can hold off for a few days," Leslie smiled.

"I don't think I can, but I don't want to jeopardize this case against Michelle Fost. As you can see my dick is about to burst from the seam of my pants. I'm hot and I need to use the bathroom so I can jerk off."

"You two need to leave," Toxic said. "I'll be in touch."

Justin and Leslie stood up. "Let's go to my office and maybe I can suck your dick," Leslie pointed out, and you can suck my wet pussy."

Toxic had never been so stunned at the way Leslie was acting. She was so professional in the office, but today she was acting like a whore, reminding him of Michelle Fost. "You two need to be discreet," Toxic pointed out.

Leslie walked to the door. "Let's go, Justin because your dick is aiming for my wet cunt."

Justin shook his head as the passion was enveloping him. "Let's go," he whispered.

Toxic stared at the two of them as his door closed. He shook his head because life was funny as hell. Now Leslie didn't have a man in her life, and Toxic thought she was into women, but now she was all over a complete stranger. Did the two of them bring out the whorish nature?

He shook his head again feeling the sexual vibes in the room. All he could think about was sucking Madison's pussy and hearing her scream out his name repeatedly. His dick reacted to his thoughts, and he felt like masturbating himself. What was happening in the world? Was sex the only answer? He wanted to pick up the phone and find out if Madison was available for some sex. He was hot and ready, and he did not want to jerk off. He wanted to suck that sweet pussy of Madison's and feel his hard dick inside of her wet cove of pussy. He reached for his cell phone.

Madison Johnson

M adison found herself sitting in the elaborate conference room of the Lyon's mansion as she stared across the table at Tanyann and Beverly Bonds, a famous editor. She was stunned at the two lovely white and black women. Beverly Bonds was a black supermodel, and she edited on the side. She loved editing writers, never finding the urge to write for herself. She was lovely reminding her so much of Tyra Banks. The two could be sisters.

Beverly Bonds was a size ten, and she wore it well in her long maxi blue dress with accessories to match. Tanyann was wearing jeans and a halter top, and Madison was in a long top with shorts. She loved wearing shorts, and working from home afforded her these options.

"Are you okay?" Beverly asked.

Madison came back to the present. "I'm just in awe of this. You are publishing my first book of short stories. I can't believe it."

"This is happening," Tanyann stated. "I'm officially your agent once you read and sign the contract right in that blue folder in front of you. The red folder is a contract with Lyons Publishers. We're going to publish your first book."

Madison was stunned. "I didn't know you had a publishing house."

"We do, and Beverly works there as a head editor," Tanyann stipulated. "The offices are in New York, and I have a ready staff running the place. I'm the agent who brings in the staff."

"You Lyons must be in the billions," Madison exclaimed.

Tanyann laughed. "We are and then some. We own restaurants, hotels, stores, banks, and the list is endless. Your fiance is worth more than you think possible, and you never have to work again."

Madison frowned. "That's not an option. I love my work as a paralegal and writer. I'm never going to stop working. I like having my own money and independence. Toxic is the love of my life, and he enhances my life. I don't need his money."

Tanyann laughed. "My brother is finally lucky to have found the woman of his dreams and then some."

"I'm very lucky," Madison cried. "What's the next step?"

"You need an attorney to read over the contracts with you, and then sign them," Beverly stated. "We also need to come up with a name for your first book. Since they are mostly written in the first person, what about, I Confess?"

Madison smiled. "I like it, and the covers have to be green which is my stipulation."

Beverly smiled. "It's going to be nice working with you. Now you have sixty short stories so far, so we're going to put forty in "I Confess," and then forty more in "I Confess 2.""

"Wonderful," Madison cried. "I'll get my attorney to go over the contracts with me, and we're on our way. Thank you both so much. I can't believe another dream is coming true for me."

"We thank you," Beverly said. "I'm going to get together with the cover designer and send you some cover samples. I know you want everything green, so we're work on it. What do you want on the cover?"

Madison smiled. "I want a woman and man on the cover, but not real people but amination. I want an unforgettable cover."

"I also need a recent photo, and for you to write your bio and email it to me," Beverly stated. "It's August now, but I want to have your books online and in the stores by October or November, but sometime this year. You need to be available also for the media. I'm going to turn your life into a media circus."

"I don't know if that's good or bad," Madison said.

"It's going to be great," Tanyann said. "I know you're not a media hound, so we're keep it down a peg or too. But we have to circulate you and your books to make people want to buy it, so you will do a few talk shows. Which one interest you?"

"Steve Harvey, The Real, Ellen, and Wendy Williams," Madison cried.

Beverly smiled, writing on her Samsung note 4. "Your wish is my command."

Madison's eyes opened-wide. "Are you serious?"

"Of course," Tanyann said. "The Lyons know all of them, so I'm going to make another dream of yours come true. Madison your writing is going to explode. You're talented enough."

Madison felt the tears forming. "I love writing, but I never thought I'd do anything with them. They were just journal writings when I had a situation I couldn't deal with like having no money, or not being able to eat."

"This could be good publicity," Tanyann pointed out. "If you tell your story about the poverty you encountered, you can help others overcome and make their dreams come true too."

Madison frowned.

"It's giving others a chance to make their dreams come true," Beverly said. "If you could do it, then so could they."

"I'm all for helping others," Madison stipulated.

"Then we're on the same page," Tanyann said.

"I do have a wedding to plan," Madison said.

"I'm excited about that," Tanyann said. "Mother is happy about the flowers and the catering service. Her second born is getting married, and then two more to go with Toniann and Tammyann."

"I love your brother so very much," Madison cried.

"And he loves you so very much," Tanyann cried.

"Love is in the air," Beverly added.

The three ladies laughed.

The ringing of a cell phone interrupted the laughter as all three stared at their phones. "It's me," Madison smiled. *She stared at Toxic's smiling face.* "Hi honey."

"What are you doing right now?"

"Talking with your sister, Tanyann and Beverly about my writing career."

"I want to suck your cunt right now," Toxic said.

Madison was stunned as she stared at Beverly and Tanyann, and then she blushed. "I can't talk right now, honey. Why don't you take me to lunch in twenty minutes, and we can exercise that fact."

"I'll see you in twenty minutes," Toxic laughed.

"Okay, honey." *She clicked off the phone.* "Sorry about that."

"You blush very well," Tanyann said. "Let's go so you can spend some quality time with my brother. Beverly and I will be in touch the minute you sign the contracts and have them sent over to my office in the Lyon's Restaurant. I'm on the tenth floor."

"I will, and thank you both so much," Madison cried. "It's nice to finally meet you Beverly, and I look forward to working with you."

"You too," Beverly said. *The three women embraced, and then Madison walked them to the door as they rushed out, and then she did a twirl around the conference room. Her career was booming, and she had the man of her dreams. What more could she want? She hurried into the elevator and pushed the button for the fourth floor. She had to take a quick shower and get ready for some love making, and she wanted to be clean and smell good. She couldn't believe Toxic calling her in the middle of the day informing her that he wanted to suck her cunt. What is going on with her man? She was about to find out.*

She exit off the elevator and hurried into her bathroom, turning on the shower, and stripping naked as she got into the warm water, making sure her hair didn't get wet this time. She grabbed the body wash, Cherry, and cleaned her body about five times, and then she stepped out of the water, and added her Cherry lotion and spray to her body. Then she nakedly walked into her bedroom closet to find a sexy negligee. Madison remembered buying these negligee's, a size smaller to parade around the house in them when she lost the weight, and now she was able to make another dream come true. She knew she had to get to Church. God was so good to her. She'd talk to Toxic about Church.

Madison walked to the bedroom mirror and sat down at the vanity table, not having one when she was poor, and making up her face, adding blush, eye shadow and then lipstick, and then combing her hair down her back. She had gorgeous long hair, and all she had to was wash it, blow dry it, and then roll it up or let it hang straight. She was blessed, and that's why she needed to go to Church. God was so good to her, and she needed to show her appreciation by giving God some of her time. Church was this Sunday with or without Toxic.

She went to stand at the full-length mirror, and smiled looking at herself from back and front. Madison Johnson was the most gorgeous woman in the world. She remembered seeing all the gorgeous woman on television, and in person, and wishing that she looked like them, and now she was beautiful. She walked back over to her vanity table, and reached for her wind song perfume, and prayed herself, and then she smiled. She was ready to rock her man's world, and then some as she sat on the bed to wait.

Twenty minutes later she heard the door and she got into bed and posed with a smile on her face. Madison laughed to herself because this episode was in one of her romance novels, and to think that she was living a romance was funny as hell.

Toxic's handsome ass walked into the bedroom, staring at her in shock. He was speechless as he noticed her fine ass. "Wow!" he said.

"Hi yourself and remove your clothes."

Toxic began removing his clothes and soon he was naked as he joined her on the bed. "You're the most beautiful woman in the world."

Madison stared at his large dick. "You're all ready for me."

"I need you to get naked with me."

"Why don't you make me," she laughed.

Toxic laughed, and then he took her lips, adding his tongue, and then began removing the skimpy negligee, and soon she was naked. Their hands moved over each other's bodies as their moans entered the room, and then Madison grabbed his hard penis, and went to work on licking it like a lollipop. She loved Toxic's moans as she took his hard dick into her mouth which excited Toxic.

"Honey, I'm about to explode."

"Let it come," she cried. *She took him all the way into her mouth, and in less than five minutes he screamed out as his body rocked with pure pleasure.*

Madison felt his semen down her throat, and she welcomed it as she licked her lips and watched the satisfaction all over him. She was laid on her stomach and Toxic was between her legs as he played with her clit and exciting her to her moans of pleasure. She rocked her body and then screamed out as multiple orgasms played with her senses. She was seeing spots and she never wanted this pleasure to end. She continued to rock until she couldn't rock anymore, and then she laid spent. Her breathing was all over the place and when Toxic grabbed a condom, and entered her, she felt the sensations heat up her body again. The two of them rocked as he thrust and pounded into her. The smacking of their bodies made noise as they went for more pleasures, and the pleasure exploded into action. Madison and Toxic screamed out as their thrills electrified them. After a few minutes, they went back into action, and it was an hour later before their breathing came back to normal.

It was a few minutes before Madison spoke. "Wow!"

"I'm still on a high," Toxic said.

They laid beside each other naked and high on their sexual episode. "What brought this on in the middle of the day, honey? It's only noon this Monday morning."

Toxic laughed. "I guess I can discuss a case with you since you're a paralegal, and I know it's not going out of this room."

"Cross my heart," Madison laughed.

Toxic laughed at her. "My client is Justin Barnes."

"The producer," she cried.

"Yes, and he needs me to get rid of a pest."

"Who is the pest?"

"Michelle Fost," he stated.

"What?"

"I know, but she gets around. Anyway, Justin dated her for six months, and she began stalking him, so now he wants her ban from Chicago and Los Angeles. I didn't want to work on the case with her, so I called in my associate, Leslie.

She came into room, and the minute she walked into my office, the two of them were like in a romance novel. It was chemistry all over the place, and they couldn't stop staring at each other. I felt the sexual vibes in the room, and if I wasn't there, they would have had sex in my office."

"Are you freaking kidding me?"

"I'm not, and the two of them left to fulfill their lustful natures."

"I didn't think Leslie was a freak but looks are deceiving."

Toxic laughed. "She surprised the hell out of me. Leslie was just like another person to me. She actually seduced my client. I told her to be discreet and not jeopardize this case."

"This is unbelievable," Madison cried.

"I can't get rid of this Michelle Fost."

"She's dangerous," Madison cried.

"I'm going to ban her from Chicago and Los Angeles."

"Good luck with that, Toxic. Michelle is a smart and clever attorney. She knows the ropes, thank you very much."

"She's not going to win, Madison. I'm going to handle this. How are the wedding plans going?"

He was changing the subject, and Madison wasn't stupid. "Sylvia and Helen are on it, and your mother too. I'm so blessed, and I was thinking about going to Church on Sunday. God has been so wonderful to me, and I want to give him more of my time. Do you belong to a Church?"

Toxic laughed. "I do, and we can go on Sunday. The entire family will be there."

"Wow!"

"The Lyons are eager to thank God for their blessings. We sing and praise the Lord, and tithe too. I'm so glad you'll be joining us. I knew you were the right woman for me. God told me."

Madison blushed, staring at her naked body. "I need to find my negligee and put on some clothes."

"Don't you move," he stated. "I love your naked body."

Madison touched the hairs on his chest. "You're fine, Toxic Lyons, and your body is all muscled, and perfect for me. She circled his chest with her hands. "I love touching you."

"And the electricity is mind-boggling."

"I feel it too, Toxic. I'm so confused why this is happening to us."

"Me too, but I'm not going to fight it. I love you."

"I love you more."

Toxic laughed. "I got to get back to work."

"I know, and so do I. I need to call let Fink look at my contracts. I have one for the publishing house, and Tanyann as my agent. Why didn't you tell me that you have a publishing house?"

"I don't usually work at it, and it's Tanyann's baby."

"I write stories honey."

"It just never crossed my mind, Madison. We have hotels, stores, restaurants, real estate, computer stores, etc."

"You don't trust me," she frowned.

Toxic stood up. "I'm going to take a shower and then go back to work. Stop being stupid. Do you want me to bring you some McDonald's home? I know you love your fish fillet."

"I think Amy cooked dinner for us, but thanks."

"Don't be mad at me, Madison. It's a lot we don't know about each other."

"And this is why we need to wait to get married."

He stopped at the entrance to the bathroom, as his long dick stood up at attention. Madison couldn't stop staring at his huge penis. "We're getting married January 1st so don't change the plans."

"I know this," she frowned. "Don't you dare threaten me?"

"Of course not." *Toxic walked into the bathroom. Five minutes later Madison heard the water running and she stared at the ceiling. Toxic loved her, and she wasn't about to doubt his love for her. She was getting married the 1st of next year, and her last name will be Madison Johnson-Lyons. She was definitely going to keep her maiden name, of course. She had to get back to work, but she felt so happy and settled in bed all in her naked glory. She remembered when she could never look at her naked body. Things had definitely changed for the better in her life.*

Ten minutes later Toxic walked back into their bedroom with a towel wiped around his middle. Madison stared at his fabulous chest, and she wanted to tear off the towel, and make love again to this wonderful man, who had this wonderful body. He walked into the closet and grabbed jeans, underwear, and a polo shirt. "You're wearing underwear," she laughed.

Toxic stared at her naked body. "I need to get back to work so cover yourself."

Madison laughed. "Do I have too?"

"Yes," he said.

Madison pouted, but she reached for the blanket and covered herself all the way up to her chin. "Is that better now?"

"Yes," he laughed. "I love your body, but I'll be coming straight home, and as for the underwear, I should wear them to work."

"I love you Toxic Lyons."

Toxic put on his blue polo shirt. "Where did that come from?"

"I just felt the need to say it."

"I love you more," he confessed. "How is your day going?"

"Wonderful since you're here, and your sister and Beverly is going to make me a house hold name. My first book of short stories is called "I Confess."

"I'm so proud of you," he stated, adding his blue underwear and then jeans to the mix. I can't wait to have a signed copy in my hands. You're going to busy at the end of the year."

"I know, but I'm a super woman and I can do it all," she laughed.

"Maybe you can, but in all your careers, remember marriage is our number one spot, and you also need to call my mother and get the name of her therapist, and start talking to her."

"Are you going to see her too?"

"Yes, I will," he stated.

"Okay, then I will."

Toxic laughed. "I'm not going to be bored with you."

Madison rolled her eyes. "I love you too."

Toxic walked over to the bed, sat down, and grabbed her. He kissed her on the lips and then stood back up. "I love you, and I'll see you after six."

"I'll be here," she cried. "I love you more."

Madison stared at Toxic getting into the elevator, and then the doors closing. She then got out of bed in her naked glory and got on her knees to pray. "Dear. God, thank you for bringing this wonderful man into my life, and please let us get married next year, and continue to love each other until you come down from heaven and take us with you. Please keep this Michelle Fost away from us, and let her move on. Thank you for my new writing career, and the people in my life. Bless everyone, God, and I'll see you on Sunday at Church."

Madison got back into the bed and covered herself. She was going to take a quick nap, and then wake up and get back to her paralegal cases, and fax over the contracts so Fink can read them. She wondered how he was doing.

She yawned, and then she closed her eyes and slept with a smile on her face.

Toxic Lyons

Toxic was back at work singing to himself as he focused on the rest of his cases. He was so happy after spending time with Madison and the lovemaking they shared. His body was still feeling the electricity. He was in love and proud of it.

A knock sounded on his door.

Toxic looked up at the door. "Come in."

He smiled as he stared at his brother. "Hi Tumor, and what's up?"

"Just checking the books, and making sure the numbers are in order." *He closed the door, and sat down in the chair across from Toxic.* "I see you're in a good mood."

"I feel great and loving my new life."

Tumor laughed. "Marriage isn't all it's cracked up to be."

Toxic frowned, focusing on his brother. "What are you babbling about?"

"I'm beginning to hate being married."

"What's going on with you and Tricia?"

"My wife wants to model and do the news. I haven't seen my wife for the entire week. She's meeting with Sylvia and she's in New York City. Mom is keeping the children."

"Wow!" he said. "This is great for a full-size woman."

Tumor frowned. "Of course, you wouldn't be on my side."

"I'm not involved in this," he snapped. "You're hopefully not about to ruin your marriage because your wife has a life, I hope."

Tumor frowned. "I want my wife at home," he snapped.

"Then you should have married someone who didn't want to work."

"If Tricia loves me, then she's going to honor my wishes."

Toxic laughed. "Tumor, you need to see mother's shrink."

"I'm not crazy. I just love my wife and want to come home from work and she's there in the kitchen cooking dinner for me and our children. I don't want her in New York City."

"You have a big problem, Tumor."

"I hate this."

"I don't know what to say."

"I like her independence and working on the weekend was the plan we chose. I asked her to have another baby, and she refused. She also told me that she got her tubes tied."

"What?"

"I know, and she didn't discuss this with me at all."

"Are you tired of a fat woman, and you want someone skinny?"

"I should kick your ass for that remark. I dated fat women when I was in elementary and high school. That isn't the issue, and you know this. I think you need to see mother's shrink."

"As a matter of fact, Madison and I will be doing just that."

Tumor shook his head. "You two are a romance novel."

"I thought you and Tricia were a romance novel."

"So, did I but the hero is unsatisfied. I haven't made love to my wife in weeks, and she wonders why men cheat all the time."

"You're not thinking about cheating on her with a skinny woman, are you?"

"What is your problem with weight, Toxic?"

He shook his head. "I don't know."

"You need to work on it."

"And you need to focus on your marriage, Tumor. There's no other woman out there for you, who will love you like Tricia loves you. They just want our money and our name. God brought Tricia into your life, and you're about to fuck it up."

"Watch your language, Toxic."

He laughed. "My bad! How come you didn't go to New York City with her? You have a flexible schedule, of course."

"I was angry that she left, and I thought after we argued that she wouldn't go, but she left, and I was furious."

"You need to surprise her and join her in New York."

"I guess you're right. I know she's not cheating on me."

"Go see your wife, and have a good time."

Tumor laughed. "Here's the report for the numbers, and I'm going to New York City to surprise my wife, and spend some quality time with her. Thanks so much for reasoning with me."

"I'm glad to do it."

"I thought you hated Tricia, but I'm glad the two of you called it a truce."

"She loves you like a woman should love a man, and I'm all for love. You four have a wonderful family, and this is what I'm aiming for when Madison and I get married."

"I'm still shocked about my brother getting married."

Toxic laughed. "I'm stunned myself, but when the right woman comes along, marriage is the next step. I'm ready to marry Madison yesterday, but she insists on marrying the first of the year, and I can reason with that. I'm not happy about it, but when you love someone you have to compromise. This is what I'm doing."

"You're definitely in love because I never thought I'd see the day that you compromise on anything." *Tumor walked to the door.* "I'm going to see if the private plan is ready so I can go to New York. I'll be there for probably two weeks, or however long that Tricia is there."

"Have fun, and good luck."

"Thanks again, and I love you."

"I love you too."

Toxic stared after his brother glad that he was trying to save his marriage. Tumor was fine as wine, and he could have any woman he wanted, and didn't have to settle for a career woman, but deep down inside, Tumor loved his wife, or he'd never have married her. We Lyons don't get married for the hell of it. We make sure that the woman we're going to spend the duration of our lives with is the one. I plan on never getting married again. Madison is the one.

He smiled.

Madison Johnson

Madison headed back to her office at the mansion and smiled as she pushed the button for Fink's number. She waited patiently until he answered her call, staring at her desktop computer.

"Hi Madison, and what's going on?"

"How are you doing?"

"I'm good and yourself?"

"So am I. Did you call me about the five cases?"

"I did, but I wanted to fax you two contracts and have you go over them with me."

"What are the contracts?"

"One is for an agent, and the other is a five-book deal with Lyons Publishers."

"I'm impressed," Fink replied. "Are you leaving me?"

"Of course not, Fink. I'm here forever."

"I hope so when you get married next year."

"Don't be silly. Toxic knows I'm a paralegal. I'm not going to law school since my writing career has taken off. I work at home, so I am okay. I'll be there on Fridays for the weekly meetings."

"I hope you're dressed properly," he laughed.

Madison frowned. "Don't remind me of that ridiculous time in my life. I told Toxic, and I almost lost him because of it. I want you to give me away at my wedding."

Silence took over the room.

"Hello," Madison sang.

"Are you sure?"

"Fink, are you crying?"

"Of course not. I'm honored."

"You gave me a job, and I'm devoted and you're like a father to me. I can't believe I slept with my father, but that's done and over with, so let's just move on. Will you do me the honors on the happiest day of my life?"

"Are you sure that Toxic Lyons is the man for you?"

Madison frowned. "Do you have doubts?"

"I love Toxic and the Lyons, and I'm just making sure he's the one for you. I don't want you rushing into anything you can't get out of. Is he making you sign a prenuptial agreement?"

Madison frowned. "That never came up, Fink."

"If it does will you sign it?"

"I hope it doesn't come up. I have my own money, but I'm not as rich as the Lyons are. I'm conflicted with this issue Fink, and I never thought about it until you just mentioned it. Are you deliberately trying to ruin my happiness on purpose?"

"Of course not."

"Then why bring this up?"

"It might come up, and I'm advised to bring it up."

"You better not, Fink. Just let it be."

"Why not, you don't want his money?"

"I don't mind signing it, but it brings up a trust issue with me, and what's Toxic should be mine. He bought me this very very expensive engagement ring, and I told him to take it back and get me something cheaper, but he thought it was funny."

Fink laughed. "Toxic has more money that he's going to spend in this lifetime believe me, and he's very generous. They have tons of charities they give too. I just want you to be aware of it."

"If Toxic doesn't bring it up then why should you?"

"I won't bring it up," he laughed.

"Good," she stated. "I'm not sure about it."

"I do understand."

"How you and Rita doing?"

"I'm falling for her, and she's everything I need in a woman."

"Are you about to propose?"

"I'm not in a rush to get married, Madison."

"But Rita is in her forties and she might be ready."

"She hasn't mentioned it to me, and we're just taking one day at a time. Life is short, and I want to spend the rest of it with Rita, and vice versa. We're having fun without all the commitment."

"As long as she makes you happy."

"Very much so."

"I'm glad we found happiness."

"So am I. Fax me the contracts so I can go over them."

"I'll do it now. How is Jasmine doing?"

"I haven't heard from her. Why don't you call her?"

"I'm going to do that now, and good luck."

"I don't need any luck," he cried.

"I love you, Fink. You saved my life in so many ways."

Silence again took over.

"Hello," she cried.

"I love you too," he whispered.

"Fink, you're crying," she exclaimed.

"Men don't cry," he snapped. "I'll fax you my opinion after I read the contracts."

Madison laughed. "Thank you so much, and I'll email you my five briefs in an hour."

"I need that soon and get to it. I will have more cases to follow."

"Your law firm is very busy."

"The best is the best."

"Of course," Madison laughed. *She ended the call, and smiled to herself. Fink was like a father to her, since her parents were in heaven. The fact that she slept with her father was music to her demented mind and maybe she did need to see someone. She wanted to be sane when she got married, and not insane.*

She grabbed her iPhone again and went through her contacts to find Jasmine's number. She wanted to follow up with her client. She found her number and dialed it.

"Hello," Jasmine replied.

"Hi, Jasmine, this is Madison."

"Hey girl, what's up?"

"I'm good, calling to see how everything is going with you."

"I'm just waiting for my large settlement check and figuring out what I'm going to do with the rest of my life. I'm not about to be an assistant again. I'm about to model for Sylvia."

Madison smiled. "So that's coming along."

"It is. I went to New York for a week, and I'm going back next week. Everything was so nice. I met Tricia Lyons, and she's still in New York, but I had to come back on business, so I'll be back next week. She's a very nice woman and she loves her husband and children."

"Did you tell her you slept with her husband?"

"I did, but it was before she met Tumor."

Madison was stunned. "Why did you confess?"

"I felt guilty, and she was flabbergasted at first, but she couldn't fault me for having good taste in men. It was before they met, and she was thrilled that he kept the tradition with the big women. We had a nice time."

"I'm glad you met a friend."

"We're going to be great friends, but I think she's sad about her marriage. Tumor wants her to be home more, and now she's modeling and doing the news on the weekend, it's taking a toll on her marriage. She doesn't want her husband cheating on her with a skinny woman."

"Tumor will find another fat women, believe me, and he loves his wife too much."

"Men cheat," Jasmine snapped. "Max told me I was great in bed, and the next day he had skinny women coming out of his office left and right. I can't stand men like him."

"In my experience as a fat woman, it's a curse. We're invisible, and men don't look at us. I hear men like women with meat on their bones, but they don't live in Chicago. I never met anyone. Do you know that Toxic dated a fat woman?"

"Really," she exclaimed.

"I'm still learning about my fiancé, believe me. Her name is Michelle Fost."

"Are you freaking killing me? She used to model for the plus-size model, but she lost her contract and her agent when she lost the weight. She had bypass gastric surgery. I was so in admiration of her, and she defeated, of course. I'm never going to be skinny, and probably lonely for the duration of my life. It's okay as long as I have money and can do what I want to do in this life. I don't give a damn. I do have my fingers and my vibrator."

Madison laughed. "I know about those fingers."

The two women laughed.

"Maybe we can all get together when everyone is in Chicago for the holidays, you me, Sylvia, Helen, and maybe Tricia. The more the merrier, and I believe we will have some fun."

"I'd like that."

"You're invited to the wedding in Las Vegas."

"I'm so happy you said that, and I'll be there."

"It's going to be a day I'll never forget. I'm getting married on New Year's Day. It has been a dream of mine, and now it's happening. Jasmine, I still think I'm reading one of my romance novels, and I want to pinch myself more than one time. I still can't believe that Toxic Lyons, a white man with lovely green eyes wants to spend the duration of his life with me. It's unbelievable."

"He's blessed that you love him."

Madison smiled. "I like you."

Jasmine laughed. "Keep up the confidence. Toxic Lyons is a billionaire, and he needs a woman who is confident in herself. Don't let him win, and be yourself."

"I will, and thanks for the advice. If this can happen to me, then you're next in line. It happened to Tricia, and you just have to pray and believe. Maybe God wants you to be alone for a reason."

"I heard my pastor say that to me one day. I'm not ready yet."

"We have our seasons."

"That's for sure."

"So you have a great day, and we'll be in touch."

"Thanks for calling, and you have a blessed day too."

"I will." *Madison clicked the red phone button on her phone and sat her phone down. She smiled as she thought about her new life, and the friends that have come into them. She was truly blessed. And now it was time to get to work because she wanted to be done when Toxic came home. She was living with him, and she didn't like it, so maybe it was time that she went home. She didn't want to do anything to spoil her happiness. Madison knew that Toxic was going to hit the rooftops when she demanded to go home to her condo. What in the world was she going to do?*

Toxic Lyons

September and October flew so fast Toxic didn't know it was here and gone. Now it was November and getting closer and closer to their wedding in Las Vegas. According to Helen, Sylvia and his mother, everything was set. His hunter green tux was ready and waiting. Now he needed a best man, and Tumor was going to be his best man.

Tumor found his wife in New York, and the two of them made up for lost time, and was back on the right track. Everything was going as planned, and now he had to talk to Michelle again and her lawyer to get her ass out of Chicago and Los Angeles. Justin couldn't make it because he was shooting a movie in an undisclosed location. Toxic knew where, but he couldn't let Michelle know his whereabouts.

Toxic wanted to get this over with. It was almost Christmas, and he didn't have time to deal with Michelle and her theatrics. The woman needed to find a man and settle down and stop whoring around.

The knock came on his office door, and he took a deep breath and his secretary opened the door, and Michelle and her attorney Benny walked in. Benny had plenty of gray hair, but he was skinny and very debonair as they took a seat in front of his desk. He should have met them in the conference room. He stared at Michelle looking lovely as ever, but she didn't have big legs, and her ass wasn't that big, but her dress was short as hell, and he saw her black panties when she sat down and cross her legs.

"Hi Toxic, looking fine as ever. I hear you're getting married."

Toxic frowned. "How did she find out about that?"

"It's none of your business, but let's get down to your business."

Michelle frowned. "I want to stay in Chicago and Los Angeles, so I told Benny that I don't want to make a deal. Let's just go to court."

"Are you stupid, Michelle?"

"I don't think you should be talking to my client like that," Benny stipulated.

"I heard you can't go to New York either."

Michelle frowned. "Benny is working on that."

"Justin has a girlfriend, and he has moved on." *He was off the market and dating his associate, Leslie. He was thrilled about that. The two met in his office, and he felt a part of that.*

"I can't go to Las Vegas," she barked, but Benny is working on that." *She stared at her attorney with seduction as she winked at him, and then she ran her hand down his left arm.*

Benny brushed her hands off with an evil eye, staring at her. "Will you act professional?" he shouted.

"You were screaming all over the place when I was sucking that hard dick of yours," Michelle seduced.

"Cut it out," Benny snapped.

Toxic shook his head at the antics of the two of them. How could someone as famous and highly looked upon attorney let someone like Michelle Fost get in his pants? The woman still had it going on, and her ass did look big as he stared at her, and then shook his head.

"Do you still want me?" Michelle purred.

"I want us to reach some kind of settlement?" Toxic snapped.

Michelle shook her long, black weave, almost hitting her ass. The woman was fine and then some, not having a big stomach, and now a little waist. She was definitely keeping the weight off. "What about two million dollars?"

Toxic laughed. "You need to see a shrink."

Michelle frowned. "I'm going to make your life a living hell, Toxic."

He stared daggers at her. "I want you out of Chicago and Los Angeles, and two million dollars isn't on the table as you're the stalker. You should be paying Justin for the way that you beat his ass. You need to be locked up and the key thrown in the river."

Michelle laughed. "I know you want this fine ass. I'm sure that fiance of yours doesn't have this fine black ass, and kinky ideals. I bet you're bored as hell in bed, Toxic. I can't believe you settled for a black woman, when this white woman can continue to rock your world and then some. Does this fiance of yours ride the broom?"

"Will you get a grip?" Benny shouted. "I'm going to fire myself from your case, and let you find another attorney. You're acting like a slut, and you're not listening to my advice. Take the settlement and move the hell on."

Michelle focused on her attorney as she stared at him. "Do you want me to tell your wife about our sexual appetites? Your frigid, and rich wife will divorce you so fast, she's going to leave you with the money that you make, which don't compare to her millions."

Toxic stared at the two of them. Benny was a fool, but he was one as well, Justin also, and the other sick men who was in Michelle's web. She crossed her legs, and he saw that she didn't have on any panties with her short dress. The woman had no scruples. "We need to reach some kind of monetary award, but it's not going to be the amount that you quoted. You're going to prison if we can't. Justin has photos of what you did to him. Do you really want to go to court? I'm going to get a woman judge and you're not going to be able to seduce her with your wanton seductive moves. I'm thinking about Judge Judyann."

Michelle frowned.

Toxic smiled. "Did I hit a nerve? I remember Judyann informing you that if you came into her courtroom again, she was going to punish you with the law on her side. Do you want to take the risk?"

"I need to speak with my attorney alone," Michelle snapped.

Toxic stood up. "I'm going to get a diet soda, and I'll be right back. I hope when I do get back you won't be wasting more of my time. I need you to stay out of Chicago and Los Angeles for two years."

"I'll do one year," Michelle snapped. "I have a contract with Justin."

"We'll handle the contract," Toxic said. "I'll be back."

He left the conference room, closing the door behind him, and breathing left and right. Michelle's perfume was intoxicating, but he wasn't attracted to the woman any longer. The fact that she didn't have on any panties didn't make his cock stand up at attention. He smiled because he was very relieved that Madison was definitely the only woman for him.

Toxic walked to the cafeteria to get a diet soda. He was thirsty as hell for some reason. It was November and he couldn't believe how fast the time has flown. In less than one month he was going to marry the woman of his dreams, Madison Johnson. As he put his two doctors into the vending machine, and pushed the button for a diet coke, he waited for it to drop down, and smiled to himself. He was truly the luckiest man in the world and then some.

After the diet coke dropped and he grabbed the bottle of diet soda from the vending machine, he turned the top and took a long sip. He was in heaven as he almost drained the entire bottle, but caught himself. He sat down at one of the tables in the cafeteria to give Benny sometime to talk to sense into his crazy client. He took another sip of his diet soda, thinking about the love of his life, Madison Johnson.

Twenty minutes later he walked back into the conference room and took a seat. He stared at the angry look on Michelle's face. "Did we come to some kind of agreement?"

Benny smiled. "My client will leave Chicago and Los Angeles for a year, but two years is out of the question. She will have to come back to Los Angeles to shoot movies, and only movies."

Toxic smiled. "Let's sign the contracts and remember if she shows up before the movie, she'll be arrested, and no attorney will be able to help her. This is serious business."

"Michelle will follow the rules. She doesn't want to go to jail or prison for that matter. She's too fine to sit up in prison, and she's not into women. I don't think Michelle is stupid."

She continued to frown, staring daggers at the two of them.

Toxic opened the folders, and slid the papers to Benny, who stared at them for a few minutes, and then handed them to Michelle, informing her where to sign them as he handed her a pen.

Michelle stared at her attorney, who shook his head, and then she signed the papers, pushing them back toward Toxic. Toxic smiled as he stared at her signatures, and then he stood up. "This meeting is over, and you should be glad we reached this peaceful settlement. My client wanted money damages also, but I talked him out of it. Please don't go around beating up people, or you're going to find yourself locked up or in jail."

Michelle stood up. "Fuck off!"

Toxic laughed. "You do the same."

"Let's go, Michelle," Benny snapped. "I told you about your mouth."

"It's hard controlling your client," Toxic laughed.

Benny rolled his eyes at Toxic.

"I'm not going to suck his dick for a very long time," Michelle pouted. "He's going to miss my mouth."

Toxic stared after the two of them, and then he reached for his Samsung to give Justin the news. He had Justin's private number and could call him in case of emergency, and this was one. He dialed his number and waited for him to pick up.

"What's going on Toxic?"

"Michelle signed the papers, and she's out of here."

"I'm so relieved to hear that," Justin cried.

"When she due is on set for her next movie is when you two will meet again?"

"She'll be making her third movie in May of next year."

"So we can get her on a plane, and she can go to New York for the moment."

"Yes, keep her away from me, and I might be shooting in New York so that works for me, but I still want the restraining order to stay in affect. She'd be mostly working with my assistant, Darlene and Michelle won't be seducing a woman."

Toxic laughed. "Keep me posted so I can make sure that she doesn't breach her contract. Michelle is a clever woman, and she knows the legal system. Why she signed the papers without any theatrics is news to me, but I'm not going to contest it."

"I'm just glad she's out of my sight for the moment. I just don't trust the bitch. I'm moving on with Leslie now, and we're getting along very nicely. I can't believe the electricity between the two of us. It's like a romance novel. I've been told the electricity between couples, but I thought it was lust, or they were deluding themselves. I do understand now."

"Did you two exercise the lust?"

"We did," Justin confessed. "Leslie is a sex kitten."

Toxic was surprised. "I'm shocked."

"Looks are very deceiving. Leslie has skills."

"Wow?" Toxic exclaimed. "Everyone calls her a cold fish around the office."

"She has a professional side, but the personal side will blow your mind. My body is still feeling the aftereffects of our sexual escapades, thank you very much."

Toxic shook his head. "I wish the two of you the best, or is it just sex?"

"Not on your life," Justin snapped. "I think about her all the time day and night, and I want to spend time with her. She's the woman I've been waiting for my entire life, and then some. This is no romance novel."

"I do know the feeling about the electricity. How are you two going to work out the relationship? Leslie lives in Chicago, and she does go to Los Angeles on business too."

"It's going to be a long distance relationship for the moment, and when I'm free, I come out there and when she free, she comes out here. Leslie would like to take her four-week vacation now since she never takes them."

Toxic frowned. "Four weeks."

"She's entitled to them, thank you very much."

"It depends if she has any cases pending."

"She has one she's about to win, and then I want her out here for a month. I'm sure you can give her some time off. This is a new romance, and since you're about to embark on a marriage, you should have the same romantic tendencies to help another new couple out."

"Make me feel guilty, why don't you?" Toxic laughed.

"I have to do what I need to do," Justin laughed.

"Are you two sure about this?" Toxic asked.

"Are you two sure about this?" Justin asked.

Justin laughed. "I am with bells on."

"And so am I will bells on. Her vacation for four weeks is granted. I'm going to miss her, and the firm is going to be shocked because Leslie never takes a vacation. She's working all the time."

"It's always a first time for everything."

"Wonders never cease," Toxic barked. "Good luck."

"If the two of us get married, you will be my best man."

"You're moving way to fast, Justin. Slow down."

He laughed. "I'm happy, and it's so nice to find someone that's not after my money or name."

"I agree," Toxic stated.

"I have to get back to my movie, but thanks for the good news, and Leslie will be thrilled. I'll keep you posted, and good luck with Madison. I wish you the best."

"Do you think you and Leslie will be able to come to Las Vegas for the wedding?"

"We'll be there with bells on, and thanks for inviting me. Leslie was going anyway, since she works for you."

Toxic laughed. "Of course, and I'll talk to you later."

"You too."

Toxic hung up and smiled. Love was definitely in the air.

Madison Johnson

— ❖ —

Madison was thrilled to be sitting back at Lyons Restaurant with Sylvia, Helen, and their two new friends, Jasmine and Tricia. It was a very wintry day in November. Everyone was wearing boots with fall maxi dresses and jeans. Sylvia, Helen and Madison wore maxi dresses in their favorite colors. Jasmine was wearing jeans and so was Tricia, and they looked gorgeous in their fabulous plus-size arena.

"This is so nice," Madison cried. "My two best friends, Sylvia and Helen are back in Chicago. I'm so thrilled."

"It's great to be back in Chicago," Helen said.

"And adding two new friends, Tricia and Jasmine," Sylvia pointed out.

Jasmine laughed. "I'm having the time of my life."

"I am too," Tricia cried.

"Let's order our drinks," Madison said.

The waitress, Jackie appeared out of nowhere. Madison smiled at her. "I want a Matai."

"I do too," Jasmine agreed.

"Give me a rum and coke," Helen cited.

"I'll have a long island tea," Sylvia said.

"I want a beer," Tricia said.

Jackie smiled, and left to get their drinks.

"So, your wedding is coming up very fast," Jasmine stated. "Is everything ready?"

"It's ready and waiting," Helen replied. "I booked the Lyon's Hotel and restaurant, and it's going to be the bomb and then some."

"The dresses are ready, and you two need to try on yours," Sylvia said.

"Why?" Jasmine asked.

Madison smiled. "I'm going to make you two bridesmaid too."

"Are you serious?" Tricia exclaimed.

"Of course," Madison cried. "We have two new friends added to our group, and the more the merrier."

"I'm so touched," Jasmine said. "I hope you find something that will fit me."

"Me too," Tricia said. "I'm a size eighteen."

"I'm a twenty," Jasmine confessed.

"I have the two dresses ready for both of you, and stop putting yourselves down?" Sylvia snapped. "My fashions are for all sizes, shapes and colors. I don't discriminate. I designed a fashion line for Madison, but she lost weight."

Madison laughed. "I'm sorry."

"I have Jasmine and Tricia and their photo shoot was perfect," Sylvia cried. "I love it and the way the two of them posed for the camera was perfect. My photographer, Jason was so happy and thrilled that he didn't have to give a lot of direction. He informed me that the two of you are pros."

Jasmine smiled. "I actually had a great time doing it."

"I never thought I'd like it," Tricia said. "It was fun."

"Are you two ready for the fashion show in December?" Sylvia stated. "I have a feeling you two are going to sell out all my fashions. You have beautiful faces, hair and a bombing body."

"I hope so," Jasmine said.

"Keep the faith," Madison said. "I know how it feels, but you two are meant to model so go with the flow, and have fun doing it."

"I agree," Helen said. "Right now we want to get Madison married off to her prince charming, and then wait for the babies to come."

Madison laughed. "I want to spend at least two years with my husband."

"I said the same thing," Helen said, and it didn't work out that way.

Madison focused on Sylvia. "Let's focus on something else."

Sylvia laughed as Jackie passed out their drinks, and she took a long sip. "That was good, and stop beating around the bush with me. I'm getting a divorced, but I'm not dead. I'm really happy for Madison, and we can talk about it. Helen and I are doing the planning, and Maggie is ready too. You're going to love the flower arrangement, and the food. We have the entire restaurant and the ballroom in the hotel, so only invited guests are present, and a few media circuits."

Helen frowned. "I gave exclusive rights to Good Morning America."

Madison was stunned. "Is Robin Roberts doing the interview? I love her."

"She is," Helen said. "The Lyons are famous."

"Wow," Jasmine cried. "This is unbelievable."

"I agree," Tricia said. "I'm used to the media circus being married to Tumor Lyons, and it's not an easy feat, but I'm handling it. I love him, and love conquers all."

Madison stared at Tricia. "So, you and Tumor are okay."

"We had our moments," Tricia said. "I went to New York and Tumor refused to go with me since he's self-employed. I was angry about that, but then he surprised me and we made up for lost time. I think my husband is insecure, and I don't understand it. What does he think I'm going to do? Leave him for another man. It's out of the question. I'm in love after all these years. I don't want anyone, and there's no other man out there for me."

"You two are the perfect couple?" Jasmine stated.

Tricia focused on Jasmine. "Tell me about you and Tumor."

Everyone was silent.

Tricia laughed. "I'm just curious."

Jasmine frowned. "I don't want this to become a problem with you. It was a long time ago. I was very insecure about my weight and I ran Tumor away. I couldn't believe this white, very handsome man, wanted a fat woman, but he assured me that he dated fat women before. When he finally got tired of me, took me to a nice dinner, and broke off with me, I regretted it, but I wasn't all sad about it. I knew I wasn't the woman for Tumor."

Tricia smiled. "I almost lost him too with my fat issues, and I acted the same way. I came to my senses, and called him, and he made me wait for three weeks. I was livid with rage when he finally called me back, and I ignored him for another two weeks."

"The games we play," Sylvia declared.

"I wanted him to suffer the way I did," Tricia said.

"And the rest is history," Helen said. "I'm famished."

"Me too," Jasmine said.

"Do we want to order a pizza or individual meals?" Sylvia said.

"I heard the pizza was to die for," Jasmine pointed out.

"Let's have pizza, and then appetizers," Madison said.

"A great ideal," Helen said.

Jackie appeared, and the ladies ordered pizza, and then Buffalo wings, fries, rolls, and muffins for appetizers. Ten minutes later they were feeding their faces as silence came upon the room for the moment. Of course, they rented out the restaurant, so no one was in their business or anything.

It was twenty minutes before Madison broke the silence. "Toxic is paying for everyone to come to Las Vegas for the wedding, and practically everything included."

"He's so generous," Jasmine cried. "I can't believe I'm a part of this."

"Me either," Tricia said. "It's so much fun to hang out with the girls."

"I don't have any girlfriends," Jasmine said. "I'm so blessed."

"We are friends for life," Helen said. "Let's try not to keep secrets."

Madison and Sylvia frowned at her. "Helen has a problem with secrets," Sylvia said. "She wants us to tell her when we go to the bathroom and shit. I don't think it's necessary."

Helen frowned at them. "I just don't like secrets."

"Why?" Jasmine asked.

"My husband kept a lot of secrets from me," Helen confessed. "Now I'm invading his privacy to make sure that he's leveling with me. I know it's not sane, but when you've been lied to most of your marriage, you do what you have to do?"

"Why don't you just divorce him?" Jasmine asked.

"I love him," Helen said. "When you love someone, you deal with the problems. I'm never getting married again. I know Joseph loves me, but he's a male whore, and I have women to thank, and his looks. My husband is very handsome, even in his old age, and women don't give a damn that he's married."

"But your husband needs to resist them," Jasmine said.

"Most of the time he does," Helen pointed out. "His penis gets in the way at other times. I should tell you and Tricia about the woman who almost broke up my marriage. Her name was Sable, and she was my husband's paralegal. The two worked together constantly and one day, they got drunk and ended up in bed together. Sable recorded everything, of course, and made sure I got a copy of the video. They were doing all kinds of kinky things, and it sicken me. I took the children and we left for three months. My husband begged me to come back."

"Where did you go?" Tricia asked.

"I went to Las Vegas, which is my favorite place," Helen said. "It did me some good because I was going to divorce my husband, and take him for everything he had and then some."

"I'm glad you two worked out," Tricia said.

Helen frowned. "We have our moments."

"My husband prefers a man over me," Sylvia confessed.

Jasmine and Tricia stared at Sylvia with their mouths wide-open.

Sylvia laughed. "I'm sorry, but it's the truth."

"I'm so sorry," Jasmine said.

"Me too," Tricia replied.

"It's a done deal," Sylvia said, but thanks you two. "I'm still in shock, and it's something you just don't dismiss from your life as if it never happened. My husband wanted his best friend and now the two are probably getting married when the divorce is final."

"Wow," Tricia cried. "I can't imagine the pain."

"It's difficult when your husband is cheating on you with a woman," Helen said. "It's more upsetting when he's cheating on you with a man. I can imagine the pain since I've been through the cheating, but not with a man."

"I hate it," Sylvia cried. "I did know something was wrong with my marriage, but I, like every other woman, ignored the signs. My husband was spending too much time with George, his best friend. The way their eyes met when I left the room, or the way they causally touched each other. I stood in the kitchen one day and spied on them, and I saw the signs."

"Was your husband good in bed?" Jasmine asked.

"He was, but he always wanted to make love from the back, and he liked me sucking his dick. I think he pictured George doing it to him, and he didn't see me at all. I almost caught them one time when I went out of town to Las Vegas, and came back, and the two of them broke apart real quick when I walked in. I think they had been kissing in my house. I was livid, and asked Jose was something going on with him and George and he called me all kinds of names."

"He was being defensive," Madison said.

"And he blamed me for finding out the truth, but Jose denied it over and over, and I brought into it," Sylvia cried. "I loved my husband, and this wasn't a lifetime movie. I couldn't believe this was happening to me. It wasn't happening to me. I denied this over and over, but when I caught them at George's house in the pool, and seeing my husband moaning with his dick fucking George, I wanted to die."

"Wow," Tricia cried. "The pain must be heart-breaking."

"It's the most horrific pain in the world," Sylvia cried.

"I'm sorry," Madison cried.

Sylvia laughed. "I know, so let's change the subject. Jasmine, what are you doing with your settlement? I know you don't want to still be an assistant."

Jasmine smiled. "I love modeling, but I know I need to make a living. I have been thinking about going back to school. I want to be a counselor or something, especially for women and men who have low self-esteem, and think they don't matter."

"Wow!" Madison said. "I like it."

"I've been looking into online classes and so far I'm on my way," Jasmine said. "I still want to model too."

"Good luck with that," Helen said. "It's nice."

"I agree," Sylvia cried. "You can definitely counsel me."

Jasmine and Sylvia laughed.

"That's reminds me I need to call Maggie and hook up with her shrink, Toxic and I before we get married," Madison stated.

"It's a healing experience," Sylvia said. "I don't think I'll be sane if I wasn't talking to a professional. It helps to get closure."

"It does when you start a new marriage," Helen said. "You don't want all the issues coming along to hurt you and Toxic."

Madison nodded.

"Do we want cheesecake ladies?" Jasmine asked. "I still love eating."

"Bring on the cheesecake," Sylvia cried.

Jackie appeared, and soon they were munching on three favorites of cheesecake----plain, strawberry and chocolate. "This is the bomb," Tricia cried.

"I agree," Jasmine stated.

"I can't remember the last time I had cheesecake," Madison cried. "This is definitely the bomb and then some. I'm all for this."

"You have to indulge in the sweets from time to time," Helen said.

"I agree," Sylvia said, which is my exercise and the gym was invented.

"Or diet pills," Madison cried.

Helen cried. "I don't believe in diet pills, and I'm a nurse."

Madison frowned. "I do, which is why I look like this."

"And why I look like this?" Jasmine laughed.

The four women laughed as they enjoyed their cheesecake over more laughter, and getting to know the new members of their group. Madison was having the time of her life. She had two best friends, Sylvia and Helen, and now the three of them had two more best friends, Jasmine and Tricia.

Madison felt the tears forming.

"What is going on with you?" Helen asked.

"We see the tears," Sylvia cried.

Madison wiped her eyes with a napkin on the table. "I'm sorry, but I'm just so glad. I remember having no friends or a boyfriend and feeling so lonely. I prayed for someone to spend time with me, male or female, and now I have two best friends, and two new best friends, it's just overwhelming."

"We love you too," Helen cried.

"Let's take our drinks, and make a toast," Sylvia cried.

Everyone gathered their drinks. "To new and old friendship," Sylvia cried.

"Amen," Madison cried.

"Amen," Jasmine said.

"Amen," Tricia replied.

"Amen," Helen declared.

Their classes clicked, and the four laughed for the next two hours, and then they left and went their separate ways. Madison was so blessed because she had the best time hanging with her friends. It was fun as hell.

Toxic and Madison

M adison stared out the window this cold November afternoon. It was after one o'clock, and the weather was getting cold as hell. She wished she could leave Chicago and come back when spring was on the horizon. Madison smiled, she could now do that and more.

Toxic smiled. "What's happening in that pretty head of yours?"

Madison focused on her handsome fiance as she watched him drive to their destination. It wasn't a lot of traffic, and that was good. They were on their way to meet with the counselor Maggie, Toxic's mother recommended for the two of them. She really couldn't believe she was seeing a shrink.

"Madison?" Toxic sang.

Madison laughed. "I was just thinking about leaving Chicago for a warmer climax and coming back in the spring."

"Sounds like a plan to me," he agreed.

"I remember having so many dreams, Toxic. I can't believe most of them are a reality now. I still think I'm dreaming. I'm about to marry a Lyon, and make all my writing dreams come true."

"This is no romance novel," he laughed.

"Are you sure about us?"

"Are you sure about us?" he asked.

"I asked you first."

"I'm positive that you're the woman for me. I'm not interested in another woman. They could stand here right now naked in my face, and I wouldn't give a damn, and neither would my cock. It only gets hard for you, and I heard the voice. I hope this shrink gives you more confidence in yourself and us."

Madison smiled. "I'm just afraid."

"So am I, and anyone who gets married, but if the love is there, we're going to make it."

"I should be saying those words to you."

"You should, but I'm here for you, and as long as we have each other's back, then there's nothing that the devil can pull apartment. I love you Madison Johnson, and I've been waiting for you my entire life."

"I love you more, Toxic Lyons. I'm the happiest woman in the world."

Toxic squeezed her hand with his free one, not on the steering wheel as he mingled into traffic. "Now this is the woman I love. Everything is going to be perfect. In two months you and I will be man and wife, and then we're begin our new life." *The light changed to red, and Toxic reached over to give Madison a passionate kiss. As their lips and then tongues met, Madison knew she was making the right decision.*

A car horn blew, and Madison and Toxic broke apart, and they laughed as Toxic turned left at the light. They were so blessed.

As Madison and Toxic sat in the waiting room, they were both nervous, but when the door opened and the lovely black woman walked into the room, Madison was speechless.

Toxic stared at the woman.

The woman smiled as she took her seat. "I get this reaction all the time. I'm forty years old, and not sixteen, thank you both very much. You can pick your mouths off the floor," she laughed, reaching for her pad and tape recorder. "Is it okay to tape this session?"

Madison laughed. "You have good genes."

"It runs in the family," she laughed. "My name is Dr. Reynolds, and I've been a psychiatrist for fifteen years now. I started young, and knew what I wanted to do at an early age. I have many books out there for review, and I counsel five days a week. I love what I do and that's the bottom line. Now let's get this two hours going. The two of you are lovely together, and you make a lovely interracial couple. Toxic, what is your views on interracial dating?"

He frowned. "I never really thought about it."

"And you, Madison?" Dr. Reynolds asked.

This doctor doesn't waste any time. "I wrote short stories about it, and most of my heroes were white."

"Why did you write white heroes?"

Madison shrugged. "I don't know. The plot just took off."

"Did you see yourself with a white man?"

"Maybe or maybe not," Madison said. "I don't know."

"A lot of times what we write is reality," Dr. Reynolds pointed out.

"Toxic, did you think you were going to date and marry a black woman?"

"I did think about it because my parents are mixed," Toxic confessed. "My father is black, and my mother is white."

"And when you were old enough to understand, how did this effect you?"

"It was very difficult," Toxic stated. "My parents were ignored, and ridiculed, and my father suffered the most. I was bullied and talked about in school as my siblings also. We had to bind together and look out for each other. Tumor and I fought all our sister's battles and won too."

Dr. Reynolds smiled as she wrote diligently on her memo pad. "So being with Madison isn't a big deal to you."

"I'm following in my parent's footsteps as my sister Tanyann. She's married to the famous producer, Guy."

The doctor nodded. "You two don't have any issues being black and white in this relationship?"

"None at all," Toxic said.

"No," Madison cited.

"You two will make beautiful babies," the doctor stated.

Madison and Toxic exchanged glances and smiled.

"So Toxic, why are you in love with Madison?"

He laughed. "I don't understand the question."

"There's a lot of women out there for a handsome man as yourself," the doctor pointed out. "What made you choose Madison?"

Toxic focused on Madison. "I was instantly attracted to her, and the voice told me so. I believe that God told me that Madison was going to be my wife, and I'm happy."

"It could be the devil telling you this also," the doctor stated.

Toxic frowned. "I think about Madison day and night, and when I'm around her the electricity almost blinds me. I've never felt this way about a woman before. I dated a lot of bimbos, but no one as beautiful, intelligent and exciting as Madison. I have no doubt that we're going to spend the rest of our lives together."

The doctor smiled.

"Madison do you think Toxic is the man for you?"

"I do," she confessed. "I love him, and I think about him night and day. There's no other man for me, and I've never felt this way with other men."

"Your profile tells me that you haven't dated a lot of men."

Madison frowned at the doctor. "I haven't, but the men that I did date never made me feel the way that Toxic makes me feel. I know he's the man for me, and the only man for me."

"Have you ever been in love before?" the doctor asked.

"Only with Toxic," Madison cried.

"So how do you know he's the one?" the doctor asked.

"I just know he's the one for me," Madison sang.

"Toxic have you been in love before?"

"No," he said.

"So how do you know this is love?"

"I just know. I'd die for Madison."

"And I'd die for Toxic."

The doctor smiled. "You two are passing my test with flying colors. So the wedding is on January 1."

Madison and Toxic nodded their heads.

"Who chose this date and why?"

"I wanted to get married yesterday?" Toxic stated.

"And why did you want to get married so fast?"

"Madison has a lot of fat issues."

"Yes, she does according to her profile that the two of you completed before this session, and Madison and I will discuss that in your individual sessions. Anyway, you want to rush into marriage in fear of Madison changing her mind?"

"Yes," Toxic said. "I love her."

"I chose January 1 because it's a new beginning and it gives us time to adjust to each other," Madison pointed out.

"So. it was love at first site," the doctor stated.

"Yes, it was," Madison cried.

"Absolutely," Toxic agreed. "The electricity almost electrocuted us. I get hard as a rock, and I can tell it's different this time."

"Let's get ready for our individual sessions," the doctor said. "We're going to begin with Madison. Toxic you can wait in the cafeteria and relax for a few minutes."

They stood up, and Madison and Toxic kissed, and then Toxic left the room. He was going to get him a diet soda. For some reason why was he so damn thirsty all the time. It was winter in Chicago for heaven sakes. He pushed the button for the elevator and waited as he frowned.

Madison Johnson

※

M adison twisted her fingers together as she stared at the doctor. What did she have to worry about? She was going to pass all the tests, and that was the bottom line. Toxic Lyons was the man for her.

The doctor smiled at her. "Are you truly and really in love with Toxic Lyons? Do you see him as your husband for life, or the man you want to spend the rest of your life with because of his fame and fortune?"

Madison was stunned as she stared at the doctor. Was she for freaking real?

"I see the anger on your face, so talk to me."

"Doctor, I love Toxic for him. I don't care about his fame and fortune. He's the lighting to my rain, and peanut butter to my jelly. I love him, and I do want to marry him and be with him."

"Where are the two of you going to live?"

"In Chicago, and he has a condo and I have a condo."

"I'm still waiting for the answer."

Was she a bitch or what? "We haven't discussed it."

"But you're about to get married the first of the year."

"It's either his condo, or mine, or the mansion."

"Where are you staying now?"

"The mansion."

"Why are you living with Toxic now?"

"I want too," she shouted. "Is that a problem?"

"I'm a bitch, but I save a lot of marriages, and marriages from happening. When I'm done with you two, you're going to get married next year, or end the relationship. I'm here to make sure that the two of you are destined to be together. It's my job to save relationships and lives. Are you going to work?"

"I am as a paralegal and writer."

"What about children?"

"I don't want any for two years."

"And what did Toxic say about this?"

Madison frowned. "I can't remember."

"What is Toxic favorite color and television show?"

"I don't know," she shouted.

"Does he like the right or left side of the bed?"

Madison frowned.

"Is he allergic to certain foods?"

"I don't know," she cried.

"Then why are you marrying someone you don't know."

"I love him," she cried. "I know he's the man for me."

"And how do you know this?"

"My instincts are always right."

"Why don't you wait until next May and get married?"

"Are you crazy?" she blurted out.

The doctor smiled. "I don't think so, but let me check."
Madison found herself smiling at her remark.

"I think it's for the best. You don't really know that much about him. You can find out on the internet, but everything on the internet isn't true. I think you're rushing for some reason. Are you pregnant now?"

"Of course not," Madison shouted. "Are you for real?"

"I think I am. I met my husband at a party a friend was giving, and it was instant attraction for each other. We talked for five hours, and then I ended up at his place where we made love for three days straight. I knew I had finally found the man of my dreams. We exchanged numbers, and I didn't hear from my husband until five years later."

"What is your point?"

"It wasn't met for us to marry at that time. Now our marriage is stable and tolerable."

"Life is a bitch, and we need to marry now."

"What is the rush?"

"Doctor, you need to move on. We're getting married."

"Give me five adjectives you like about Toxic?"

"Handsome, kind, loving, romantic, and attentive."

"Describe each of them for me in Toxic terms."

"Toxic is gorgeous with the green eyes. He's very nice to me, and gentle, he knows how to treat a woman in a romantic setting, and he caters to me and only me."

"Give me five negative words about Toxic."

Madison stared at the doctor wanting to kick this bitches' ass. What in the world? "I don't have anything negative to say about Toxic. He's everything in a man I want."

The doctor shook her head. "Houston, we have a problem."

Her ass needed kicked, Madison thought to herself, and she was about to stand up and get ghetto up in here. Who did she think she was?

"I'm waiting," the doctor replied.

Madison rolled her eyes at the doctor. "He's controlling, rich, white, silver spoon, and fat issues."

"Explain your answers."

"I guess I resent Toxic for being rich, when I couldn't even find money to go to work or eat; I might be bias with white and black---I don't know. Toxic never had to suffer for anything and everything. He saw something he wanted, he bought it. He has fat issues, and he blames them on me. I think someone fat in his childhood bullied him."

"You think, but you're not sure."

"I don't know," she snapped.

"Do you and Toxic just sit down and talk?"

"Most of the time, but not a lot."

"So is it only sex between the two of you?"

"It's not lusting after each other doctor. We have much more than that in our relationship. I'm new to finding love."

"My point exactly. Do you think this is a romance novel? What are you going to do when the last page ends, and you have to move on? You resent this man for being born with a silver spoon in his mouth, but you're about to marry him."

"I love him," she cried. "I have money now."

"Are you signing a prenup?"

"No," she cried.

"Would you if he mentioned it?"

Madison thought about the question real hard. Would she sign a paper giving her no rights to Toxic's fame and fortune?

Would she walk away from the marriage with nothing? "I don't know," she honestly replied. "I have no damn clue. I hope he doesn't ask me to do it because I don't know how I will respond. I know it frustrates a marriage for doom."

"So true, but your fiance is worth billions."

She frowned. "I don't give a damn about his money. I have my own and about to sign a publishing contract with Lyons Publishers. I have over fifty thousand dollars in my bank account. I'm good."

"You used to be fat, and I saw the pictures. Why did you lose the weight?"

"I didn't want to be invisible? I wanted a man to flirt with me, desperately fight for me, and probably would die for me. I would get into uber and the driver would speak, and then tune me out. If I was skinny, they would be flirting with me, and it has happened. I couldn't look in the mirror, either, and I just hated myself. I couldn't find clothes to wear, and I wanted to wear jeans and short skirts. I hated being fat."

"Are you happy now with your new body?"

"Yes, I am because now I stop traffic."

The doctor shook her head. "And this is a good thing."

"When you have been ignored most of your life and have to wear girdles to keep your stomach in, it's a very good thing."

"Why was food your crutch?"

"I don't know," she cried.

"Think about the question."

Ten minutes passed as Madison focused on the doctor. "I guess I didn't want men talking to me. I don't know."

"Were you afraid of men?"

"Yes," she nodded. "I didn't want to kiss or fuck them."

"So you use food to get so fat they wouldn't look at you."

Madison nodded.

"But they look at you all the time."

"It's okay now because I can reject the bastards," Madison shouted. "I especially rejected the men who ignored me when I was fat like that uber driver. I'm not invisible."

"So you have the confidence now."

"Yes," she laughed. "I can get any man I want, and I can reject them too. I can look in the mirror, and my clothes fit perfectly on me now. I don't have to hide with jackets and vests. I remember wearing a vest and sweater with all my outfits, and it got on my nerves. I hated covering myself up."

"Give me five adjectives about you."

Madison smiled. "Skinny, fine, beautiful, gorgeous and pretty."

"Sounds like a diva to me."

"Whatever, it's how I feel."

"You're just getting to know that new skinny body of yours, so why would you want to settle down with one man? You can have any man you want now, and you should ride the freedom wagon."

Madison frowned. "I love Toxic, and he's the man for me."

"So, you're going to turn the other men away when they flirt with you?"

"Of course, doctor. I only see Toxic."

"And he's the only man for you."

"Yes, doctor, he's the only one I want."

"Who is Tony?"

Madison frowned. "What?"

"I investigate my patients before I take their cases because I don't want anyone killing me. Most patients who see me are insane, and I'm not saying you and Toxic are, but I have to protect myself. You dated someone name Tony when you were fat."

"I don't wish to discuss him."

"But we're going to discuss him. He was a married man."

"So what?"

"What happened and how did you two meet?"

Madison stood up and paced the room. "We met at a bookstore when he sat down at my table, and I ignored him, of course, but he kept staring at me. I was fat and working on a paralegal assignment because my computer had crashed. I was wondering why he sat down at my table when there were so many empty ones with prettier woman, and even they wondered to by the frown on their faces. Tony was handsome and black, and he wanted my fat ass. I couldn't believe it."

"So you let him have your fat ass."

"It took a while, but he kept coming back to the library and he practically harassed me. I finally gave in because a fat woman craves a lot of attention, and Tony was a pro. He wined and dined me, and soon he got my fat ass in bed, and we made passionate love. He never told me to lose the weight. He liked women with meat on their bones. I fell so hopelessly in love with him, and I told him, and this is when I found out he was married, but separated from his wife."

"So you ended the affair."

"I did for a few weeks, but Tony was fine and he insisted that we continued our relationship. He showed me papers of a pending divorce, so I continued to see him. One day his wife paid me a visit at my office and she had a gun in her hand. She pointed the gun to my head and informed me that if I continued to fuck her husband, she was going to blow my brains out, and no one would ever find my body. She had connections and his name was Ice."

"So you ended the relationship?"

"I did, and it almost killed me. I loved him."

"So do you love this Tony like you love Toxic?"

"I know what real love is now, and Toxic is the one."

"I see," the doctor said, still writing diligently in her memo pad.

"I loved Tony because he was unconditional. He made my fat body come to life, and I sucked his dick, and the two of us talked for hours, and fucked for hours. When I found out that he was married I wanted to die."

"Tony is single now and living here in Chicago."

Madison was stunned. "Why are you doing this to me?"

"I'm here to make sure that you're marrying the right man."

"Toxic is my future, and Tony is my past."

"I think you need closure with Tony before you marry Toxic."

Madison took a seat on the black sofa. "I don't want to see Tony. It's over and how dare you invade my privacy and bring up Tony. I haven't thought about him in years."

"He's been searching for you too. I have a lot of friends in high places."

"What do you mean searching for me?"

"He's been trying to find you for a long time. He was truly in love with your fat ass."

Madison was flabbergasted. Tony was a fine Morris Chestnut and she was so thrilled to be with him. She was a size fourteen at the time, and Tony was so proud of her big ass and large breasts. Why was he still searching for her? It was over when his wife threatened her life.

"I think we should move on. I don't want to see Tony."

"You should and I can make it happen."

Madison shook her head. "No!"

"What are you so afraid of?"

"Nothing," she cried. "Doctor leave this alone."

"You can't get married until you get the closure. It's not fair to Toxic. You need to meet up with him and see if the sparks are still there. You're skinny now, and it might be a problem. He likes big women."

"Where were the men when I was fat?"

"You lacked confidence in yourself and they can spot a woman with low self-esteem in a heartbeat. It's the right thing to do. Get the closure you need."

"No," she cried.

"Do you think you're going to fall back in love with Tony?"

"I don't know," she cried. "Just leave it alone."

"I wouldn't be a good shrink if I left it alone. Do I have your permission to give him your number? Maybe he needs closure so he can finally move on with his life. You owe him that much."

"I don't know," she cried. "Tony is my past."

"And Toxic is your future, but until you take care of the ghost of Tony, you're not going to have the right kind of future with Toxic. Our session is over, so think about it and call me, and I will release your number to Tony. I do know what I'm doing."

Madison shook her head as she walked to the door. She was wearing jeans, and they were tight, and she loved the feel of jeans, remembering when she couldn't wear jeans. Dammit, why did she have to bring up Tony? Why was he still searching for her after all these years? "Thanks for the session."

"You two need many more so I'll see you next week, same time, but call me if you change your mind about Tony."

Madison opened the door and walked out, heading to the cafeteria. She needed something to drink. What in the hell was she going to do? She had a feeling that if she laid eyes on Tony all her feelings will resurface, and then Toxic would be left in the cold. Dammit! She cried.

Toxic Lyons

⸻ ❧ ⸻

*T*oxic *smiled as he took a seat on the black sofa and stared at the gorgeous doctor who was staring at her memo pad. Madison didn't look happy as she walked into the cafeteria. She smiled at him, and kissed his cheek, and then she ordered something to eat.*

"Hello, Toxic," Dr. Reynolds replied.

Toxic focused on her. "Hello."

"Have you been in love before?"

She didn't waste any time, but his mother swore that she was the best. "I don't believe I have ever been in love. I do know how it feels to be in love, and Madison makes me feel brand new in love."

The doctor smiled. "How would you know what love is if you never experienced it?"

Toxic frowned. "I watch my parents, Tanyann, and the way they love their spouses. I want that kind of love, and Madison and I are on our way to that kind of love."

The doctor shook her head. "Give me five positive adjectives about Madison."

"Beautiful, loving, sweet, kind and ambitious," he replied.

"Why those adjectives?" the doctor asked.

"You can look at Madison and see her beauty; she's very loving toward me, and she's sympathetic and a nice person to me and others. She's also a paralegal and she's about to become a writer. I love her so very much."

"Give me five negative adjectives about Madison?"

"She's insecure, fat conscious, cautious, leery and negative."

"Explain," the doctor asked.

"Madison used to be fat, and sometimes I think she sees herself still as fat, and the insecurities come in. She's on this crusade to help all fat women overcome their insecurities and lose the weight. She loves me, but she thinks I'm going to leave her. I also fear that she believes she's going to gain her weight back. I know she doesn't want any babies."

"Did you ask her about babies?"

"We haven't discussed it."

"You two are ready to get married, but don't even know each other."

"We'll learn about each other as we go along."

"What's her favorite color?"

"Green," he laughed.

"She doesn't know your favorite color."

Toxic frowned. "What is her favorite television show?"

"She likes the soap operas on channel 2 I believe."

"You two need to wait another year."

"It's not going to happen, doctor, and why are you so negative?"

"I counsel a lot of couples before they get married, and I saved a few of them from making the biggest mistake of their lives. I'm not here to be negative, but practicable, thank you both very much."

"I want us to get married ASAP."

"I feel the chemistry between the two of you and the tension, so maybe you are met for each other. If this is the case, why rush it? You two are attracted to each other, so you can afford to wait and get it right this time. I think you both need to date and court each other. There's no way you shouldn't know her favorite television show, or the things she likes and dislikes and vice versa."

"January 1st is our wedding day, doctor. Maybe you need to recommend someone else who is going to be more positive. My mother sings your praises, but I'm having my doubts right now."

"Why are you two in counseling if you don't want to listen to my advice? I'm an expert and I know what I'm talking about. A few couples are grateful to me for saving their lives."

"We can continue to learn about each other as we connect with you, Dr. Reynolds, but nothing or no one is going to stop this marriage. I've been waiting a long time to find someone like Madison, and the voice told me so, and it's not the voice of the devil. The electricity is electric when our hands or bodies touched. No other woman in my entire life has made me feel this way. I know Madison is the only woman for me. She's my soul mate."

The doctor smiled. "Okay, then?"

"Are we on the same page?"

"I guess we are. I want you and Madison to have a date night this week. I don't care what day it is, but I want the two of you to spend some quality time together and see me twice a week starting next week. My job is to make sure you two are ready for marriage, and right now we have our work cut out for us. We're going to talk about your date night." *The doctor reached for her black appointment book, and opened the page.* "Let's meet on Tuesdays and Fridays. I need you both to clear your schedules and make this a priority. I think four is good."

"I'll make sure Madison and I are here."

"Great, and good luck to your both. I do want to continue with you two because when I tried to persuade you two from getting married right now, or prolonging it until May with Madison, the two of you didn't back down. This makes me believe that you two are destined for each other."

Toxic smiled and stood up. "Doctor, we're on the same page."

They shook hands, and Toxic left to find Madison with a smile on his face.

So, it was now Monday and Toxic and Madison decided to go out on their first official date before their meeting with Dr. Reynolds. They decided to go to Lyons Restaurant and rent out a private table and talk. Madison was wearing a gorgeous long maxi green dress, and Toxic had on jeans and a green polo shirt, so the two of them were in sync with each other.

Madison smiled as Toxic held her seat and she sat down. The table was set for two with pretty red flowers on the table, and it was a gorgeous setting. "This is nice," she said.

"You look very nice yourself."

"And you don't look so bad yourself, Mr. Lyons."

Toxic laughed. "Let's have some red wine."

"Sounds like a plan."

Toxic poured the wine and handed her a glass.

"To us," Madison said.

"To us," Toxic agreed.

Madison took a sip of her wine. "This is good."

"Only the best for us. Tell me about your day."

Madison smiled as she took another sip. "I completed two more short stories, and Beverly is the best editor in the world. She took one of my stories and changed it, but not a lot, and it sounded much better when she did it. I got a deposit in my bank account."

"Wow," Toxic replied.

"I was stunned when I saw the amount for ten thousand dollars."

"You go girl," he laughed.

Madison smiled. "I can't believe I'm finally getting money in my account for something I love doing." *She shook her head.* "I wept when I saw the check. I just couldn't believe it. I dreamed so long for my writing to take off."

"Your dreams are a reality."

"I owe it all to Tanyann."

"Honey, you have the gift, and Tanyann is just the messenger."

Madison smiled, and then the tears started falling. She picked up a napkin off the table and wiped her eyes. "I'm so sorry," she cried. "I thought my weeping days were over."

Toxic was touched by his fiance as he stared at her. "It's okay, and I love to see your emotions running amok."

Madison laughed. "Thank you. How was your day?"

"I won two of my cases, and it's time for me to take a vacation. I think I'm going to take a month off and focus more on my new wife. I also want to do some architecture work. I have clients just waiting for me to design their dream homes."

Madison stared at him. "How long have you been thinking about this?"

Toxic took a long sip of his wine. "For a very long time. The law I love, but it's getting very boring to me. I want to do my hobby now. I'm not quitting the law because it pays my bills, but I need a vacation like maybe three months."

"I think you need to do what makes you happy, Toxic. You don't really have to work. You're a billionaire, so I don't understand your comment about law paying the bills."

"A billionaire has to keep working, Madison. Money don't grow on trees, thank you very much. I feel you resent me for being a billionaire."

"I do, but I'm getting over it. We can't help who we are born too."

"I didn't tell God to make me rich," he snapped.

"Why are you getting angry?"

"Your obsession with money is a nuisance."

Madison frowned. "When you never have any, then you can talk to me about it. I struggled for years remembering not having enough money to pay the bills or go to work to make to pay the bills. I had to take out payday loans, and they ruined me. I filed bankruptcy twice and ended up taking out payday loans again. It's never enough money," she cried. *The tears fell again.* "I just wanted to buy or pay bills without worrying about an overdrawn."

"God is good because my money is your money."

"I don't want your freaking money," she snapped.

"I'm a package deal," he snapped.

The two of them stared at each other with angry expressions. The waiter cleared his throat, and Toxic stared at him. "I'll have the meatloaf dinner."

"Give me the barbecue ribs dinner," Madison stated.

The waiter smiled and left. Silence took over their table.

The food came in seven minutes and Madison and Toxic focused on their food as silence continued to take over the room.

It was ten minutes later when Toxic broke the silence. "Do you want to wait on getting married? You have a problem with my money and it's the opposite of the other women in my life. They wanted my money to pay their bills."

"I'm not other women, and do you want to call off this relationship? I need to go back to my condo. I didn't want to continue to live with you until we got married, and this is the best time. We need space from each other."

"What about the counseling appointment?"

"I'll take Uber and get there," she cried. "Can we just take our food to go?"

Toxic motioned for the waiter. Ten minutes later they were back in the car, driving to the mansion where Madison packed her bags and use her app to call Uber. She was out of there in ten minutes.

Toxic stared at her getting into the car, and the uber driver staring at her as if he hadn't seen a woman before. He waited for the driver to drive off, and then he got back onto the elevator. What was going to happen now? How could someone resent him for having money? It wasn't his fault that he was born rich, but he wasn't. His parents worked their asses off to make billions, and he, and his siblings followed in their footsteps. No one put a spoon in his hand. He resented the implications. He stared around his room, and he felt as if his life was taking a turn for the worse.

He sniffed still smelling Madison's perfume, Wind song. How was he going to survive without having Madison in his space? He sat down on his bed and just stared around the room. She was gone, and he did not know if they were getting married. Maybe the doctor was right about them waiting. Madison had money issues, and she needed to stop resenting him and move on with her life. He shook his head.

Toxic and Madison

Dr. Reynolds stared at the two of them as she noticed the tension in the room, and the fact that Madison was staring at her phone, and Toxic was looking out the window.

"Okay, you two what's the problem?" Dr. Reynolds asked.

Silence between Madison and Toxic continued.

Dr. Reynolds laughed. "Someone needs to talk. Toxic why don't you begin."

Toxic focused on the doctor. "Madison resents me because I have money."

Madison laughed. "I don't resent him for having money."

"Yes you do," he snapped. "You blame me because you were freaking poor."

Madison rolled her eyes at Toxic. "He doesn't understand why I feel the way I do about money. I never had any, and it makes me sick that some people had too much of it."

"And that's my fault how?" Toxic snapped. "You have plenty of money now so why do you keep bringing up the negative?"

"You don't freaking understand my plight with money," she snapped.

"I do understand, but God has blessed you with a man who has plenty of it, and what's mine is yours," Toxic demanded. "I love you, and I want to make your life better, but how can I do that if you keep harping on the past. Let the past go."

"You don't understand," she cried.

"I guess I don't understand," he snapped.

Dr. Reynolds listened to the two of them as she wrote on her memo pad. It was ten minutes as silence was golden. She stared at Madison and then she stared at Toxic. "Madison, Toxic is right about this. You can't blame him for your past. He's put into your life to make it better, and you need to focus on what the two of you can accomplish with the love that you have for each other."

Madison rolled her eyes at them. "I would if I could."

"It's like drugs or gambling," Dr. Reynolds stated. "You have to stop taking the drugs, and spending money gambling, so now you have to stop blaming Toxic or anyone for your lack of money. You have a better life now, and money won't ever be an option for you as long as you invest well, and stay married to Toxic. You also have an opportunity to make your own money. Don't let this continue to be an issue for you. Tell me about the date, Toxic."

He frowned. "We went to Lyons restaurant, and I rented us a private table, and it was good. We had good wine, and I asked her about her day, and then she asked me about mine."

"And how did the issue of money come up?" Dr. Reynolds asked.

"I explained to her that I wanted to take a break from law for a while and focus on the hobby in my life which is architecture, but I implied that the law paid my bills, and she basically went off on that comment into something negative. The fact that she moved out and went back to her condo is another factor with us."

"I agree with Madison about moving out until you two get married. It's not good to live together without the institution of marriage. I'm from the old school in that regards."

"He basically wanted to call off the wedding," Madison snapped. "I don't appreciate his words."

"And what else did you expect me to say?" Toxic snapped. "You told me that you hated me because I had money after I told you my money was yours. I know you're not with me because of my money, and it's okay to share it with my future wife. Why can't you just move on?"

"It's not going to happen overnight," she yelled.

"So true," Dr. Reynolds stated. "Madison you need to make the effort. God put people in our lives for many reasons. Some are there for a short period of time and then they move on, and others are there for a lifetime in Toxic's case. Are you willing to ruin this relationship in lieu of your deep-rooted money issues?"

"I don't know," Madison cried. "Are we ready for marriage?"

"I am," Toxic said.

"Then we have to work on Madison," Dr. Reynolds pointed out. "You don't give up on someone that you claim to love, Toxic. Madison has issues, but she's seeing me, and that's the bottom line. I want you two to write a love letter to each other. I'm going to give you thirty minutes to make this happen, and you can stay right here and do it. Here's the paper and a pen, and don't share it with the other person until I get back. Just give me one or two paragraphs."

Dr. Reynolds left the office, closing the door behind her.

Madison reached for the pen and paper as did Toxic and silence was the contributing factor as the two focused on their love letter.

Thirty minutes later, Dr. Reynolds walked back into her office and took her seat behind her big desk. She stared at the two of them, and then smiled. "Madison, why don't you begin first?"

Madison stared at the doctor, and then her piece of paper. "Hi Toxic, you light up my light with your smile, and those green eyes of yours. When I'm in your presence I feel that everything is going to be okay, and you and I will become that power couple and knock this world off its rocker and then some. I love you so much, and I can't imagine my life without you in it. Please be patient with me, and know that I'm the only woman for you, and you're the love of my life. I don't resent your money. I resent me for having to live that way. I feel responsible for my own actions. I love you more than life itself. You rock my world in so many ways. I love you."

Madison wiped the tears from her eyes.

Toxic smiled and stared at his piece of paper. "Madison, my love, when I saw you sitting at the table with Sylvia and Helen at Lyons Restaurant, I thought I had died and gone to heaven. My entire insides were burning with heat and love. I felt something inside of me turn when I saw you, and

I knew you were going to be in my life for the duration. I heard the voice, and I knew you were my soul mate. Finally, I had found the most beautiful woman in the world, and her name is Madison Johnson. Despite your insecurities, I love you more than life itself, and together you and I will work out our demons. I know this relationship seems unreal, but this is reality, baby, and you and I will be that power couple now and forever. I love you Madison, and you never have to worry about your bills getting paid or overdrawing on your account. I got your back, always."

Madison was in tears now, but Toxic got up and took her into his arms, and the two cried together as Dr. Reynolds, wiped a tear from her eyes. She smiled as they embraced each other for five more minutes, and then they kissed passionately showing how much they love and adore each other.

Dr. Reynolds cleared her throat as they broke apart in embarrassment. "You two need a room or something, but let's get on with this session. We have a few more minutes so sit down and relax."

She smiled as Madison and Toxic sat close to each other, and Toxic put his arms around Madison. "You two definitely love each other and the letters were beautifully written in such a short period of time. Go out again on Friday as a lunch date, and we'll talk about it later that afternoon. Let's get it right this time. Maybe go to a movie or something different than dinner."

Madison wiped her eyes. She just couldn't stop weeping. "Okay."

"Okay," Toxic replied.

The doctor chatted with them for twenty more minutes, and then the bell rang ending their session for the evening. Everyone embraced and then Toxic and Madison left the doctor's office and headed to their cars.

"I want you to come home with me at the mansion," Toxic replied. "I want to make passionate love to you. I need you now Madison."

She blushed. "I'll follow you since I have my car."

He smiled. "Let's go."

The two got into their separate cars, and Madison followed Toxic because right now she was hot and on fire. She wanted Toxic's hands all over her hot body, and this time she was going to get it right and spend the night. What was she thinking moving out? Maybe it was the right thing to do until they got married, but tonight she wasn't going anywhere.

Forty-five minutes later they reached the mansion and hurried inside as they ran to the elevator, hand in hand, and Toxic pushed the button for his floor. When the two were inside his apartment, their clothes fell to the floor, and they ran to the bedroom where their bodies danced together until the wee hours of the morning. Moans and screaming were heard in their bedrooms, as Madison and Toxic made love like they had never made love before. It was exciting and intoxicating all at the same time as their bodies meshed together thrust for thrust and climax for climax. It was definitely a great day after all.

Madison Johnson

$\diamond$

Madison smiled as she stared at herself in the mirror. Christmas was over and it was the best Christmas in the world and then some. She spent it with her best friends, Sylvia, Helen, Jasmine and Tricia, and the rest of the Lyon's family. They laughed, opened gifts, and celebrate Jesus' birthday and it was wonderful. Now it was New Year's Eve, and everyone was in Las Vegas, sin city.

Madison was in her hotel room, the Lyons Hotel, getting ready for their mini reception with everyone who was here to see her, and Toxic get married tomorrow. She was happy that Dr. Reynolds accepted their wedding invitation, and they were eager to be here to see them get married. The counseling sessions went along, but, she still had her issues, and after they were married, Madison decided she was going to continue with the sessions. She wasn't healed overnight, but she was secure in knowing that Toxic loved her. She remembered, as she frowned, the conversation she had with

Tony, with Toxic's approval. She sat down on the bed in her black bra and panties thinking about her dinner with Tony.

They met at Lyons restaurants in one of the private floors. Madison was happy to see Tony walking toward her. He had not changed a bit, still fine and handsome reminding her of Morris Chestnut. She stood up as they embraced, and then Tony set down. He was chocolate, and fine. His slacks and shirt, in his favorite color, blue. He was over six feet tall, and he still had it going on and then some. "Hi."

"You look very different," Tony stated. "I didn't recognize you."

Madison smiled. "I lost some weight," she laughed.

"You lost a lot of weight," Tony laughed. "I miss that ass and those large breasts."

Madison blushed.

"I see that gorgeous ring on your finger, so you have finally found the man of your dreams. I'm really happy for you, Madison. You deserve the best. I thought I was the best, but I was very selfish for getting involved with you. I found out that my wife was cheating on me with other men, and I was so angry with her, I wanted to do the same thing to her. I used you, and it was the wrong thing to do. I did fall in love with you, but my wife found out, and it was over for us. I'm sorry."

Madison was stunned by his confession. "I thought I was in love with you, but I know what real love is, Tony and you weren't it. We worked out for the best. How are you doing and what's going on in your life now?"

He smiled. "I finally got rid of my bitch of a wife, and that's the best medicine in the world for me. She found someone that she loved better than me, and divorced me so fast, I was thrilled. Tammy has moved on with her life and now I'm free from her. I'm living in Chicago now, but I'll be moving to Atlanta in a few days. I just need to have a new beginning for myself."

"Are you going alone?"

He blushed. "I met someone, but I'm not rushing into anything. Her name is Rush and I've known her since high school. We dated, but after high school she left to act in Los Angeles, and we lost touch. She's in Chicago shooting a movie, and she called me, and the heat and the flames are still there. I feel the electricity all over the place when I'm with her, and it's the most magical feeling in the world. She lives in Atlanta when she's not working on her movies, and I'm excited about the new adventure for myself. Tell me about you."

Madison took a sip of her wine, and then she sat the glass back down on the table. "His name is Toxic Lyons, and he's the love of my life. We're getting married on New Year's Day and I can't wait to be his wife I love him so much and he loves me. The electricity is horrific, in a good way with the two of us."

"Toxic Lyons is a very rich man."

"He is, but he's also a very nice man. I love him."

"I do see the love in your eyes when you talk about him. You never looked like that when you and I were dating. I wish you the best because you deserve the best, Madison. I'm glad we got the closure we needed. I was going to contact you before I get into another relationship but you beat me to the punch. This is a good thing for everyone involved."

"I agree, so let's eat this delicious meal."

"It looks delicious."

Madison and Tony fed their faces and they talked about everything under the sun for the next two hours, and then kissed on the cheek, and went their separate ways. As Madison stared after the handsome man, she was thrilled that he wasn't the love of her life.

Madison smiled as she stood up and opened her closet door. She was at the mansion with Toxic who was taking a shower. If they didn't hurry up they were going to be late for their own party. Madison stared at the clothes in the closet. She was still living with. Toxic at the mansion but that was okay. They were going to be man and wife in twenty-four hours, so why did it matter. They hadn't decided where they were going to live, but it didn't matter because they would definitely work out the details later. Right now all she wanted to do was get married.

She pushed clothes around in her closet. What was she going to wear? After a few minutes of searching, but finding nothing to wear, she noticed the big white box in the back of the closet. She didn't remember putting it there as she reached for it, and then sat it down on the bed. She opened the box and then grasped, as she covered her mouth in shock.

The dress was beautiful as she stared at the lace black dress with ruffled hem and cap sleeves. She loved the ruffled hem, and the cap sleeves. There were accessories to match the dress and Madison knew Toxic had spoken to Sylvia because this was definitely a Sylvia original. It was short, and perfect for her new body. Madison loved it.

She hurried into the bathroom in their room because Toxic was in the one down the hall. She was going to be the most beautiful woman in the world and then some. She smiled to herself.

Toxic Lyons

⸻ ✦ ⸻

*T*oxic was dressed in his black suit with red highlights in a handkerchief, a shirt and tie. He was going to be in tuned with his bride-to-be. She was also wearing a black dress with red accessories to match thanks to Sylvia and her expertise in fashion. The girl had it going on and then some. He was a handsome dude as he stared at himself in the mirror. Tomorrow he was getting married and everyone he loved was right here in Las Vegas. He couldn't wait to marry Madison Johnson. He had never been so eager to get married. Once upon a time he told himself that he'd never get married----not being able to trust another female. But God had other plans for him.

Toxic sat in the living room to wait on Madison. They were going to their party before the wedding, and he was glad it wasn't a lot of people here. Madison didn't want a big deal wedding and he couldn't blame her. His siblings were here, and Guy, who was going to be his best man, and Jasmine, Sylvia, Helen and Tricia were Madison's maid of honor and bridesmaid. It was *going to be a short ceremony and then they were going to party in the Lyons den ballroom until the wee hours of the morning.*

Toxic smiled because he was stunned when Madison confessed to him about a married man she dated, but didn't know he was married. She needed closure, and he wasn't going to stand in her way. He didn't want anyone to come between them on their special day. He even thought his ex-girlfriend was going to give him some problems, but she was exclusively dating her attorney, Benny, who was divorcing his wife for her. Toxic shook his head. He forgot that Dr. Reynolds and her husband was here for the wedding, and Leslie and Justin.

He just wanted to get married and the media was going to play a role too. He was a Lyons for heaven sakes. The media hounded them all the time, and today wouldn't be any different.

Thirty minutes later, Madison walked into the living room all dressed in black and read, and Toxic was speechless. She was definitely the most gorgeous and beautiful woman in the universe and then some. The dress was perfect for her body type and it fitted like a glove. Sylvia was the best fashion designer in the world.

Madison blushed at her handsome fiancé. "Is something wrong?"

Toxic finally found his voice. "Words can't describe how lovely you look."

Madison blushed. "You are the most handsome man in the world," she cried.

"And you are the most beautiful woman in the world," he cried.

Their eyes met as the electricity charged up the room in one flick. It was five minutes before Toxic cleared his throat. "We should get going before I take that dress off of you and make passionate love to you right here in this living room. I didn't know your legs were so thin and long."

Madison laughed. "Me either. Let's go. This dress is the bomb and then some."

"Sylvia has excellent taste."

"My man has exquisite taste"

"Can I get a kiss instead?"

Madison reached for her man. "My lips are all yours."

Their lips met in a very passionate kiss, and then they broke apart as the electricity almost blinded them into a heating inferno. "Let's get out of here," Toxic replied.

"I'm pushing the elevator now," Madison laughed.

Madison and Toxic

I t had been two hours now and the party was in full swing. Madison and Toxic were having the time of their lives with Lyons parents, and their friends. For some reason the men had centered on one part of the room, and the ladies were all sitting together in another part of the Lyon's Den ballroom.

"I'm having a great time," Maggie said.

"Me too," James said.

Madison smiled at her future mom and dad.

"This is the bomb and then some," Sylvia cried.

"I agree," Helen chorused.

"You look so gorgeous, Madison," Jasmine cried.

"Yes, she does," Tricia said. "Your legs are forever."

Madison laughed. "You all should have seen pictures of me with my big legs and fat pockets. I don't look nothing like I used to look believe me. I'm taking pictures all the time and posting them on Facebook. I never did that before when I was fat."

Jasmine frowned. "I do it all the time. I'm not ashamed of my fat body. I'm modeling a lot and I'm getting more positive feedback than negative feedback. Most of the negative want me to lose weight, but I don't give a damn about the comments. I respond to each, and every one of them, and when I'm done, I feel good about myself, and I hope they feel bad about themselves."

"You go girl," Tricia said. "I hear it all the time about Tumor marrying the wrong woman. How could his handsome ass be with a fat woman? I'm so used to the negative remarks I don't give a damn. I'm having the time of my life modeling, and Tumor loves me more than life itself. I have no insecurities."

"I'm getting there," Madison said.

"It takes time for you," Sylvia said. "You were so negative I stopped complimenting you."

"Madison is a soul in progress," Maggie laughed. "James let's dance."

"Of course, "James said. *He took his wife's hand, and the two of them walked onto the dance floor. A slow song was playing, and they snuggled close. It was the prettiest picture of romantic love that Madison had ever seen. She wanted to find that kind of peace with Toxic. She drained her diet soda.*

"I can't believe you're not drinking a glass of wine," Sylvia said.

"I don't want to be tipsy on the eve of my wedding," Madison exclaimed.

Sylvia and Helen eyed Madison, as they stood up and grabbed her. "Ladies, the two of us will be back."

Madison found herself in the fabulous ladies room as Helen pushed her into a chair, and Sylvia and Helen sat down next to her. "Are you pregnant girl?" Helen stated.

"Don't lie to us." Sylvia said.

Madison stared at her two best friends. She didn't want anyone to know because she was going to surprise Toxic on their wedding night. But she could never fool her two best friends. "I am," she cried.

"I knew it," Helen said. "Lies and secrets."

"She didn't lie," Sylvia pointed out. "She just kept the information to herself."

"Thank you," Madison said.

"I hope you don't plan on getting an abortion," Helen cried.

"What?" Madison cried.

"You're going to get fat pregnant," Helen said.

"I'm not going to get fat," Madison replied. "I'm going to gain enough weight for the baby, and then exercise as much as I can. I'm never going to be fat again."

"We're going to be Godmothers," Sylvia cried.

"I guess we are," Helen said. "Why did you feel the need to keep it from us?"

Madison rolled her eyes at Helen. "I'm still in shock myself because Toxic and I have been so careful with condoms, but I'm pregnant and my doctor confirmed it after I took a home pregnancy test. Girls, I'm going to be a mother. A little baby is going to depend on me. I'm so afraid."

"You never have to be afraid," Helen cried. "Sylvia and I have your back, and you have Jasmine, and the Lyon's family.

You have nothing to fear. Your son or daughter is going to be the most blessed baby ever."

"I should have told my best friends," Madison cried.

"You should have," Helen snapped. "Maybe I need to find new friends who don't see the need to keep secrets."

"I'm sorry," Madison cried.

"We forgive you this time, "Sylvia said. "I know you're scared."

"I am," Madison cried. "I'm going to need my best friends more than ever."

"You have us always," Sylvia cried.

"As long as the secrets stop," Helen stated.

"We know," Madison said. "I want to surprise Toxic first on our wedding night."

"Your secret is safe with us," Helen snapped.

"Let's go back before we're missed," Sylvia said.

When they walked back into the room, Madison smiled at her siblings-in-law, Toniann, Tanyann and Tammyann as they sat down at the table. "I'm glad you three could make it."

"We wouldn't miss it for the world," Toniann said.

"That's for sure," Tammyann said.

"Sorry we're late," Tanyann replied.

"I see mom and dad are showing off," Toniann laughed.

"I love seeing the two of them," Madison cried.

"They are so loving," Toniann said.

"There's plenty of food and drink," Madison cried.

"I'm famished," Tanyann said. "I'm big as a house and this baby is hungry."

Madison stared at her. She'd be due in a few months. She watched as her new family of sisters walked over to the buffet

table and filled up their plates with chicken, barbecue, shrimp,
pizza, and the list was endless. They had plenty of food to last
into next week.

Madison still found it difficult to believe that tomorrow she
was going to marry the man of her dreams. The Lyon's family
was so nice, and they welcomed her with open arms. She felt the
tears forming, but she controlled her tears. She didn't want to
be a baby, but they were tears of joy.

"Are you okay?" Tanyann asked?

Madison smiled at her. "I'm overwhelm with happiness."

"Welcome to our family," Tanyann said. "We're so happy
to have you in our family. Our brother is so happy and you
make him happy and that's the bottom line. We love you so
much."

"I love you all too. Tomorrow is the big day."

"Where are you two going on your honeymoon?"

"It's a surprise," Madison laughed. "You know your
brother."

"We do, and you're a very lucky woman."

"And he's a lucky man."

Tanyann and Madison embraced.

Two hours later Madison and Toxic were sitting at a table.
"How are you doing?" Toxic asked.

"As usual, I'm having the time of my life."

"Is your favorite color green?"

"It is, and what is yours?"

"Mine is yellow."

"Wow," she cried. "I'd have never guessed."

"What is your favorite television show?"

Madison laughed. "I have a few, but my soap operas are the most favorite, The Young and the Restless, and The Bold and the Beautiful."

Toxic laughed.

"And what is yours?"

"Major Crimes, the Game of Throngs, Law and Order."

"I like Law and Order too," Madison cried.

"Dr. Reynolds is talking to your parents."

"I see," Toxic said. "Are we going to sleep together tonight?"

"No, we're not," she laughed.

Toxic frowned. "I'm going to miss you."

"Me too, but it's only for one night."

"One night is to long for you."

Madison laughed. "I love you too."

"So you will be with Sylvia, Jasmine, Tricia and Helen."

"I'm going to bond with my sisters."

"I can live with that."

"Guy is very handsome in person."

"And he's very nice too."

Madison smiled. "Are you jealous?"

"Yes, I am," he pouted.

Madison kissed him on the lips, and then released his lips after a few minutes. "Does that make it all better?"

"If you kiss me again, I'll tell you."

Madison gave him a more passionate kiss, and then tongue. After the kiss, she stared at him. "I love you so much," she cried.

"I love you more," he cried.

"You two need to get a room," Tammyann said.

"I agree," Dr. Reynolds laughed.

Everyone laughed as the celebration continued for another four hours. It was the wee hours of the morning when Madison went home with her girls. They'd be over Sylvia's house until it was time to get married.

Toxic left with his brother Tumor, who was spending the night with him. Tomorrow was the biggest day of their lives.

The Marriage

M adison was dressed as she stared again at herself in
the mirror. She was always glancing at herself in the
mirror. The wedding gown was perfect for her size six body,
and she wanted to weep as she stared at herself.

"You are gorgeous?" Maggie cried.

Madison turned toward her almost mother-in-law. "Thank
you so much. I feel so pretty."

"You're beautiful," she cried. "I want to give you
something old."

Madison was stunned.

"This is my mother's necklace and she gave it to me.
When I got married, and I loaned it to Tanyann when she
got married. Now I think it's your turn to have it. I don't
want you to give it back. I have more special Jewelers for my
other daughters."

Madison felt the tears forming. "Are you sure?"

"This gold necklace fits perfect with your shades of green
wedding gown. Let me put it on."

Madison was in tears and she couldn't help herself. The necklace was as gorgeous as she stared at it in the mirror. "I love it."

"It looks perfect on you. Welcome to the Lyon's family."

Madison embraced her. "Thank you so much."

"It looks beautiful on you."

Madison let the tears fall.

"Honey don't mess up your makeup. I want to get a picture of you for the photo album for the house. I have pictures of everyone in my living room. I'm having the time of my life adding new photos. Imagine the gorgeous babies the two of you are going to have."

Madison smiled. "Can I tell you a secret?"

Maggie smiled. "You're pregnant."

"I am."

"This is very exciting news, but you haven't told Toxic yet."

"I'm waiting for the honeymoon."

"I'm so thrilled for you and Toxic, and my lips are sealed."

"You can spill the beans after Toxic and I leave."

"I will give you today and tell everyone tomorrow."

"Thank you for welcoming me into your lovely family."

"Thank you for loving my son. I prayed for him to find the right woman, and God has answered my prayers."

The two women embraced as Sylvia and Helen burst into the room.

"I'll see you later as Mrs. Toxic Lyons," Maggie cried.

"Thank you, "Madison cried.

Maggie embraced Sylvia and Helen and then she closed the door.

"That necklace is gorgeous," Sylvia cried.

"And it looks very expensive," Helen pointed out.

"Maggie gave it to me."

"She's very generous."

"All the Lyon's are," Sylvia pointed out.

"I know," Madison cried. "You two look beautiful."

"You look out of this world," Helen cried. "Green is definitely your favorite color. It looks perfect on you."

"I can't believe this is me, staring back at me."

"This is real life," Sylvia said. "And in five minutes your life is about to change."

"Girls, let's do this."

"Let's pray," Helen said.

Helen, Sylvia, and Madison all held hands as they closed their eyes and prayed to God for a blessed day.

"You look very handsome," Tumor laughed.

Toxic smiled at his brother. "You look handsome yourself."

"I know," he said. "My lovely wife will appreciate me."

"You and Tricia are okay?"

"We're in the best place now."

"I'm glad for the two of you. I like Tricia."

"So, the counseling is working for you."

"Madison and I both are in counseling, and it's working for both of us. She's not cured from her insecurities, but she's calling a truce about the negativism today and on our honeymoon. She's been tired lately, so I'm going to pamper my baby, and give her the best honeymoon she'll remember for the duration of her life."

Tumor smiled. "Las Vegas is the city."

"Yes it is. Green is such a pretty color."

"It's Madison's favorite."

Tumor stared at his watch. "Let's get you married."

"I'm ready as I'll ever be, Tumor."

Tumor patted his brother on the back, and the two walked out of the room, and headed to the chapel in Las Vegas. It was time to get married, Toxic thought to himself, and then he smiled.

"It's time for the vows," the minister replied. "You may begin Toxic."

Toxic stared into Madison's hazel eyes. "I take you as you are, Madison Johnson," Toxic began. "I love you as who you are, and what you're destine to become. I am going to listen and learn from you. I will support you, and take your support for me. I will love you and have faith in your love for me for the duration of our lives."

Madison smiled as she peered into Toxic's green eyes. "I love you unconditionally and without hesitation. I vow to trust, respect, and encourage you. As man and wife we will laugh and give compassion to each other in the good and bad times. I choose you as my husband, Toxic Lyons," she cried. "I accept you just as you are, and I offer myself too you in return. I will always care for you, be there for you right by your side, and share the trials and the tribulations. You are mine forever."

"Today, I promise you this," Toxic sang. "I will comfort you in times of sorrow and laugh with you when joy surrounds us. I will honor your dreams, and be there for you when you celebrate your goals. Today, we begin our new lives on this New Year's Day. Let us partner with each other as friends, and lovers for the rest of our time on this earth."

Toxic, you are my soul mate," Madison cried. "I will cry and laugh with you, and we will grow together. I promise to support your architecture dreams, and to love you and be by your side forever."

"I, Toxic take you, Madison to be my wife. I promise before God and these witnesses, to be your loving and faithful husband."

"I, Madison take you, Toxic to be my husband. I promise before God and these witnesses, to be your loving and faithful wife."

"For better and for worse, or richer, for poorer, in sickness and health, until the end of the world do us part," Toxic cried.

"For better and for worse, or richer, for poorer, in sickness and health, until the end of the world do us part," Madison cried.

"With this ring, I declare," Toxic replied.

"With this ring, I declare," Madison cried.

"I now pronounce you man and wife," the minister announced. "You may kiss your lovely bride."

Madison and Toxic's lips met in a passionate kiss. They were married. They broke apart as the room applauded. Madison and Toxic was so happy.

"Everyone, let's welcome Mr., and Mrs. Toxic Lyons."

The room applauded with cheers and happiness. Toxic and Madison was about to embark on their new lives as man and wife.

"I love you so much," Toxic cried.

"I love you more," Madison cried.

As they headed to the ballroom for their wedding reception, the two held hands, kissed and walked into a room of applause. This was definitely just the beginning.

The Honeymoon

As Madison stared out the window of their private airplane, she smiled. She had a private airplane, and it was Toxic, but now it was hers. She thought she was going to die from the shock, of owning an airplane. Toxic gave it to her as a wedding gift, and she was still flabbergasted. He also gave her jewelry and a visa gold card with thirty thousand dollars of credit. Madison had never been so stunned in her life.

Toxic also opened her a joint bank account for them, and they had to get approval from the other person before any money was withdrawn from the account. She couldn't believe it, and they had keys to somewhere, but she wouldn't find out that gift until they got back to Chicago.

She yawned, watching Toxic on the phone. Who was he talking too on their honeymoon? Where in the hell were they going? As she continued to stare out the window of the airplane, all she saw was clouds and nothing more or less. She closed her eyes and yawned again. She was so freaking exhausted mentally and physically. Now that she was a married woman, the stress of getting married was finally over.

Madison smiled because she was pregnant, and going to be a mother. The baby was making her tired as she yawned for the third time. She was only four weeks for heaven sakes and all she wanted to do was take a nap. How could she be sleeping when she was on her honeymoon? Love making was the next stop in her itinerary.

Finally, Toxic got off the phone and took a seat next to Madison. "Honey, are you okay? You're the most beautiful woman in this world, but you look exhausted for some reason."

Madison smiled. "I'm good, baby. Who was on the phone and where are we going?"

"We don't want to start of our marriage with lying."

"I'm not lying, Toxic, I'll joyous." *She yawned again.*

Toxic laughed. "Baby did you get any sleep?"

"I was too high on getting married. I'm good."

"I was just finalizing the details of our trip."

"Where are we going, Toxic?"

He frowned, and then she smiled. "I guess I can give you the surprise now."

"Are you freaking killing me, Toxic? You gave me so many surprises for my wedding gift, and I haven't given you yours yet."

He laughed. "What are you waiting for?"

Madison laughed, and then she yawned for the fourth time. "I'm so sorry, honey. I'm going to give you your surprise very soon."

"I want you to go in the back and lie down, Madison. It's an order."

Madison laughed, covering her mouth as another yawn took over. "Are you going to end this marriage before it starts, Toxic? You don't give orders to me, and I don't obey them."

"I didn't mean it that way, love. Just go and rest."

Madison shook her head. "I can't go to sleep on our honeymoon."

"You're going to sleep on the plane, Madison. Why do you have to be so stubborn?"

She smiled. "Where are we going?"

"What is your favorite place in the world to visit, but you've never been there before?"

"It's Hawaii," she cried, but only Sylvia and Helen know this about me. "The three of us decided we were going to take that trip this year."

"We're going to Hawaii," Toxic exclaimed.

Madison opened her mouth, and no words came out as she stared at her husband.

"Is that okay?"

Madison jumped in her husband's lap and began kissing his face. "I love you so freaking much," she cried. "Are we really going to Hawaii?"

"For three long weeks," he cried.

"This is the best wedding present ever. I love you so much."

"I love you too," he laughed.

Madison yawned again.

"Please take a nap because we have a long trip."

"I can't do that to my new husband."

"I'll wake you up when we get near Hawaii. Besides, I don't want you sleeping or tired when I make love to my new wife. I need you to have a lot of energy for what I have in mind for that hot body of yours."

Madison yawned and blushed at the same time. "I don't know why I'm so tired, honey. I'll just close my eyes for a few minutes. I can't believe you have a bed on the airplane."

"Go back there and get it in and relax."

She stared into Toxic's green eyes. "Are you sure?"

"I'm positive."

Madison gave him a very passionate kiss and then she jumped off his lap and went to the back of the airplane where she found the bed and happily leaped on it, and smiled as she curled up in a ball and closed her eyes. She was asleep in five minutes.

Toxic stared at his wife. What was going on with her? Was she sick? He stared at his wife for the next ten minutes and then he walked back to his seat. They were going to talk when she woke up.

Eight hours later, Toxic walked back to the bedroom of the plane and stared at his wife. She was still sleeping like a baby. He sat down on the bed, and began shaking her. They were in Hawaii, and Madison slept through the rest of the flight. Something was definitely going on with his wife.

He shook Madison a few more times, and she finally opened her eyes. She stared at him. "Hi honey," she yawned.

"Madison are you sick or anything."

She laughed. "Why do you ask?"

"You've been sleeping for eight hours, and now it's time to get off the plane."

Madison yawned again and covered her mouth in shock. "Are you kidding me?"

"No, let's find a hospital and see what's going on with you."

Madison sat up in the bed. "Honey, I'm mentally exhausted, but I'm fine now. Are we in Hawaii? I'm so excited for this trip."

"I can't believe you're lying to me."

"Honey, I'm good."

"I want to know why you're so exhausted."

Madison knew she had to tell him or he was going to carry her screaming to the nearest hospital. She stared into his lovely green eyes, and she saw the pain he was in. "Toxic, I'm pregnant. I didn't want to tell you this way, but you insisted." *She stared at the shock on his face.* "We're going to have a baby. I'm four weeks, and my doctor confirmed it in Chicago. For some reason, I'm just exhausted."

Toxic was speechless.

Madison laughed, touching his face. "Are you going to say something? I'm so sorry----I'm spoiling our honeymoon with my exhaustion, but I'm going to make it up to you. Do you think we can take a tour or something?"

Toxic was still speechless.

"Honey snap out of it. Are we here?"

Toxic stared at Madison and then he touched her stomach. "You're pregnant?" he finally said, finding his voice.

"It's my wedding gift to you, honey. Sylvia and Helen figured it out and I told your mother because she was so nice to me, but she's not going to tell anyone until the next day. Let's go visit this island of Hawaii. This is another dream of mine, honey."

"I love you so much," he cried.

Madison flew herself into Toxic's arm and embraced him. "I love you more," she cried. "Now can we get off this plane and see Hawaii."

"Do we need to find a hospital to get you checked out?"

"No," she cried. "I'm not spoiling my dream in Hawaii sitting in a hospital all day. My doctor confirmed that everything was fine. I'm stressed out with the wedding and everything, honey. If I get tired again, I'm going to rest. I want to see Hawaii right now, and then make love to my new husband. Are you game?"

Toxic held her tight. "I love you so much."

Madison smiled. "I love you more."

It was three hours later when Madison and Toxic walked into their hotel on Kaanapali Beach hotel. As Madison took pictures of their hotel she couldn't believe the luxury of the place. It looked like a mini mansion to her. They were on 11 acres of tropical gardens. They were going to take hula lessons before they left.

"This is so beautiful," Madison cried.

"You're so beautiful," Toxic replied. "Are you okay or hungry?"

"I'm famished," she cried. "I had a ball touring the islands, honey. I took so many pictures."

Toxic laughed. "We're going to the Kupanaha Magic Dinner Theater tomorrow, and they have so many activities that will keep us busy for the three weeks we are here. Do you want to dine in or out?"

Madison smiled. "I'm not tired, so let's check out their award-winning restaurant."

"Please let me know if you get tired."

Madison frowned. "I don't want you treating me like a fragile doll, Toxic. I'm pregnant not sick with cancer. I'm healthy and taking my prenatal vitamins. The eight hours of sleep rejuvenated me. I'm ready to go five more hours. Let's get something to eat, and then sit on the beach. I love this hotel. How did you know?"

"I did my research with the help of Helen and Sylvia."

"I should have known they knew where I was going before I knew. Helen is always fretting about keeping secrets and she kept a big one from me. I'm going to let her have it the next time I see her."

"Let's go eat, and then I want your body. Is it okay?"

"We can make love, honey. I'm only four weeks." *She shook her head at him. Toxic was going to be a pain in her ass with this pregnancy.*

After their dinner, Madison and Toxic came back to their hotel where they showered and made love for hours. Madison was on fire, and Toxic was so gentle with her, she had to take the lead and bang his ass with her pussy juices. As she sucked his dick, he was screaming out her name, as the two of them got sexual nasty. It was an hour or more before they laid spent.

"Are you okay?" he whispered. "I'm so satisfied."

"I'm fine, Toxic, and don't ask me that again," she snapped.

"I'm sorry," he said. "I'm concern for the baby. We were banging each other from the front and the back. I don't want us to hurt the baby."

"I'm sure they have a bookstore or two in Hawaii, and I'm going to buy you a book or two on pregnancy and how it enables you to have sex without hurting the baby. I need you to do your homework, thank you very much."

"I'm being a pain in the ass."

"Yes, you are, husband," she laughed. "Stop it."

"I will try," he laughed. "I just can't believe we're going to have a son or daughter. It's the most remarkable feeling in the world."

"It's very exciting, and you and I will share every moment of this experience, Toxic. I want you to go to my doctor's appointments with me and be there when we take our first ultrasound. Your mother is a doctor, and your sister is a nurse. We're good."

"I love you so much," he cried.

"I love you more," she cried. "Toxic what is this key for?"

Toxic stared at the key on the nightstand near the bed. "I bought you a range rover in your favorite color of green."

Madison stared at her husband in shock. "What?" she cried.

Toxic sat up in bed, all in his naked glory as he reached for his cell phone of the night stand on his side of the bed, the left side, and searched for the photo of the range rover, and handed her his phone.

Madison stared at the hunter green car, and she screamed, as the tears blinded her. "Oh honey, it's the most beautiful car in the world. I don't drive that much, but I'm going to be driving now. It's so pretty."

Toxic laughed. "I take it you love it."

"I'm going to show you just how much I love it, and I love you." *She handed him his cell phone, and then she reached for his dick and began playing with it until it was hard in her hands, and then she took it into her mouth, and showed Toxic just how much she appreciated his gift.*

Toxic moans and screams satisfied her sexual expertise in more ways than one. When his semen ran down her throat, Madison licked her lips in excitement, and then she position his hard again dick inside of her wet cove of pleasure and she rocked his world, and hers. Their screams confirmed their sexual pleasures. Let the honeymoon continue.

Three months later, Madison and Toxic found out, at their first ultrasound that they were having twins, a boy and a girl. The two Lyons were happy, as the rest of their family were for the first twins in the family. Madison was stunned, and so was Toxic, but they were very ecstatic, as their family was now complete in the Lyon's Den.

Printed in the United States
By Bookmasters